ROMANCE ON THE TRAIL

KAY STUART

WESTERN ROMANCE BY KAY STUART

UNDER WESTERN STARS
OUTLAW'S DAUGHTER
BANDIT RANCH
COURTING FAITH
COURTING HOPE
GALEN'S FEUD

RELUCTANT BRIDES
COURTING GRACE
COURTING WISDOM

Copyright ©2016 Kay Stuart
All Rights Reserved
ISBN 13: 978-1539029519
ISBN 10:1539029514

CHAPTER ONE

Casper Van Holland climbed the stairs of his tenement building weary after a day in the warehouse loading and unloading freight. He stopped on the top landing, stretched to release sore muscles, and knocked on the plain wood door in front of him.

An elderly woman's voice bid him to enter, "It is open Mr. Van Holland." A little girl left playing and ran into her father's arms. He caught the child lifting her high above his head. She squealed in delight then wrapped her small frail arms around his neck.

Another long day was ending, Casper thought as he lowered his body onto the only cushioned chair in the small room. The chair's seat was old and lumpy. Molly, his daughter, sat on his lap resting against his chest. Was he providing for her as her mother would want? His long days away from his daughter left little time for him to see to the child's needs. Mrs. Fuller though kind and motherly was crippled with arthritis and unable to walk up and down the stairs which left Molly to play in the one room tenement day after day.

Casper took the evening addition of the local newspaper from inside his winter coat. "There's talk on the docks about opportunities in the west," he told the old woman.

"There is talk every year about the great and wonderful west," Mrs. Fuller replied. "Didn't your brother up and leave after hearing wonderful things about this place called Oregon."

"It's what got me thinking" Casper answered. "Jorge is married now and Molly needs a mother's care."

"It is a fact that I am old and can give her very little care. Wee ones need a mother and rightly so," Mrs. Fuller replied. She had advised Casper to remarry and give Molly a mother. Something the young man was reluctant to do.

1

"Molly loves you," Casper quickly assured. "And I know you do all you can."

"Aye, still a body can do only so much with crippled hands," she lamented.

Casper handed Mrs. Fuller the newspaper and watched as her faded blue eyes brightened. "Talk is," he continued, "there's a family heading for Oregon Country and needs a driver for one of their wagons. It is suppose to be in the newspaper. Would you mind looking for me?"

"Aye," the woman said, spreading the newspaper over her well scrubbed wooden table. She found the section she wanted and began slowly and laboriously to read through each advertisement. One crooked finger pointing to each printed line as she read.

Casper leaned back in the chair and closed his eyes as he waited. "It is here," Mrs. Fuller said at length. Then, she read the short advertisement aloud to the young man.

"Doesn't say much does it," Casper ventured. He was weary more of heart than of body.

"Is a fact," Mrs. Fuller agreed. "Mostly, it contains the name of this lawyer, Mr. Forbes on Conley Avenue. It is that big brick building on the corner, I'm thinking." She opened the top drawer of her dresser, took out shears, and carefully cut out the advertisement Casper wanted. She handed the piece of newspaper to him and he placed it inside his shirt pocket. "Are you thinking about looking into it," she asked.

"I don't rightly know," he told her. "It is more an idea. Driving a wagon isn't something I know about," he pointed out honestly. The look in his blue eyes was intense with uncertainty.

"Aye," the old woman agreed. "Sometimes a body just has a feeling something is right. And when it is so, you best be on about doing it."

Casper considered what Mrs. Fuller said. Did he have a feeling about it? "If I decide to go and make inquiries can I bring Molly around in the morning," he asked.

The old woman patted the child gently on the head. "If you feel it is the right thing for you to do come morning, bring the wee one here," she told him.

He thanked her and rose to his feet. His height dwarfed the stooped over frail looking Mrs. Fuller. He left the apartment pulling the door closed behind him. Was it the right thing to do, he

2

wondered as he climbed the flight of stairs to his apartment one floor up. The room was cold, lonely and empty. Its furnishings were sparse. He did not look around the room for the sight of it made him long for his Mary. Brought back to his mind the last desperate days of his wife's illness, her labored breathing and feverish ravings, he watched Mary slip from this world into the next. He preferred to dwell on the peace he saw on Mary's still white face after her labor was over and the certain knowledge that she was face to face with her Lord. The hurts and sorrows of this world would not touch his wife again.

Casper placed Molly on the bed before cooking their evening meal. His mind returned again to the piece of newsprint in his shirt pocket. "If a body feels it was right," Mrs. Fuller had said. Did he feel it was right? "Lord," he called out in his mind, "Show me the right path." It was a cry of desperation that vibrated through his soul.

The meal over, the dishes washed and returned to the shelf, Casper sat holding his daughter. Her small frail body caused him concern. Molly was too small and too frail. He looked down to see her watching his face. Reaching up, she rubbed one hand across his firm chin feeling the day's growth of beard that darkened his jaws.

He kissed her forehead. "What do you think, Molly," he asked. "Should I try for the job?" She put her fingers in his mouth and felt his even white teeth. He nibbled gently on her fingers bringing squeals of laughter from the child. "You know Molly, I believe I will have to think on the job some more."

He undressed his young daughter placing her on the small cot he used for her bed and pulled the wool blanket up under her chin. "Goodnight little one," he told her. Molly smiled at him trustingly. Her eyes were heavy with sleep.

Removing his heavy work boots, Casper stretched out on his bed and tucked the pillow under his head. Closing his eyes, he listened to the sounds of the building. The Brewster boys were running up the stairs calling to each other. Mr. and Mrs. White in the apartment above were having another quarrel. Soon he heard the door slam and heavy footsteps going downstairs. The MacAfee baby was crying again, young Mrs. MacAfee hardly more then a child herself was unable to produce enough milk to feed her baby. Casper wondered if the infant would make it through the cold winter.

All this mingled with the sound of the wind. Was it snowing again? He felt a chill settle in the room and got up to check on Molly. He went to the radiator and placed one hand against the side to feel for warmth. Through the one window, he saw great white flakes of snow falling made visible by street lamps. He went back to Molly and picked the child up. He pulled back the blankets on his bed. Casper did not like sleeping with his daughter. He was afraid of hurting her during the night but the room was growing steadily colder and she needed the warmth from his body to stay warm.

Casper woke frequently during the long night. Each time he checked on Molly. Once, he went to the window and looked at the white world outside. Snow covered the ugliness of the tenement buildings, the back alleys and streets below. Later, he woke with a start and looked at the sleeping child beside him. "Molly," he said softly, "I think I will try for the job. It just feels right to me."

Come morning, Casper took extra care in shaving and brushed his blond hair until it lay smooth. He considered whether to wear his one dark suit he saved for Sundays and decided against it. He was going for a job requiring him to work out in the open. Being a teamster was hard dirty work.

He walked the first blocks knowing it would help release the tension he was feeling. Snow covered the sidewalks and the air had a biting chill to it when he breathed deeply. He stepped aboard the horse drawn streetcar and rode to the business district then walked the last block. The big brick building Mrs. Fuller had mentioned came into sight. He retrieved the clipping from his shirt pocket and matched the lettering to the plate on the side of the building. Walking through the door, he found himself in a wide entry hall. Stairs lead to a second story, doors opened off to the right and left of the corridor. Again he matched the letters to the newspaper clipping. Opening the door, he stepped into a world completely foreign to him.

A tall thin man neatly attired in a dark business suit and seated behind a desk glanced at him. "Is there something I can do for you," he asked in polite tones. His sharp grey eyes were quick in assessing Casper.

Casper handed him the clipping and wondered what he was doing there when he saw shelves of books and beige walls with gold framed paintings of country scenes. His gaze returned to

4

the man behind the desk. "I want to know if the job is still open," he asked. "And if it requires experience. I've never worked as a teamster. It will be better if I don't waste your time if experience is required."

Mr. Tibbs pulled out a sheet of paper and asked Casper his name, address and if he was employed. This Casper willingly supplied. The man stood. He had a long face and grey eyes that sized up a man at a glance. "Mr. Forbes is currently with a client. Will you please wait?" He indicated one of the comfortable chairs in the corner of the room. "I'll let Mr. Forbes know you are here. He is quite anxious to fill the position as soon as possible."

When Mr. Tibbs entered the room, Allen Beach looked up from the law books he was poring over. It was the first time the law student saw Mr. Tibbs display a sense of excitement.

"I'm sure we have him," Mr. Tibbs announced, handing Mr. Beach a slip of paper with a name and address. "Take this to Mr. Denton and ask him about Mr. Van Holland at once and report back. Mr. Forbes will be waiting." Mr. Denton worked on the docks and was Casper Van Holland's supervisor. It was luck the young man in the outer office was employed at one of Miss Warren's many enterprises. Mr. Tibbs knocked on the door a few feet away from the one leading into his office. He walked in and placed a slip of paper on top of Mr. Forbes desk.

Mr. Forbes excused himself from his client, "What do you think," he asked, knowing Mr. Tibbs to be a reliable judge of people.

"A little young perhaps, thirty I would say. Yes, I think he is the one," Mr. Tibbs replied. "Honest I would say."

"What makes you think that," Mr. Forbes asked intrigued to hear the answer.

"The young man admits he has no experience. Yes, very promising," Mr. Tibbs declared. "The right sort. I'd say hard working, independent with a sense of duty and knows right from wrong. Not like the other men who have shown up, he did not bluster or brag about his credentials. He works for Mr. Denton in one of Miss Warren's warehouses. I sent Mr. Beach around to inquire."

Mr. Forbes raised his eyebrows in surprise. Besides himself, he valued Mr. Tibbs' ability to judge a man's character above anyone else. In fact he had never known Mr. Tibbs to be wrong.

5

Mr. Tibbs' one fear was that Mr. Van Holland would leave before proper inquiries could be made. He observed the young man's nervousness. If Mr. Denton's report came back favorably as expected, Mr. Forbes could always find the young man again. After all, they had his name and address besides him working for Mr. Denton which would surely know how to reach him. Still it would be better to keep him waiting. With this objective in mind, Mr. Tibbs filled a coffee server with fresh coffee and placed a cup on one of the many trays they kept in the office and brought it to Mr. Van Holland.

"I thought perhaps you would like coffee while you wait," Mr. Tibbs said, placing the tray on the table in the corner of the room. "It may be some time before Mr. Forbes will be able to meet with you."

"Thank you," Casper said, taking the cup Mr. Tibbs handed him.

"There's cream and sugar if you use it," Mr. Forbes' secretary replied.

"No, the coffee is fine as it is."

Mr. Tibbs nodded his head. His task completed, he returned to work.

Forty five minutes later John Forbes ushered his client to the outer office, helped him on with his winter coat, handed him his scarf and hat, and said good day. He was anxious to meet the young man Mr. Tibbs believed to be right for the Oregon trip. Thus far he had only gotten a quick glance at him and noticed the man's freshly scrubbed clean appearance. His hair was blond, his face stern, carriage erect, broad shoulders and muscular built. An impression the man was not accustomed to idleness and waiting took effort on his part to control pent up energy.

Casper rose when Mr. Forbes approached him and extended a work harden calloused hand.

"Mr. Van Holland, I'm John Forbes." He felt the young man's appraisal and felt some of the excitement Mr. Tibbs must have felt on meeting him. Standing Casper was slightly taller than average, five foot eleven or perhaps an inch more. His eyes were pale blue and were intense from nervousness.

Casper followed Mr. Forbes into his office and continued standing after he was offered a chair. "There's something I must say first," he said, his voice level and serious. Mr. Forbes leaned back in his chair looking up at the young man. "I want you to know

6

I'm a widower. I have a small daughter and unless she can come with me, I'm not interested in the job."

Mr. Forbes nodded his head. "We can sort all this out later," he said. Mr. Van Holland waited a moment longer before taking the chair placed across from the desk. "If all I wanted was a driver for a wagon, I could hire an agency to find a man for me," he continued. "It's important I find the right man. Someone I feel I can trust to do the job and not leave as soon as the going gets tough. The trip to Oregon is not an easy journey with hardships and a good amount of danger."

Casper nodded in agreement. His brother's letters said the same thing. Not all those who started out on the journey to Oregon ended the trip. Some simply gave up and returned home while others died from accidents or were murdered by outlaws and Indians.

John Forbes had studied human nature all his adult life. In his law practice, he found knowing people immensely helpful. He believed he had developed a better then average ability to read a man's character. In this case he hoped he was correct. He did not take lightly the task set before him. Namely, the task of finding someone to chaperone his former ward and much loved adopted niece on her trip to Oregon. He considered Miss Warren his adopted niece because she was not by blood though she called him Uncle John. Mr. Warren had been his best friend and upon the man's death he was appointed Julia's guardian.

Mr. Forbes leaned back in his chair and thoughtfully observed Mr. Van Holland. He was younger then he would have liked. Thirty if that, he thought. Age did not make the man. On second thought maybe his age could be a plus. Mr. Van Holland could possibly understand Julia's youthful exuberance.

"First, I'll fill you in on the situation," Mr. Forbes began. He paused to sort through what facts he should reveal. "Normally, I would not undertake this type of venture. Miss Warren is a very special person and I would say more than just a friend. About two years ago her sister and brother-in-law returned from a European trip expounding on the advantages of living in the west and in particular Oregon Territory. Someone they had met in their travels had convinced them of the many opportunities for someone with ambition and money. Mr. Heywood is determined to make the trip."

7

"Miss Warren is very close to her sister and the time Mrs. Heywood spent in Europe was especially difficult for her. You can understand Miss Warren's dismay when she learns she was to lose her sister again. This time perhaps never to see Mrs. Heywood again."

Casper nodded his head when Mr. Forbes stopped talking. It was an interesting story Mr. Forbes was painting for him.

"The natural thing for Miss Warren to do is go with Annabel. Yet, she is having difficulty with her decision. Frankly, I did all I could to dissuade her. I don't like the idea of her being so far away," Mr. Forbes interjected. "We have talked quite a lot and when the Heywoods started making definite plans to go this spring, Miss Warren's decision was more or less made for her. She firmly states she is going. Charles wants her to travel with him and Annabel. Only Miss Warren has decided to travel independently of her sister. She has given many reasons for her decision all of which are valid. I believe it's really because she finds Mr. Heywood's company trying at the best of times."

Mr. Forbes selected a cigar from a box on his desk. He offered one to Casper. "No, thank you. I never acquired the habit."

Mr. Forbes rolled the cigar between his thumb and forefinger. "The trip will take about five months. You will be in Miss Warren's company for that amount of time. I need someone I can trust with the responsibility of seeing her safely to Oregon and someone I can trust...," he paused wondering how best to phrase what he meant.

Casper smiled, it changed his stern features. "Someone you can trust Miss Warren to without worrying about entanglements," Casper said.

"Mrs. Heywood has two daughters," Mr. Forbes said, deciding to continue without further comment on Julia's vulnerability in a man's company day after day. "I've been trying to remember their ages. Children grow up so fast. I believe Clara is six or seven. She is the oldest. Wilma is two years younger." He clipped off the end of his cigar before asking, "How old is your daughter?"

"Molly's two years old."

"That young," Mr. Forbes said. "I don't believe it will make a difference. You do understand though, Miss Warren will have the final say. I'm just her agent."

Mr. Tibbs knocked on the office door, opened it and crossed the room placing a folder on top of the desk.

"Thank you," Mr. Forbes said. He opened the folder taking time to read the first page. Then he glanced quickly through the remaining pages. "I had one of my law clerks talk to Mr. Denton. The warehouse where you work is owned by the Warren family," Mr. Forbes said, leaning back in his chair. "Like I was saying before the interruption, I'm more interested in who you are and not your experience. Why are you interested in moving to Oregon," he asked.

"I've family in Oregon," Casper stated. "A man with a baby to rise has a difficult time. He needs family to help."

As simple as that, Mr. Forbes thought. It fit in with what the report said. Mr. Van Holland was hard working, lived in a tenement in the poorer part of town, emigrant parents, no schooling, and never been in trouble with the law. Wife died during the recent influenza outbreak leaving an infant daughter. Mr. Forbes came to a decision. With three weeks left before the planned departure, Mr. Van Holland seemed his best choice, his only choice really. He wrote Miss Warren's address on a slip of paper and handed it across the desk.

"Miss Warren will expect you at 3 o'clock this afternoon. I'll send round a letter of introduction recommending you for the job. It will be her decision."

"Thank you, Sir," Casper said, standing and shaking Mr. Forbes' hand.

9

CHAPTER TWO

Julia Warren turned the long white envelope over in her hand. Picked up the letter opener, slit open the top, and slid out the single sheet of paper. It was from Uncle John informing her, he had found someone to drive her wagon. Enclosed was the name, Casper Van Holland. Mr. Van Holland would arrive at 3 o'clock for an interview. Then, she was to send her stable man, Johns, around with her answer.

Julia glanced at the clock on the mantel above the fireplace. It was just shy of two o'clock. She had an hour more to wait. Her hands were shaking as she returned the sheet of paper to the envelope and opened the folder accompanying the letter. Much as Mr. Forbes had done earlier, Julia read the first page carefully. In the margin, Uncle John's bold handwriting added: family man, wife-deceased-daughter about two years old.

For a brief moment, Julia's attention was centered on Mr. Van Holland's daughter. The child was two and already motherless. Her young heart went out to the child. Julia had lost her dear father three years earlier and her mother the year before. Julia leaned back in the chair getting a sense of comfort from the fact her father had occupied the same chair many times over the past. What would it be like to grow up never knowing a dear mother?

Julia sat thinking about her mother and feeling her loss all over again. She then squared her slender shoulders and picked up the file on Mr. Van Holland. She was not really interested in who the man was. She could rely on Uncle John's judgment of his character. Since Uncle John believed him suitable, she was comfortable with the decision. At eighteen, what did she know about men?

Mr. Forbes had written in the margins once again, no experience, no formal education. Oh dear, Julia thought. She had spent the past year earning her teacher's certificate. If Annabel and Charles did decide to move to Oregon Country, she wanted to be ready. She wanted something to occupy her time and make a difference. Besides, she did not want to be dependant on Charles Heywood or share a home with him and Annabel. It was said, teachers were needed in Oregon and Julia had settled on the profession.

She closed the folder and crossed the library opening the door. She wanted to talk with Perkins before Mr. Van Holland arrived. Martha, the cook, was always in the big well equipped kitchen and usually knew where Perkins was at any given time. Perkins was seated at the long table, where the staff took their meals, eating a late dinner.

Perkins stood when Julia entered the kitchen. "Is there something I can do for you, Miss," he asked.

Julia pulled out the chair across the table from him and slipped onto it. "Uncle John is sending a man around this afternoon. He will be here at three o'clock."

"I thought that was what his letter would be about," Perkins said calmly and resumed eating.

"Will you look him over and tell me what you think." Next to John Forbes, she trusted Perkins' judgment. Perkins studied the slender girl who carried the responsibility of the household and a large cooperation on her slender shoulders. "Uncle John says he's alright. I just want your opinion as well."

The elderly butler nodded his balding head. He was part of the Warren household long before Miss Julia was born.

"Is one of the servant rooms vacant," she asked next.

"Miss Ann's, she recently married the young baker that delivers bread on Thursdays," Perkins reminded.

Julia was happy Miss Ann was well placed and needed to replace the kitchen helper before her departure. "Have Miss Jordan ready the nursery."

"The nursery Miss?" He glanced at Martha who stopped stirring the pudding she was making for supper to stare at Julia in surprise.

"Mr. Van Holland has a daughter. I think she will be more comfortable in the nursery. And Miss Jordan will be delighted to

11

have a child once again, even for such a short time." Julia explained.

"Yes Miss," Perkins agreed. It would be nice for Miss Jordan to have a child about the place again. She was feeling the strain of young Miss Julia's departure. Weeping into her cup, he knew. Miss Julia leaving was troubling for the entire household. But Miss Jordan was taking the departure particularly hard.

"Is that all, Miss," he asked. Finished with his meal, Perkins rose to his feet.

Julia stood when he did. She wanted to complete her task of packing a crate of books before Mr. Van Holland's arrival. She said as they walked across the kitchen floor, "Tell Johns, he's to have a new helper. Mr. Van Holland has no experience with horses or wagons and Johns is to train him. Tell Johns I want to see him after Mr. Van Holland leaves."

Perkins knew John Forbes' main concern was finding a trustworthy individual. It would be Johns' duty to see he was also a reliable man with horses.

"I believe I'll have Mr. Van Holland come Thursday. He can always take time off if he needs to finish any last minute business." She was speaking calmly, yet Perkins knew it was because she had tight control over her emotions. Miss Julia was endeavoring to keep the household calm and functional until she departed. He thought what Miss Julia needed was a good cry. It always seemed to help Martha when she was experiencing difficulty.

Casper found himself on a tree lined avenue with large stately homes set far back off the street. He looked again at the address Mr. Forbes had given him to make sure he was on the right street. With resolve, he squared his shoulders and approached the wide front door. Putting his hand on the brass knocker, he summoned someone. He was ready to knock a second time when a tall erect older gentleman dressed in a dark suit and crisp white shirt opened the door. Casper felt the man's appraisal as his dark eyes surveyed him.

"Mr. Van Holland? You are expected." Perkins stepped aside so Casper could enter. Closing the door, he offered to take Casper's coat.

Casper felt uncomfortable but the memory of Molly's pale face and large blue eyes so trusting gave him strength. If he had to humble himself before these people it was for her sake. He

12

knew he could do anything necessary for his daughter's sake. He followed the gentleman down a hallway to the back of the house. Perkins tapped on a door. At the sound a soft voice asked, "Yes?"

Perkins opened the door and announced, "Mr. Van Holland, Miss."

The girl leaning over a wooden crate sat up and brushed a wisp of brown hair off her face. She was tall and slender with a fair complexion and soft blue eyes which studied Casper with grave intensity. Julia was not what he expected. No middle aged spinster with sharp disapproving eyes, smelling of lavender water and wearing stiff starched taffeta. He quickly recovered from the shock of meeting his employer. Miss Warren was calm and haughty but little more than a child. She looked boyishly trim in a simple dark blue skirt and shirtwaist wearing a white apron obviously too large for her. The apron she removed when Perkins and Casper came into the room placing it over the crate she was filling with books. "Thank you, Perkins," she said to the elderly butler.

"Come in please," Julia invited in a cool formal voice. Staring at Casper for a long moment before, she glanced at the clock on the fireplace mantel. It read two forty-five.

"I'm sorry I'm early. I don't own a watch," Casper explained. His statement brought her attention back to him. He was tall but not overly, blond and clean shaven. He carried himself erect with a sense of confidence and was wearing the usual clothing of the working class. His wool plaid shirt was tucked into dark cord pants and he wore heavy work boots. Much as Johns the stableman and his helpers wore.

She realized he was studying her as closely as she was him and silence stretched between them. This is awkward, she thought. Yet she had expected their first meeting to be awkward. Each would have reservations about the other. They were going to spend a lot of time together over the next four or five months.

Julia took a deep breath and let it out slowly. She had learned this calming technique for facing difficult situations from her mother. Her life was not always easy. It had not been easy for her mother. People expected too much from others. Especially from those who could afford to be charitable. Thinking of her mother brought a renewing calm. Julia managed a slight smile that did not reach her blue eyes. Walking to the desk, she sat in the

13

chair behind it and scooted the chair forward before picking up the folder placed on the desktop and opened it.

Casper was sure it was the same folder Mr. Forbes had read just hours before.

Julia looked up and was surprised to find Casper still standing by the door. "Please," she said and motioned to the chair across from her.

Casper moved with a grace that belied his powerful frame. But the thing about him that arrested Julia was his large pale blue eyes. Surrounded by long gold eyelashes, his eyes were beautiful. She stared for a moment unable to draw her gaze away. Embarrassed, she opened John Forbes' folder and ran one hand across the top of the page. "Mr. Forbes writes that you are honest, trustworthy and reliable. Are you," Julia asked frankly. She did not look at Casper when she spoke but continued to stare at the page in front of her.

"I try to be," Casper answered simply.

Julia looked at him. She gazed into his pale blue eyes. Her smile reaching her eyes as she realized what she had just asked. His honest answer striking her sense of humor.

"It is all we can do," she stated, under any other circumstance she would have laughed. She wondered if Mr. Van Holland realized how ridiculous the question was. If he had said yes or no she could not have believed him. He would not have been honest either way. No man is completely honest and to have said yes would have put a lie to his answer. If he had said no, he would have admitted to being dishonest.

"What is your daughter's name," Julia asked, coming back to safer ground.

"Molly," his voice held anguish.

Julia wondered if something was wrong with the child to put such pain in her father's voice. "Is your daughter ill," she asked even before she realized the thought had entered her mind.

"No," was all Casper said.

She stared at him again sure his daughter was not ill. The concern must be something else. There really was nothing more she wanted to know. She closed the folder and leaned back in the chair. "The questions are all just formality," she told him. "Mr. Forbes has the real say in who he hires. He will set your salary and make all necessary arrangements with you. I just wanted to

14

meet you and make sure I have no objections. You don't chew tobacco or use rude language?"

She watched his eyes brighten but he did not smile. "At least not in the presence of a lady," Casper answered.

So he did have a sense of humor buried under his sternness. "You are to move in here," Julia stated. "I thought perhaps Thursday should give you time to complete any business you might have." Casper was taken by surprise. He had not expected to live with his new employer and never considered just picking up and moving. "It will be simpler," she answered his unspoken question. "Mr. Forbes included a note to the effect you have no experience with horses or driving a wagon. Johns, my stableman, will be able to work with you if you're on the premises."

Casper nodded in agreement seeing the sense of her explanation. "And Molly," he asked.

"I've asked Miss Jordan to get the nursery ready. I thought she would be more comfortable there and Miss Jordan will love having a child to look after." There was warmth in her voice as she spoke of her former nanny. "Miss Jordan was my nurse. She has lamented the fact there are no children about the house." Now why had she said that, Julia wondered? "It's also important Molly and I get acquainted." Julia returned to the practical. "The first part of our journey will be by train. I'm shipping provisions and personal items and do not want any of them to go astray. That will be your responsibility. I've made arrangements for you to travel in the freight car. Naturally, I didn't know you would have your daughter with you. And a freight car is no place for a child."

Speechless, Casper nodded his head and wondered where she was going with her reasoning. "I've booked a private compartment for myself. Under the circumstance, I believe Molly will be better off with me."

Casper opened his mouth to protest. He did not want Molly left to her indifferent care. No, he could not protest. Going to Oregon was too important. Sensing his concern, Julia quickly added, "You will be needed only when the train is stopping at stations along the route. I don't see how even the railroad can misplace cargo while it is moving. And you will naturally want to see your daughter."

"Naturally," he admitted.

"Is Thursday convenient," Julia asked.

Casper was getting accustomed to her side tracks and then returning to the main subject. "Yes, Thursday is convenient."

Julia rose to signal the interview was over. "Please bring all the belongings you plan to take with you. Space is limited. And most of it needs to go toward supplies. We not only need to take a full five months worth of supplies but I'm told that supplies are often short once we get to Oregon. Supplies must come by ship around South America."

"There will be very little for me to take," Casper said, "Just clothing for me and Molly."

"If you need time to conclude business, make arrangements with Johns. He's a fair man."

Casper nodded his head before realizing she was not looking at him and said, "I will do."

Julia opened the door and stepped back so he could precede her from the room. The front hall was empty, Perkins having been called to another part of the house. She walked to the front door and placed her hand on the doorknob. She saw through the front window it was starting to snow. "Oh." The sound was soft barely more then a whisper, "you'll have a coat."

"Yes, Miss."

Perkins would have hung Mr. Van Holland's coat in the closet. She opened the closet door and selected the coat she was sure was his. It was lined with lambs fleece. The type of coat one wears if they worked outdoors. Or in Mr. Van Holland's case worked in an unheated warehouse.

"Do you have a hat?' She saw no strange hat among those on the shelf.

"It's in the pocket, Miss," Casper said.

She did not offer to help him with his coat. She returned to the door and opened it. He gave her one last nod and took a deep breath of cold winter air. It was final. He was not sure if he was relieved or worried about the decision.

Julia opened the door and called to him as he stood on the cobbled walk in front of the large mansion. "Mr. Van Holland."

Casper turned. She was framed by the door. A child with wide concerned eyes in a pale frightened face, he was to remember his impression of Julia often over the next days.

"Mr. Forbes has made an appointment for you at ten o'clock Thursday morning in his office."

"Thank you," he stated.

16

Julia closed the door against the cold, yet she felt the chill in her heart. She walked back to her father's study and after closing the door leaned against it. Tears streamed down her cheeks.

Casper thought of young Miss Warren as he walked home. He was having mixed feelings about her. She seemed cool and self assured. When she smiled her face brightened and her dark blue eyes sparkled with hidden lights. It had been as if he were talking with two different people. The cool haughty Miss Warren and occasionally a shy friendly girl would break through.

The tenement was cold as he walked up the stairs to Mrs. Fuller's second story room. He thought of the blazing fire in Miss Warren's fireplace. The room had been warm, not overly just comfortably warm so one could sit and talk. He wondered about the nursery, he was not sure what a nursery was. Concluding, it must be where children lived by what Miss Warren had said. One whole day he thought, today being Tuesday, then he would be in that large unfriendly house with Molly tucked away in what was called a nursery.

Well, it had to be done, he was not able to take Molly west on his own. He was barely able to keep things going. He did not like what he was doing, not that he was not thankful. No, he was thankful a way was provided him. Molly was so frail, so small and his heart was wrapped up in his child.

Mrs. Fuller heard his footsteps on the stairs. Knowing his firm tread, she had the door open waiting for him. Excitement shining in her faded blue eyes she said, "It is all over, a man has been here asking all kinds of questions."

The folder, Casper thought. Mr. Forbes was the kind of man who would want to know all about a man before he hired him. It was understandable knowing Miss Warren's age.

"It's settled," Casper said, relaxing on her one uncomfortable stuffed chair.

"Settled?" Mrs. Fuller looked at his handsome face. But she could not tell if he was pleased.

"We leave Thursday, Molly and me."

"Thursday," the old woman said, looking at Casper, "As soon as that?"

He leaned back and closed his eyes. Mrs. Fuller placed one finger against her lips telling Molly to let her father rest. She would see to a bite to eat, it was likely the last time she would see

17

father and daughter. She was happy for them but would miss them also. More then she liked to think, Casper always looked after her comfort fixing any little thing that needed to be looked to, stopping at the corner grocer to pick up what she needed, helping her down the stairs when she needed to go somewhere. Or just spending a quiet evening with her to chase away the loneliness they both felt.

Casper smelled pan fried potatoes and hot coffee. He had not intended to fall asleep. He had been unable to sleep much the night before. Would tonight be any better, he wondered.

"I want to fix you one last meal," Mrs. Fuller told him. "I'll be praying for you too." She assured as they ate the simple meal fixed from kindness.

"I've things to do," he said, pushing away his plate. "Thank you for the kindness you've given Molly and me. I'll drop by before I leave," he promised her. She kissed him on one clean shaven cheek. Tears were shining in her old eyes. He felt the lump in his throat as he pulled the door closed. Molly was in his arms.

In his one room apartment, Casper placed Molly on his bed giving her an assortment of spoons and pans to keep her busy. He emptied the bureau drawers stacking what he wanted to take on the kitchen table.

Casper took out a small box from the dresser drawer and held it in his hand. Hesitating, he opened the lid and looked at the small gold band. It had been his mother's wedding ring. The only thing he had that belonged to her. Mary had worn the ring for six short years. He was saving it for Molly in hopes that someday she would love someone as deeply as he loves Mary.

One by one, the tasks he had set before him were completed. Molly had long since fallen asleep and been tucked under the blankets on his bed. The room grew steadily colder. A gust of wind occasionally rattled the panes in the window. One thing he would not miss was the cold empty room. And yet he was not sure this was true. He and Jorge shared the room when they set up bachelor quarters.

He thought back over the years to those long ago happy days. He had always felt a sense of duty toward his brother. Often worrying Jorge would end up ruining his life. On more than one occasion it had been brought to his attention Jorge was straying from the straight and narrow path. Aside from this worry, times had been happy and the two brothers close.

Jorge was the first to notice the red haired, brown eyed sassy sixteen year old girl living on the ground floor of the tenement. He settled down then and rose early each morning to walk her to the corner to catch the streetcar. Mary worked in a factory in the factory district and Jorge worked with Casper in the large warehouses. The romance lasted about three months before a blond caught Jorge's attention. The blond caused Casper more than a few headaches. It was evident from the beginning she was out for a good time and Casper was not sure where the good times ended and promiscuous behavior began. He tried to caution his brother to no avail and was glad when the girl decided to move on to her next conquest.

Broken hearted Jorge returned to Mary. Who by then saw Jorge as a friend not someone to trust with her heart. It was Jorge who one day pointed out that Mary chose to walk beside Casper on their way to the streetcar. And it was the more dependable Casper who asked the then eighteen year old Mary to be his wife. They had been happy with few quarrels disturbing their happiness over the next six years.

He turned his thoughts back to the present. Molly would need a good winter coat. She so seldom went outside he had not bothered to buy her one before. They would also need a valise for their clothes. He would see to these tomorrow.

CHAPTER THREE

Thursday morning Casper had everything ready to move into the large house of his new employer. After saying goodbye to Mrs. Fuller he walked to the end of the row of tenement buildings. Molly looked up at him with wide blue eyes as she stood on the paved sidewalk waiting for the streetcar. The noisy car rumbled to a stop at the corner and Casper lifted Molly aboard then joined her. The ride across town was uneventful.

Carrying the two valises in one hand and holding onto Molly's small fist with the other, Casper walked along the cobblestones to the front door. He raised the brass knocker on the regal looking door and tapped it against the brass plate then waited for Perkins. The two newly purchased valises contained Molly's and his belongings. This was all the possessions he was taking with him.

Perkins opened the door and instructed the young man to follow him. They ascended the stairs, crossed the landing, and turned down a long hallway. Here they ascended a second flight of stairs and stopped before a closed door. Perkins knocked once before opening the door.

The room was large, sunny and airy. Casper stopped in surprise. The nursery was finished in bright colors to accommodate children. Shelves full of books and toys, a large round table with miniature chairs set in one corner of the room, a rocking horse, and other play things occupied another corner.

Miss Jordan was short, stout with bright blue eyes, and a warm welcoming smile. She spoke with a slight accent, her voice soft and cheerful. "It is a pleasure indeed. The old nursery hasn't had a wee one in it for too long a time. Not since Miss Clara and Miss Wilma stayed while their mama was in them foreign parts.

20

Now remember, you're welcome anytime you've a free minute. Wee ones need to see a face they know from time to time," she said to encourage Casper to visit often.

Molly went to the nurse. "A fine one she is. Not afraid at all. Had a rough time of it I hear. Miss Julia said how you've lost the Mrs. Hard times raising a wee one on your own. Miss Julia has a kind heart. I knew the moment I heard about Miss Molly why she hadn't been able to refuse your request. She'll love the wee one like she is her own, just you wait and see."

If Casper had trouble believing the haughty, cool Miss Warren would love Molly he did not say. The girl had been too remote. But had she been uncaring. She had asked after Molly's health.

Casper left Molly with Miss Jordan and followed Perkins to the rear of the house and down two flights of stairs to the main floor. "Miss Julia thought you might be more comfortable in the servant's wing. But if you find the accommodations unsuitable, I'll have Patty make up one of the guest rooms."

Perkins opened the door to a large room. It contained a bed and dresser, writing desk and chair, and one large overstuffed comfortable chair pulled close to a fireplace. "This is fine, thank you," Casper said, remembering the poorly furnished tenement he had just left.

"Very well, Sir." Perkins answered. "Then there's the matter of your service. Miss Julia wants you introduced to Johns our stableman. Mr. Forbes has given him instructions." Mr. Forbes had been very busy over the past days, Casper realized. "When you're ready, I'll have Young Tom take you out to the stable and introduce you."

Casper looked about the room, "I'd soon start right away, if it's convenient."

"Very good," Perkins answered with approval.

Young Tom was a lad about twelve years old. He was found in the kitchen sitting at the table eating. When Young Tom saw Perkins, he gulped down his last bite of breakfast and drained a glass of milk. "You want me, Sir," he asked.

"When you have finished your breakfast take Mr. Van Holland out to Johns," Perkins instructed. "Please tell Johns to have a carriage ready to take Mr. Van Holland down town at Ten o'clock to Mr. Forbes' office."

21

Casper followed Young Tom to the ante room off the kitchen. The lad sat on the floor pulling rubber boots on over his work shoes. "Better put on a pair of rubbers," he advised Casper, "pick any that'll fit. Mrs. Williams, the housekeeper, she don't like for us to track muck in from the yard," the lad went on to explain as Casper tried on rubber boots. "You'll like it here. Johns a grand chap. He doesn't take any nonsense though, but you don't seem the kind. Perkins, he's fine too. Only a little stiff if you know what I mean."

Casper nodded his head.

"And Martha, she'll mother you like you was her own. But she doesn't take any sass. The two girls," he went on indicating the kitchen maids. "I'd watch out for them. You're a nice looking chap and Perkins, he won't stand for any fooling around. If you know what I mean."

Casper smiled to himself. The lad was giving him the lay out of the household. He had noticed one of the kitchen maids flirting with him and so had Young Tom. They walked across the wide lawn on a path shoveled free of snow to a brick paved drive. Beyond was a carriage house and beyond the house were stables.

Johns was a spry man, with graying red hair and lively green eyes. He expected Mr. Van Holland and greeted him in an easy manner that had Casper feeling at ease. Their talk centered round horses and he soon had Casper sized up without seeming to do so. Knowing the young man's strengths and weakness, and knew Casper preferred walking to riding the streetcar.

"Enough for today," Johns soon said. "We'll take out the wagon tomorrow and see what you need to learn. Then we'll work on some horse sense," he laughed at his pun.

At ten o'clock Casper arrived at Mr. Forbes' office. Mr. Tibbs was behind his desk poring over a stack of papers. He rose and crossed to Mr. Forbes' office door, saying, "He is expecting you."

The lawyer greeted him by saying, "I was sure Miss Warren would find you acceptable. I've had a devil of a time though. Let's get done first things first." He named a monthly salary twice what Casper was currently making which was more generous than Casper expected. "Sounds like a lot," Mr. Forbes continued as if reading the young man's mind. "Not really considering you are taking on a twenty four hour, seven days a week job. I understand driving a wagon can be tedious grueling work. And of coarse Miss Warren's safety and her comfort will also be your responsibility." Mr. Forbes paused opening the top drawer of his desk. "Under the circumstance, you are to be paid a full six months salary in advance." Saying this he brought out a sack of gold pieces, counted the coins, and handed the sack to Casper.

"Miss Warren wants it done this way," he continued. "If she can't trust you to do the job once you're paid, she would rather know about it before leaving on her journey."

Casper placed the sack of gold pieces in one coat pocket.

"Next," Mr. Forbes said, "is between you and me. Miss Warren is not to know about our deal." Casper waited for him to continue before agreeing. "It's the matter of Miss Warren's safety." He counted out a stack of gold coins and handed them across the desk to Casper. Then he leaned back in his chair studying the young man. "I have an acquaintance wintering here with his brother. He spends most of his time out west." Saying this Mr. Forbes walked across his office to the door leading into the back room. He spoke to someone.

A tall broad shouldered, lean hipped man entered the office. His black hair was graying at the temples, darkly tanned skin was like leather, and a ragged scar followed one jaw line.

"This is the young man I told you about," Mr. Forbes said to the stranger. "Mr. Arlen, I would like you to meet Mr. Van Holland."

Casper stood when the man entered the room and extended his hand to Mr. Arlen. "Glad to meet you, young feller," Mr. Arlen greeted in a friendly fashion. Casper returned his greeting and they stood sizing each other up. "So you're going to be escorting Miss Julia out west," he stated. "Miss Julia is a mighty fine woman."

"I've asked Mr. Arlen to instruct you in the use of firearms." Mr. Forbes told Casper. "Like I said Miss Warren's safety is my concern."

"West can be mighty dangerous, son." Mr. Arlen said seriously. "If the Indians don't scalp you, the wolves and bears will tear you to threads, or the sun will bake you dry to the bone, and a blizzard will freeze you stiff. And all in the same day." He winked at Mr. Forbes grinning broadly. "Truth is you can't trust a man, even if you've known him all your life and that's a fact. Ain't no such thing as honor and mores the pity." He looked Casper over in a way that had color rising in his face. "I don't mean no offense,"

23

he told Casper. "You look like a fine feller, maybe that's what got me concerned the most." The man spoke plainly. "Just want to see your strong points. Kinda like a horse, a man has got his good and his bad points. Mr. Forbes says he believes you're honest, that's a mighty good point. But if you are skittish about killing that can sure go against you. Often the only thing in the stew pot is what you put there with a gun."

Casper said he understood city life was a lot different than life on the frontier. "I can't give you an answer," he admitted, "I've never had to kill beast nor man."

"There's killing and then there's killing," Mr. Arlen said. "Killing for grub is one thing but them that kill just for sport," the man shook his head sadly, letting Casper know he did not approve of such. "Anyhow, Mr. Heywood's a crack shot and a mighty fine hunter, you might not have a need. Just the same it won't hurt none for you to know a thing or two about using a pistol and rifle. You never know when those red devils are on the prod, neither," he finished thoughtfully.

Mr. Arlen addressed Mr. Forbes, "Are you finished with this young feller?"

After saying yes, Mr. Forbes added, "I will see you before you leave. Did Miss Warren tell you the departure date is in three weeks? Not a lot of time." He shook Casper's hand.

"Well, if you're going with me, we best be a going." Mr. Arlen shook Mr. Forbes' hand, "I'll do my best by the boy and I'll guarantee it. I ain't likely to be seeing you again before I head out. Soon as I'm satisfied this young feller can handle himself. I'm going back to Texas. I've had enough of city life. Don't reckon I'll be heading back this way again. City life ain't for me, no siree."

"Thank you," Mr. Forbes replied.

"Tarnation. I had my feet under Miss Warren's table many times when her pa was alive. Mr. Warren was a right nice feller. I know Brother Henry thought a lot of Mrs. Warren and I'm mighty glad to be able to help. Mind you, I don't know much about young Miss Warren. But the older gal, she's a crack shot. She's almost as good as her ole man. Yes, sir." He rubbed his chin with his forefinger. "I'm going."

He paused looking at Mr. Van Holland. "Well, come along young feller. Mr. Forbes done told me what he wants done." He was inching his way into the outer office. "It's one thing to get a man in your sights and another to pull the trigger," he looked around as if trying to decide what to do next. "Well, I'm going." This time he walked across the office, flung open the outer door, and with heavy treads strode into the morning sunshine. Casper followed Mr. Arlen out of the office. He stood on the sidewalk looking perplexed when Casper joined him.

"Tarnation," he said. "I sure wish I had me a saddle horse." He got into the waiting carriage and settled back against the leather upholstery. "Well, get in and settle yourself," he invited.

All the way across town and out into the countryside, Mr. Arlen expounded on the greatness of the west. Casper believed most was exaggerations, but Mr. Arlen had a way of telling a story including gory details. They arrived at a large country house, rode past the stable and outbuildings to a house located back a ways from everything.

The driver stopped the carriage at the backdoor of the house, "will that be all, Sir," he asked Mr. Arlen.

"Will take, say a couple of hours today," he told the man. "See if you can return around two."

Casper followed Mr. Arlen into the house. The whole back wall was glass windows looking out on a wooded area. The end wall was stone with a wide fireplace set in the middle. The two remaining walls were covered with hunting trophies. "Brother Henry is a member of the local Hunt Club. He's even been on safari to Africa." Indicating the stuffed animal heads along the walls. "Me, I don't go in for killing for trophies." Saying this he dropped the subject.

"Mr. Forbes didn't say how much you know. So I figure we'll start with the basics. A man's gun can save his life as well as put food in the pot. The first thing a feller needs to know is how to care for his weapons." The next hour, Casper spent getting hands on experience with a Winchester Rifle. Taking it apart and putting it back together. Cleaning, oiling and polishing the weapon. Then, he went through the same routine with a revolver. The time was punctuated with Mr. Arlen's grisly tales of Indian raids, border ruffians, and shootouts with outlaws.

"Been from south Texas north to the Canadian border," Mr. Arlen told Casper. "Rode through snow so thick I couldn't see my hand in front of my face." He scratched his chin. "One time I came across a grizzly bear. I was so hungry I skinned him and ate him raw." He laughed joyously. "Yes sir. This city life sure ain't for me. Promised Brother Henry I'd give it a try. I sure don't cotton to it, no siree. I'm heading back. I'm going to spend my last days as far away from a city as I can get."

When the carriage pulled to a halt before the backdoor, Mr. Arlen said he would see Mr. Van Holland the next day just after the noon hour. "Tell your driver Henry Arlen's place and have him drive you around back here."

The Warren house seemed friendlier when he returned in the Arlen's carriage. Maybe because he knew Molly was waiting inside? His daughter greeted him with her usual out stretched arms wanting him to lift her above his head in the familiar manner. Miss Jordan sat in a rocking chair and watched as Molly showed her father all the toys she had played with while he was away. The child rarely talked and used gestures instead of words.

The young man cuddled his child as she lay sleeping in his arms. Secure in the knowledge he was there with her. Miss Jordan asked after the things Molly usually ate, saying it was best not to change the child's food too much and then showed Casper where to lay Molly down for her nap. The bed was in an alcove off the playroom. The quilt was turned back so he could place her on the bed. He tucked her under the quilt kissing her rosy cheek. The room was warm but Casper knew he would still check on his daughter during the night just as he always did.

The evening meal was a jolly time. The men all trooped into the kitchen and took their places around the white scrubbed table. The young maids loaded the table with bowls and platters of food. Each man filled his plate as the bowls passed before him. In all there were Johns and two stable boys along with Young Tom, which Casper later learned worked in the house. A Gardener and his helper joined them.

Casper listened to the conversation, Johns was concerned about a mare which was soon to foal. The Gardener told of the new spring bulbs that were starting to appear through the ground and worried the snow might hang on to long and damage the new growth. McInroy, one of the stable boys, told Young Tom about the kittens the tabby cat had in the feed trough. The talk was all new and interesting to Casper. He soon realized it was more like a family gathering than employees sitting around the table jawing as they ate.

26

CHAPTER FOUR

A warm wind blew from the west. A bright sun overhead gave off warmth on a late winter day. The last snow was slushy under feet and robins were seen hopping along the ground or flying from tree limb to tree limb.

"Best thing about Sundays," McInroy, the stable boy, said to no one in particular, "Is Martha's fried chicken." He was still young enough to think often about his stomach. He turned to Casper and declared, "Every Sunday we have fried chicken for dinner." The way the young man said the words made Casper wonder what was significant about having chicken for dinner. "Sunday has got to be the best day of the week," the youth continued soulfully.

"I reckon I like fried chicken just the same as you. Along with thick slices of Martha's yeast bread with butter and jam spread over top," Young Tom agreed.

"I hope we have strawberry jam today," Jones, the gardener's helper, said joining in the conversation. "I like it better then grape jelly. We always seem to have grape jelly on Sundays."

Peters, the oldest of the lads, shook his head at Jones' foolishness. "If you want strawberry jam all you need do is ask for it," he reminded.

"I don't feel right asking," Jones answered, frowning at the older lad. "They never let us ask for nothing at the orphanage."

"I reckon we do have it easy," Peters agreed. "Miss Warren, she doesn't demand too much from us as long as we do the best we can. Not like some places I've worked." Peters was not from the orphanage but had heard enough tales to sympathize. Miss Warren was partial to taking in orphans and training them the way Martha calls proper. Miss Warren's mother had been the same.

"That's a fact," Jones agreed. "Only, I don't want to go back to that place. Reckon I'll have to with Miss Warren leaving us?"

"Naw," Young Tom answered, "Ain't there Mr. Stanford."

"He will go back to that University place and learn some more," Jones declared gloomily.

Casper noticed the lads all fell silent not wanting to look at him. Their earlier comradeship replaced by thoughts of Miss Warren leaving and what it would mean for each of them. "Who is Mr. Stanford," Casper asked.

The young lads were lazing away the morning in the back yard. Flowerbeds had green shoots coming through the ground. Peters lay on a concrete garden bench. Young Tom from the house lay on the cobbled walk with his hands behind his head. Jones and McInroy were seated on stone pillars which would soon have baskets of flowers placed on them, and Casper sat on the edge of a stone fountain. Miss Warren's backyard intrigued him. Growing up in a ghetto, he had never seen a backyard only cluttered back lots full of trash and waste.

"Mr. Stanford is Miss Warren's cousin," Peters replied. "His folks died some time in the past and he lives here when he ain't away at University studying. When Miss Warren leaves it will be Mr. Stanford living here. I overheard Perkins say he's getting married in the fall and there will be a new Mistress running the place. It won't be the same around here without Miss Warren," he ended gloomily.

"I ain't heard a thing about us all leaving," Young Tom said. Working in the house, he kept abreast of the gossip. "You'd think Perkins would tell us if we weren't going to be needed or the new Mrs. Stanford has plans to replace us." But he didn't sound too sure of himself.

"I have a mother and the young ones to think about," Peters said. They all nodded their heads knowing Peters supported his mother and sisters.

"Ain't going to be the same anyways," Jones retorted. "It was Miss Warren who made me stay in bed when I had a nasty cough. She brought me warm broth and soothed my head with a cool cloth when it hurt." He hung his head sadly. "It ain't going to be the same even if we do stay."

28

"Well, it can't be helped," Peters said, straightening his youthful shoulders, "she is going to this here Oregon Country and that's that."

They all mumbled in agreement.

Casper knew the lads were all down in spirit because they were not sure what would become of them once Miss Warren left. He would talk with Miss Warren. The lads needed to know one way or the other and be prepared for their future.

They came into the ante room together, unwrapped scarves from around their necks, pulled off gloves and heavy winter coats. They took turns washing up at the sink with more than a little shoving and laughter trying to appear jolly amid despair. Casper stood and watched recalling earlier days with his brother Jorge.

Miss Warren, a white apron wrapped around her dress to protect from spills, was pouring tall glasses of foamy milk. The lads each took one and found their usual place at the table. Miss Jordan sat at the end with Molly on her lap. Casper took the chair next to her and reached for his daughter.

Platters piled high with crispy fried chicken were placed at intervals along the table. Miss Warren helped Nellie, the kitchen maid, place baskets of bread and jars of jam along with bowls of butter on the table. Next came, dishes containing pickled cucumbers, Brussels sprouts and beets. Gladys, the second kitchen maid, brought bowls of mashed potatoes from the stove's warmer and placed the bowls along the table.

Peters looked at the jars of grape jelly, rose and returned from the pantry with a jar of strawberry jam placing the jar in front of Jones. Jones grinned happily from ear to ear. Martha came bustling into the kitchen with her face flushed. "Sorry I'm late," she announced before looking at the loaded table.

"We managed," Julia assured her.

"Miss Driscoll came by wanting to know about the get together next week. She talked on and on," Martha said, wrapping a large apron over her Sunday dress. "No coffee," she asked.

"I knew you wouldn't want me to make it." Julia explained. She stood next to the table to see if anything was missing. Casper listened to her soft musical voice. It was the voice of the shy friendly girl.

"You're right," Martha agreed with a smile.

Julia laughed and leaned over Casper's shoulder to place a dish of pickles in front of him. Chairs were carried in from the dining room and everyone slid closer together to make room. Two young house maids and Nellie and Gladys, the kitchen helpers, were seated at the far end of the table. A tall dark haired young man came in, put his arm about Miss Warren's shoulders, and leaning over kissed her on the forehead.

"You didn't think you were going to get away with keeping me out of this festive party, did you," he asked. "Buck-up," he said with a grin displayed on his fine young face. His eyes were dark blue and his features were on the line of Miss Warren's. Casper was sure he was looking at Mr. Stanford, the university student home due to illness. He found himself listening to Miss Warren's soft voice gentle with laughter.

Each one bowed his head thanking God for his bounty before tucking into dinner. Soon the smell of coffee brewing filled the kitchen along with talk and the larking of the lads as they sat around the table. It was an informal meal with the entire household joining in. Miss Warren served as often as the kitchen helpers, refilling coffee cups and bringing more food to the table as it was needed.

Molly leaned against her father's shoulder, asleep long before the meal was over. Egg custards were passed out with strong cups of coffee. When Miss Jordan rose, Casper joined her carrying the sleeping child. The young lads all looked at him with a new respect in their eyes observing for the first time his devotion to his young daughter.

Late in the afternoon, Casper asked Perkins if he could speak with Miss Warren for a few minutes. Perkins said Miss Julia was in the conservatory and if Casper would follow him, he would show the way. The room was light and airy with a fountain tinkling and ferns and palm trees growing in ceramic pots. Pretty flowering plants bloomed even in the cold of winter.

Miss Warren was seated in a white painted chair with bright orange cushions. She looked up when she heard footsteps. It was the cool, calm and haughty Miss Warren that looked at him. Casper was not sure he could confess to this remote young woman. When he did not speak right away, she asked, "Is there a problem?"

"Yes, no, in a way," he said. "It's about the lads."

These words caught Julia's attention. She closed the book she was reading and leaned forward on her chair. She was interested in anything that had to do with the smooth running of her household. "Please, sit down." She invited indicating one of several chairs.

"The lads are concerned about their jobs," Casper began. "Young Jones wonders if he is going back to the orphanage. I know it's none my business but the lads are worried and I thought you might want to know."

"I should have realized," Julia said, her dark blue eyes turning nearly black. She rose from her chair placing the book on the cushion. Casper rose to his feet when she did. "I will have a talk with each one," she said. "I will go and see Jones right away." She did not want the boy to fear he would return to the orphanage.

"Thank you," she said sincerely, her mind not really on Casper as they walked to the kitchen together. She asked Martha if she had seen Jones.

"I believe he is in his room, Miss," Martha replied.

Casper returned to the stable and pulled open the door. The stable smelled of fresh hay and horses. He was told Peters went home for the afternoon. The lad visited his mother every Sunday. McInroy played with the batch of new kittens. They were little more then balls of fur, their eyes still closed, and their mouths and noses bright pink. The youth sat crosslegged on the stable floor ruffling the fur of the tabby cat that purred and rubbed against his leg.

"I've been to see Miss Warren," Casper stated. Young McInroy looked at him with concern on his youthful face. "She promises you will keep your jobs. She is going to tell you later. She is with Jones now."

"For sure," McInroy asked.

"It's what she said." Casper answered. "Mr. Stanford is not going back to University but will be taking over the businesses and living here. She says nothing will change."

"If she said it, she means it. That'll be a load off Peters' mind. He is concerned about his family and all. Me," the lad stopped and turned dark red. "Guess the truth is, I was concerned too. I don't have a family. Miss Warren brought me from the orphanage. I didn't like it there and probably would have run away by now. I don't know what would have become of me. But Miss Warren, she came and looked us lads over and picked me." You

31

could hear the wonder in McInroy's voice as if being picked was the greatest thing to ever happen to him. "Right then, she brought me home and gave me this job with Johns. Told me I'd be able to someday make a way for myself if I worked hard and followed Johns' orders. But gee, it weren't hard. Johns is a swell guy and treated me fair right from the start. And Martha," he said his eyes beaming, "Martha's better than having a mother." After his outburst, he cleared his throat, "Young Tom and Jones are orphans too. I guess we're sure lucky. Miss Warren doesn't like us to say lucky," he corrected. "She says it's the will of God that we are brought here to live. And we're to grow into fine young men who will love him for what he's done for us."

Casper nodded his head in approval. "She's right," was all he said.

McInroy smiled cuddling a kitten in his hand. "Jones, he doesn't like kittens much. Says they're a nuisance. I reckon it's because they dig in the garden. I like working with horses a lot better," he continued. Then thought for a moment before adding, "Reckon if Miss Warren asked me too, I'd dig in the dirt just to make her happy."

Johns walked up while they were admiring the kittens. "So Queen has had her batch," he said, lifting one kitten in his big work calloused hand. "Going to be cold tonight," he told McInroy. "Put some extra straw in the trough for Queen and her kittens. And you might bring some scraps of meat out from the kitchen for the next few days to keep her from having to leave the kittens while she hunts. Ask Martha."

"Yes Sir."

Casper realized Johns not only loved horses but had concern for all God's creatures.

* * * * *

From early morning until noon each day, Casper worked with Johns. Soon concluding there was little the man did not know about horses. He worked alongside the lads, grooming and currying the animals. Learnt to mend harness, repair breaks and the best way to stitch for the strongest hold. He learned to maintain a wagon, greasing axles, fixing a single tree and reinforce wheel rims. He went for long drives in the countryside returning sore and stiff. His dinner, he took in the common room then spent a few minutes with Molly.

Afternoons he spent with Mr. Arlen, the first few days learning to fire a rifle and revolver accurately. He went hunting and learned to clean his kill. Learning all he could in the short time allotted him. Mr. Arlen was anxious to leave what he called civilization. Casper was given the use of a carriage which made it convenient to visit the Arlen Estate. Upon returning each afternoon, he attended the horses and checked over the carriage. He knew after the short distance he drove to visit Mr. Arlen, it was not necessary to check the carriage and grease the axles but his goal was to develop a habit. Once on the trail he would need to be vigilant.

After the nightly meal, Casper spent the rest of the evening with Molly. His daughter's health was improving under Miss Jordan's kindly care. He could already see a difference in her thin face and arms. Miss Jordan was faithful to take Molly outside each day for a short romp in the fresh air. Along with nurturing meals Molly was growing.

He had not seen Miss Warren since Sunday. But knew she too was busy preparing for their trip to Oregon Country. The ante room off the kitchen was filling with crates and barrels.

Sunday afternoon Casper took Molly to visit Mrs. Fuller. The woman was excited when she greeted them and happy Casper remembered her. He stayed late into the evening not wanting to cut short his last visit with his dear friend. He told about the Warren household. Mrs. Fuller nodding her head as if she could see it all from his detailed description. When he got ready to leave, he hugged the old woman presenting her with a package.

"Now, what can this be," she asked, her faded eyes tearing.

"I remember you once said if you had only one wish to come true." Casper did not need to complete what he was about to say. She hugged him with tears spilling from her eyes and running down her cheeks.

"You don't mean," she asked. He smiled at her, the first real smile she had seen on his lips in a long time. With trembling fingers she removed the wrapping paper and pulled out the black leather book with gold lettering. "Oh my," she whispered, "ain't it pretty." Casper watched the way she held it tenderly pressing the book to her breasts. "Each time I read it, I will think of you," she said. "To think, I've wanted one my entire adult life. My own book of God's words." Mrs. Fuller was so overcome with emotions Casper was afraid to leave her. "You don't know what it means," she said through her sobs of joy.

"I reckon I do," he assured her.

"You're a good boy," she said, drying away her tears. "I won't be lonesome now."

Casper smiled and kissed her paper thin cheek. "I reckon I know about being lonesome."

CHAPTER FIVE

It was one of those beautiful spring days that appeared in late winter. The weather turned surprisingly warm and the snow of the previous days quickly melted. Julia dressed in a dark brown suit, wearing a severe hat to cover a crown of neat braids, entered the stable yard. Casper was with Peters. She crossed to where they were working. One of the draft horses had somehow cut his hind leg. Peters was helping Casper clean the wound in preparation to apply a stringent.

The horse was side stepping straining against its hobbles. Peters shouldered his weight against the animal's flank to bring the horse back to where Casper could apply the salve. Julia waited until he had the animal back under control. Peters wiped his forehead with a clean handkerchief still breathing hard from his exertion.

"Are you ready, lad?" Casper asked not seeing Julia from where he was standing. "All hell will break loose when I apply a layer of salve so be prepared."

Julia looked at Peters whose face burnt a bright red. He choked on what he was about to say, coughing and gasping for air. The horse lunged forward and twisted as it kicked back. Casper jumped as the horse's buck nearly knocked him down.

"What the…" adding a few colorful imperatives, Casper gripped the horse's halter stretching the animal out until he was unable to maneuver. The horse tried kicking again. "Peters?" He started to say more then stood stock still. He was gazing at Miss Warren's shocked face. Her blue eyes were wide and her cheeks flushed. Peters was looking at the ground his face burning hot. He coughed trying to bring his breathing under control.

"Sorry Miss," Casper's voice was regretful, his face too burnt from a flush of heat. He tried to remember just what he had said. He only knew it had not been acceptable for the ears of Miss Warren. "Is there something I can do for you," he asked. He could only brave it through. He had apologized there was nothing more to be said.

"Would you tell Johns to have the closed carriage ready in fifteen minutes, please?" She was trying to bring order to her chaotic senses. She had heard the words before only somehow they seemed different the way Casper said them. She witnessed his embarrassment and heard his quick apology and the regret in his voice.

After Julia left, Casper raked fingers through his hair, shook his head as if to clear it. "Miss Warren was here the whole time," he asked.

"Yes Sir," Peters said.

"Well, there's nothing I can do about it now," he said with finality.

"Miss Warren is going to the orphanage," Peters volunteered. "She always takes the closed carriage when she goes to the orphanage," He watched as Miss Warren walked out of sight. "And she always wears that plain brown suit."

Casper watched Peters and saw a mixture of emotions crossing his fine young features. "It ain't a fit place for a lady like Miss Warren to visit," he muttered.

"Where's Johns?" Casper asked.

"He's with McInroy. He said earlier he believes the mare will foal today."

"Show me which carriage and which team of horses. I'll get them ready while you find Johns." Peters nodded his head bringing his attention back to the task at hand.

Casper had the carriage ready and waiting at the side entrance to the kitchen when Johns arrived. "It will be some hours before the mare will foal," Johns said gruffly. "Peters and McInroy can handle things until I get back."

Miss Warren did not look at Casper when she approached the carriage. "I want you to come, Mr. Van Holland," she stated.

"Yes Miss," he answered. He opened the carriage door and helped Julia inside by taking hold of her elbow.

"You might as well drive," Johns said when Casper joined him on the seat. Casper picked up the reins and called to the team. Johns gave him directions and soon they were in the poorer section of the city. The streets were dirty, the houses poorly kept, and the smell of soot and garbage hung in the air.

The orphanage was located in the part of the city where Casper had grown up. It was a rambling three story building in need of repair. Paint was peeling and the tall windows shuttered so no one could see inside. The yard was full of children getting a few hours of sunlight and warmth. The children if not dirty, were not clean.

Casper jumped down, opened the carriage door and helped Julia as she stepped into the sunlight. "I want you to come with me," she said. Julia turned to him holding out her hand. He could see it was shaking. He was not sure what she wanted or expected of him. She laid her hand lightly on his arm when he stepped beside her. She opened the gate to the fenced in yard then turned to close and secure it behind her.

The children all stopped in their various tasks to watch the young woman in her neat brown suit and the tall man with her. The young woman they knew, she was one of the ladies that came to the orphanage to select children to take into her home. Each secretly hoped to be one of the children she chose. Miss Myers told them she loved the children she took home. Some wondered what the word love meant. Only knowing it must be something special because of the look on Miss Myers face when she told them.

Miss Warren did not look at the children. She kept her eyes straight ahead as if she did not know they were there.

Miss Myers, a short wry looking spinster with salt and pepper hair and a sad face, greeted Julia. "Good day Miss Warren," she said in a formal voice, "You've come for another child? Do you what a boy or a girl this time?"

Miss Warren stopped and addressed the woman in a tight controlled voice. "A girl. I need to replace Miss Ann. She has made a suitable marriage. I want a kitchen helper."

"Aye, your dear father chose Miss Ann. I remember the day well. Married, you say and to a suitable young man. I do hope she will be properly taken care of."

"There's no question on that account, Miss Ann was supplied with ample dowry for her years of satisfactory service."

"Aye, I hear you are generous to your young people. Most admirable that is," Miss Myers went on to say.

37

Miss Warren did not reply to the comment, only nodded her head respectfully. They entered the large rambling house through the front door. The entry hall was wide and dimly lit. A staircase on the left lead to an upper floor, to the right was a large room where chairs were placed. A fire burnt in the wide fireplace. A desk stood in one corner positioned where the light from the tall windows fell across it.

The room was empty.

"I'll inform Miss Wayne you are here," Miss Myers said, escorting them into the room.

Miss Warren did not sit on one of the wooden straight back chairs but stood before the open fire as if she was cold. "Thank you," she told Miss Myers in a cool voice. Her chin tilted at an angle added to Julia's look of haughtiness.

It was a few minutes before a pinched face sour looking Miss Wayne joined them. She studied the tall blond man wondering if Miss Warren was making a match. The thought of the young woman finding happiness added to her own discontent. Bitterness welled up inside of Miss Wayne at the unfairness of life. Miss Warren had everything she did not, a fine standing in the community, wealth, poise, a beautiful speaking voice and real beauty of face and character. Miss Wayne resented the happiness of others even though she felt beyond such foolishness.

Miss Wayne spoke abruptly, her voice high and nasal. "Miss Myers informed me you are interested in a kitchen helper."

"Yes." Miss Warren did not add any details but clamped her jaws together.

"You usually prefer a girl of Twelve to fourteen. We have several strong willing girls."

Miss Warren did not reply. She waited unbuttoning her cotton gloves then pulled them off revealing well cared for hands with long slender fingers.

Miss Myers escorted in a dozen-plus girls in single file. The children knew the routine. They turned to face Miss Wayne, stood erect with hands at their side, and eyes forward. Casper could feel their excitement though they strived to conceal it. He watched as Miss Wayne's lips tightened, a cynical look came into her eyes as she checked over the appearance of each girl. She made sure they obeyed her every instruction. Then her eyes narrowed in a flash of hate, her lips curling back against her teeth. He saw Miss Myers move to stand behind a frail looking child with a pretty pixie face and large dark eyes. The child's dark hair tended to curl about her small face. It was this child that incurred Miss Wayne's hatred.

Miss Warren walked to the first girl, asked her name and her age before continuing to the next girl. She paused as if considering the suitability of the girl before asking the same questions. Her task completed, she stood facing Miss Wayne with her back to the assembly of girls. In a soft pleasant voice Julia told Miss Wayne which girl she had chosen, "Jenny," she said pleasantly.

"Jenny? Oh, surely not. I don't believe she will be suitable," Miss Wayne protested. Color rushed into her pale cheeks and her eyes blazed.

"I have decided on Jenny," Miss Warren said with finality.

Miss Wayne was indignant as she continued to point out Jenny was much too small and frail to be of any use around the kitchen.

Miss Warren turned to Casper, "stay with Jenny and see she has all of her belongings." He noticed her firm 'stay'. Miss Warren was not requesting but commanding. He nodded his head without speaking. There was something in Miss Warren's words he did not comprehend but he would do what was requested.

The other girls walked from the room leaving the frail looking child behind. She nervously shifted her feet looking at him with fear. Her dark eyes searched for Miss Myers.

"If you will follow me, we'll get Jenny ready to leave," Miss Myers said with satisfaction in her voice. Casper was sure she had wanted Miss Warren to take Jenny. Then, he wondered if Miss Myers standing behind the child was to signal Miss Warren her wishes.

Jenny was trembling. He laid a hand on her shoulder giving her an encouraging look. His eyes smiling, assuring her everything was alright. Miss Myers noticed the exchange, thinking what a fine man he was to take pity on the frightened girl.

The room on the second floor was large with rows of iron bedsteads along the walls. Jenny went to the one she occupied for the last two years. Since the time, she was moved into the dormitory for older girls. Before, she had lived in the room with the younger girls and before that the room with the babies. Jenny had been days old when she was left on the orphanage's front steps.

39

Jenny knelt down and pulled a box from under her bed. It contained all her earthly possessions, a nightgown, comb and a change of under clothing. It was apparent Jenny's only dress was the dull gray one she wore.

Miss Myers spread a square of fabric on the bed which the girl used to bundle her belongings. Casper stood at the foot of the bed and watched while Jenny did up her belongings. He noticed two bruises on the girl's arm and another discoloration on her cheek and wondered if they were the reason Miss Warren had chosen the child.

Miss Warren waited at the bottom of the stairs. Miss Wayne's high pitched nasal voice sounded strident. "You can not truly desire to bring a child like Jenny into a good Christian home. What would your father think or your sainted mother. I believe it is my duty to forbid it."

Casper took Jenny's hand stepping between Miss Wayne and the child. The light of battle was in his blue eyes and his jaws held rigid.

"There will be a generous donation made to the orphanage. I'll see to it myself," Julia told the headmistress, who looked coldly on the child. Julia knew the thought of a sizable donation would prevent any further outburst on the part of Miss Wayne. And she was correct. The woman clamped her thin lips tightly together to prevent any further protest from escaping. Her eyes hot with feeling.

Casper helped Miss Warren into the waiting carriage, picked up Jenny by lifting the child with his hands under her arms and placed the girl inside the carriage. The girl was as light as a feather, much to light he thought.

He took his place beside Johns. "I see you met Miss Wayne," the man said at the look on Casper's face.

"Aye," Casper replied and let it go at that.

Casper had expected to see Jenny at supper. He wanted to know the child was alright. But the girl was not among those who assembled around the kitchen table. Only Nellie and Gladys were in the kitchen helping Martha.

It was not until he came into the kitchen the following afternoon that he saw Jenny. She was dressed in a new light green cotton dress and wore a white apron. Her hair had been washed and fixed into a short braid down her back. The girl looked clean and as shiny as a new copper penny. Casper nodded at her, his features brightening at her appearance. He poured coffee and took his place at the kitchen table.

McInroy came from the pantry with a pitcher of milk in one hand and his other hand holding the tail of his shirt. He grinned at Casper before placing the pitcher of milk on the table. Three apples rolled out of his shirttail. Then, he fetched two glasses pouring milk into each glass.

Jenny carried the coffeepot across the kitchen and refilled Casper's cup spilling coffee on the table. Her eyes were wide with fear as she gazed at him.

"It's alright Jenny," he assured her. He brought a cloth from the sink and wiped up the spill while she looked on with fear in her dark eyes. "Why don't you put the coffeepot back on the stove and join us," Casper said.

"Sit," McInroy told her less formally.

She obeyed his command then gazed at Martha with questioning eyes.

McInroy moved a glass of milk and an apple in front of Jenny. She looked at them in surprise. Were they really for her?

Casper picked up the apple the lad had passed to him and took a bite. He really was not hungry but figured Jenny would be more comfortable if he ate. She watched until he had finished his apple and McInroy was halfway through his and on his second glass of milk. Casper wondered if McInroy ever really got full. Jenny picked up her apple and took her first bite. She wiggled from side to side as she ate with her eyes downcast.

McInroy got up and walked to the pantry. He brought three more apples and placed one before Jenny. Another he tossed to Casper who set it on the table in front of him. "My name's Sean McInroy. This here is Mr. Van Holland, he's Miss Warren's special driver." It was the first time Casper heard he was Miss Warren's special driver. So this is what the household called him.

"What's your name," the lad asked.

"Jenny," she answered shyly.

"Jenny what," McInroy wanted to know.

"Just Jenny, because I ain't never had no father," the girl answered.

"Sure you...," he stopped when Casper signaled by shaking his head no. McInroy scratched his head thoughtfully but said no more.

41

Nellie came in from the servant's quarters and sat down across from Jenny. Casper passed her his unwanted apple. She smiled shyly thanking him.

"Miss Wayne," Jenny spoke to no one in particular, "she told me not to come downstairs saying Miss Warren wouldn't want no clumsy girl like me."

"Ah, she told us all the same thing," McInroy informed her dismissively.

"She did," Jenny asked, looking doubtful.

"Yes," Nellie said, "Miss Wayne said Mr. Warren wouldn't want an ugly child like me in his home." Nellie was a plain looking girl but was not ugly. Nellie finished her apple then reached to take Jenny's hand. "It's nearly time to start supper. I'll show you what to do."

Jenny drank the last of her milk, looked at the apple on the table in front of her, and after picking it up put the apple inside the pocket on her apron. After all, McInroy gave it to her so she supposed it belonged to her.

Casper finished his coffee and carried the cup to the sink. McInroy followed him carrying the two glasses. Jenny watched in horror, she had forgotten to put the dishes away. Yet, no one seemed to notice. McInroy gave her a lopsided grin as he followed Mr. Van Holland to the stairs leading to the upper floors. The youth took the steps two at a time.

"Why'd you stop me," he asked Casper at the top of the stairs. "Everybody has got to have a father."

"Jenny doesn't," Casper answered, looking at the lad. "Her parents were never married."

"Oh," McInroy said, "Miss Wayne treats them differently. But it weren't Jenny's fault. I'm surprised Miss Wayne let Jenny come. Of course, Miss Warren can be stubborn when she's a mind to be. She must have promised Miss Wayne a pile of money."

Casper agreed. The lad knew Miss Wayne and he also knew Miss Warren. McInroy started down the stairs. He turned and looked up at Casper before saying, "Someone needs to give Jenny a last name." McInroy has a compassionate heart, Casper thought as he watched the lad continue down the stairs and through the door.

42

CHAPTER SIX

With only a few days left before Miss Warren's departure, Johns decided it was time Casper learned the fine art of horseshoeing. Sometime during their journey a horse's shoe would need replacing. Likely there would be someone experienced along on the wagon train to see to the matter, yet Johns in his methodical thinking reasoned Casper should know a few tips of the trade. So he fired up the forge, brought in a team of horses that sooner or later would need re-shoeing and began his instructions.

Along about noon, Stanford Warren strode across the stable yard. He was pale, underweight with hair the color of Miss Warren's, and blue eyes. "Johns, will you have Red saddled," Stanford asked.

The stable man looked perturbed, "Mr. Stanford, are you sure you're up to riding Red? I can saddle Star; he's had his morning romp. It took the edge off him."

"I'm feeling better this morning," the young man replied. "Julia's had me cooped up in the house long enough."

"The reason I am speaking is only concern," Johns quickly reminded the young man. "We nearly lost you and it'd break the Miss' heart if you over do and become ill again."

"A bunch of old hens," this Stanford said to Casper as Johns moved away to saddle Red. He extended his hand, "Stanford Warren, I take it you're Mr. Van Holland. We haven't been formally introduced."

Casper shook his hand, "Casper," he replied.

"I see Johns is putting you through your paces," he said good-heartedly.

"Then some, I would say," Casper agreed, moving the iron horseshoe back and forth in red hot coals.

"Julia means a lot to us. I wish she would give up this fool notion about going to Oregon. But I know she won't. She's a stubborn ass at times and I should know," he laughed, his fingers rubbing a small scar on his forehead. "If it wasn't for this bout of influenza I would go with her. I had to come home from university last semester," he added. "Why Charles can't wait another year is beyond rational logic. You would think they just discovered the place or something. We're all glad John Forbes has found a reliable man to accompany her."

Johns returned with the big red stallion Casper had admired a few times. The horse was high spirited and more than a little troublesome. He sidestepped as Johns led him across the cobblestone yard.

Peters followed leading Early Dawn. "Since you're riding Red," Johns began, "Peters is riding with you. If the horse throws you, Peters can haul what's left of you home."

Stanford Warren laughed good-naturedly, slapping Johns on the back. "If this fool horse throws me, tell Peters to leave me lay. I won't be worth dragging home for Julia will just grind up what's left of me."

"Aye," Johns agreed, "After she rips off my hide."

Red backed off as Stanford brought his foot up to the stirrup. Then the horse reared as Stanford threw his leg over the saddle. The man's firm grip on the reins soon had the horse standing with his muscular body quivering.

An hour later the riders returned to the stable yard. Miss Julia banged the backdoor shut and crossed the cobblestones in long easy strides. "And what do you think you're up to," she asked Stanford. The look she gave the young man would have cowered lesser men into submission.

"I'm not up to anything, it's done," he told her with a teasing note in his voice.

"That, I can see for myself. Did the doctor say you can go riding," she demanded, placing her hands on her hips as she glared at her cousin.

"He said it was time I got out of the house for a while each day," Stanford answered. Dismounting, he threw the reins to Johns. "Well, I'm out of the house," he leaned over kissing Julia on the forehead.

"Don't think you can butter me up and get around me," Julia chided.

"I wouldn't even try," Stanford assured her.

"Well," she began, a smile slowly breaking across her face. "I saw Martha taking an apple pie from the oven when I came through the kitchen." She hooked one arm around his elbow. "If we hurry we just might get the first pieces." She hooked her other arm around Peters' elbow and glanced back at Johns. "Is it alright if I steal Peters for awhile," She asked grinning.

"Sure," Johns called as the trio headed for the house. He shook his head as he led the horses away. "We might as well see if there's any pie left for us after we attend to these animals."

Casper learnt baking apple pies was a big event in the Warren household and a monthly ritual. Everyone dropped what they were doing and headed for Martha's kitchen. He also learnt it entailed not one pie but a half dozen with flaky crust and oozing filling. Miss Julia sat at the well scrubbed table with everyone else laughing and joking as they ate pie and drank coffee.

Perkins walked into the kitchen and said, "I wondered where everyone got to." He sniffed. "Apple pie day," he said smiling. Casper had never seen the man smile and was intrigued by the man's lapse in protocol.

Julia stood and all the young men scrambled to their feet. "Stay seated," she told them. With one accord they looked at Perkins for confirmation who nodded his head in approval. "Sit here," she told Perkins. Walking around the table, she picked up the coffeepot and began refilling coffee cups.

Miss Jordan came in pushing a buggy. "Well Molly, it looks like we've finished our outing just in time." She lifted the child into her arms.

Casper rose to his feet. "Take my place," he offered. Molly reached for him and ran cool hands over his chin.

"Thank you," Miss Jordan said somewhat breathless. Julia brought her pie and coffee. "I'm not as young as I used to be," the middle age spinster complained. "Either that or distances are getting longer." She smiled at Julia. "Thank you, dear," she said.

Johns rose, thanked Martha and left. Soon afterwards the room began to empty. Everyone returned to his or her duties. Casper remained watching his daughter eat. Miss Jordan was attentive to the child's needs. Julia poured him another cup of

45

coffee and placed the coffeepot on the table in front of him. She soon left.

As Casper watched Molly, his thoughts were on Miss Warren. The young woman had been different this afternoon. Not the haughty Miss he had been privileged to see on so many occasions. And to his surprise he understood the difference in Miss Warren. The haughty young woman was a cover, a way for her to deal with difficult situations and the quiet friendly girl he had witnessed a few short minutes ago was the real Miss Warren. It also explained the love and devotion the lads as well as the rest of the staff had for her. Miss Warren was really a gentle loving person.

CHAPTER SEVEN

Thursday evening before departure, Julia arranged a gathering so everyone could meet. She sent word by Perkins for Casper to be present at eight o'clock in the large parlor.

After spending the morning shoeing a team of horses, Casper spent Thursday afternoon driving a loaded freight wagon into the country with Johns seated at his side. "There's no more time," Johns lamented with regret as Casper turned the horses toward town. "You know how to handle a team well. You can take care of a wagon and groom horses. Still, I wish I had more time. The rest you will learn along the way. You probably know more than the average man heading west. Still…well, I will be frank. It is Miss Julia I'm worrying about. I promised her father I'd look after her and now she's off to Oregon Country and I can no longer protect her."

Casper understood Johns' worries. "I promise to do my best, Sir," he said.

"Aye lad, I know you will. It's Charles Heywood I'm worrying about. You would think with all the money the man has, he wouldn't be traveling by covered wagon. That's the crux of my worry. I hear it takes three or four weeks to get to the west coast by train. Yet Mr. Charles wants to travel by wagon and spend five months on the trail." Johns sat thoughtful for a long moment. "You will be watchful of Mr. Charles," he instructed soberly.

"Yes sir," Casper replied.

"Martha says I'm an old hen," Johns declared after clearing his throat. "She says I'm worrying over nothing."

"I will be watchful," Casper promised. The lads did not like Charles Heywood and said as much on more than one occasion.

The spacious Warren House came into view preventing further talk. Peters was waiting to take the horses. "You'll be wanting a few minutes with Molly," the young man said. "I'll see to the horses and put away the wagon."

"Thank you," Casper called. He hurried to his room and washed before changing his clothes. He looked at his black suit then discarded the idea of wearing it. He was not one of the family and did not feel he should put on airs to try and impress everyone.

He took the backstairs two steps at a time. Molly was seated at the round table with a supper plate in front of her. Mrs. Jordan had her rocking chair moving back and forth as she watched Molly eat.

"I thought you would show up soon," Miss Jordan said. She dapped at the corner of her eyes with a white lace handkerchief. "I'm going to miss Molly," she admitted. "If I wasn't so old I'd go along and watch out for the child."

"Molly and I will miss you as well," Casper replied. He sat in a chair near Molly and watched his daughter eat. Miss Jordan had worked miracles in a very short time.

"The day has finally arrived," Miss Jordan lamented. "I had hoped time would stand still but it never does. Mr. Stanford insists I stay on and look after the nursery. He says someday it will be put to use again." Miss Jordan took a deep breath and wiped moisture from her cheeks. "It's Miss Julia I'm worrying about. Oregon is way on the other side of the country."

"I will look after Miss Warren," Casper promised.

"Aye," Miss Jordan said. "You're a good lad with a kind heart. Not like some I know," she made a sour face.

"Johns is worrying about Mr. Charles' influence," Casper confided, sure Miss Jordan already knew Johns opinion on Charles Heywood.

"Aye," Miss Jordan said. She did not put her worry into words.

"I'm to meet Mr. Heywood at eight o'clock tonight," Casper replied, taking Molly onto his lap. His daughter leaned against him as Miss Jordan washed her hands and face. Casper stayed in the nursery until Molly was sleeping.

Casper was thoughtful as he went to find Perkins. He followed Perkins down the long hallway to the back of the house. Perkins knocked before opening the door. "Mr. Van Holland," he announced.

Julia was standing before a large open fireplace talking with John Forbes. She came across the room, hooked an arm inside his pulling him into the room. "You know Uncle John," she said. "And this is Aunt Clara, John's wife. Mr. Van Holland," she told the petite woman standing beside John Forbes. The woman was dressed in a soft grey evening gown. Not what the fashion conscience woman would call fashionable. But it suited Mrs. Forbes who did not believe in parading about like a horse on display. Her smile was friendly and her voice soft as she greeted Mr. Van Holland. "John has told me so much about you, I feel we are acquainted," she said. There was graciousness in her manner that reminded Casper of Miss Warren. Mrs. Forbes made him feel comfortable as if there were no differences in their social status.

Miss Warren crossed the room to where a couple stood before long windows. Drapes were pulled letting in the last rays of sunlight. They turned when Julia approached. "My sister, Annabel Heywood and my brother-in-law, Charles Heywood" she said by way of introductions. "Mr. Van Holland and his family are going with us. It is my good fortune to get him to drive my wagon," she said pleasantly.

"Are you still harping on that," Charles Heywood said sharply. "There's plenty of room in our wagon without going to the extra trouble and expense of having a second wagon along."

"I've explained already," Julia said softly. "The extra supplies will come in handy. I'm told the prices in Oregon Country are outlandish." Charles glared at Casper without speaking, dismissing him as a peasant unworthy of his attention.

Charles Heywood was not what Casper had expected. He was not overly tall but muscular built with a ruddy complexion from spending hours out of doors. He was also older than expected with white hair in his sideburns. He had sharp dark brown eyes and a small mustache. Mrs. Heywood was an older version of Julia though more endowed and dressed to show off the differences. She was fashion conscience and had the money to indulge her whims in what was considered the latest styles. Of the couple, she was the one to engage Casper in conversation and was as gracious as Clara Forbes. She could not by any means of the imagination be called outdoorsy but had a great wealth of knowledge about horses, hunting, and what could be termed, 'men's interest'.

49

"Coffee Miss," Perkins said, entering the parlor carrying a serving tray.

"Are you still following your antiquated ideas? It's time you started serving cocktails," Charles scolded, looking disgusted at the prospect of being served coffee. He ignored Perkins and went back to looking out the long windows. Spring bulbs were in bloom. Dainty crocus and tall regal tulips, white star flowers, and yellow forsythia bushes grew along the walks or were tucked into corner flowerbeds.

Stanford entered with a tall slender young woman on his arm. "Sorry I'm late," he said, kissing Julia on one cheek. "Uncle John," he greeted, shaking John Forbes hand. He kissed Clara Forbes on one cheek.

"It was all, my fault," the girl explained, blushing. Julia took both of Sherry's hands leaning to kiss her on one cheek.

"You know everyone except Mr. Van Holland." Julia said, "And I'm sure Stanford has told you about him. Mr. Van Holland, I'd like you to meet, Miss Waters."

"I do remember Stanford saying he knew the prettiest girl in town," Casper said. Miss Waters' blush darkened and she turned shining eyes toward Stanford.

"Now that everyone is here," Julia said, not sure why she was peeved Casper called Sherry Waters pretty. She turned to John Forbes hoping no one noticed her reaction. "It is time to get business behind us so we can enjoy the rest of the evening," she announced.

"Business," Charles Heywood demanded, coming across the room to glare at Julia. "What business are we to conduct and why do it tonight?"

"Because, tomorrow we leave for Oregon Country," Julia replied. "Have you brought the papers to be signed," she asked John Forbes. "I want Charles to witness the signatures." She moved gracefully to the fireplace and took the chair placed before the hearth. She motioned for Charles and Annabel to join her.

Stanford and Sherry Waters took chairs across from Julia while John Forbes, still standing, opened a briefcase and took out files. "Julia and I have discussed her move to Oregon Country and the family businesses." He picked up the top file and opened it. "Julia is signing the house over to Stanford," he said without further preamble.

50

"This is nonsense," Charles Heywood declared his voice rising in fury. "Why, half the house belongs to Annabel. We were not informed of any changes."

"Annabel sold her half of the house to Julia before she left on your European tour," John Forbes replied politely, knowing Charles was aware of the fact.

"Still," Charles declared belligerently, dismissing John Forbes' comments about Annabel selling her half of the Warren home to Julia. "Julia might decide she doesn't like Oregon and return in a year or two. It is nonsense her signing the house over to Stanford. He's not really one of the family."

Julia smiled as she looked up at Charles. He stood with his back to the fireplace his face red with scorn. "You know how I dislike traveling," she said calmly, dismissing Charles' statement Stanford was not family. "I get ill riding the train to New York City. I can't imagine what sailing around the tip of South American in a Clipper Ship would be like. No, once I get to Oregon I plan to stay. Therefore, it is only wise to give the house to Stanford. It should not remain vacant and there are the servants to consider."

"There are trains," Charles Heywood retorted angrily. "And stagecoaches where there are no trains."

"I have thought it through," Julia replied calmly though Casper noted the look she gave Charles Heywood was the haughty Miss Warren. She turned to Annabel waiting for her sister to comment.

Annabel gazed at Charles before returning Julia's look. "I don't know what to say," she admitted. "You should have consulted me. I dislike the thought of my home going out of the family."

"Stanford is family. He has lived here since his parents' death," Julia reminded. "My mind is made up. Uncle John insisted I wait until tonight knowing I might change my mind about going to Oregon. As we are leaving in the morning, I want all the papers signed before I go."

"I won't sign," Charles declared. He gave Julia a superior look. One that suggested Julia had lost her mind.

"Then Perkins can sign as witness," Julia replied. It was the haughty Miss Warren speaking. Charles noted her complexion was pale and her blue eyes glowed angrily. She picked up the fountain pen and signed her name where John Forbes indicated.

51

Knowing he did not have a say in the matter, Charles grudgingly signed his name. "I say it is a mistake," he declared.

"Next," John Forbes said after signing his name to the document, "Is the Warren businesses."

"You're not giving Stanford the businesses," Charles declared ready to do battle. His face turned purple with rage. "John, you mustn't let Julia give away her fortune on a whim."

"I'm not giving away all my wealth," Julia replied calmly. "Stanford will naturally take over the responsibility of running the many Warren enterprises. He is to have half ownership in the companies. It is fair since he will be doing the work. After all, he is a Warren," she emphasized.

Charles sputtered incoherently. "Annabel, don't let your sister do such foolishness," he demanded when he got his anger under control.

"Annabel does not have a say in the matter," Julia reminded. "I bought her shares in the companies when she decided to sell. Uncle John did not want someone else buying into the businesses and taking over. You wanted the money to finance your European trip. What shares remain, Annabel controls and can do with as she pleases. I am dividing my shares with Stanford."

"I say old girl, this is mighty generous of you but are you sure. Like Charles is suggesting you might not like Oregon and return someday," Stanford said awkwardly. Sherry Waters turned pale after hearing Charles raging against what Julia purposed.

"If ever I do return then we will discuss the house. As for now, I am giving it to you knowing you will keep the lads on and see the girls are cared for properly until they decide to marry," Julia said.

"You know I will do as you request," Stanford replied. "I'm a bit overwhelmed. You never said anything before now."

"Like Charles, I felt you would try and argue me out of my decision," Julia replied.

Charles was furious but resigned to Julia's decision. He signed his name to each document John Forbes handed him. "Now that business is completed, we can have a nice evening together before you leave in the morning," John said, folding the papers and returning them to his briefcase.

Clara Forbes turned to her husband saying, "I know I promised no tears." She smiled brightly though her eyes shimmered with unshed tears.

"If you will all excuse Mr. Van Holland," Julia said crossing to where he stood. "He has a full day ahead of him tomorrow."

John Forbes shook Casper's hands wishing him luck and God's blessings. Clara asked him to look after her girl and placed a kiss on his cheek.

After the well wishes, Julia went with Casper into the hall. "Johns is to have the freight wagon at the backdoor by ten o'clock tomorrow morning. I want to go over everything with you before you start loading. Hopefully, you will be able to recognize all the crates, barrels and boxes once everything is aboard the train. I don't know what Annabel has decided but more than likely you will be expected to look after her shipment as well." She stopped talking and looked at Casper. "I want to thank you," she said shyly. "The train leaves at twelve thirty. Johns will take you to the train station and oversee the loading." She paused and ran her hand over the front of her stomach nervously. A gesture Casper had seen her do before. "Perkins will bring Molly and me, as we won't need to leave as early."

Julia looked up and Casper saw she was struggling against tears. "You will be there," she asked unexpectedly.

"Yes Miss," Casper assured her. To change the subject and give her time to get her emotions back under control, he said, "I didn't know John Forbes is your uncle."

Julia's smile was watery, "he is my father's best friend. He sort of inherited Annabel, Stanford and me after my father died. He's my legal guardian, but since Perkins and Martha are here, he allows me to live at home."

Casper nodded his head, not sure what to say.

"Good night," she said.

CHAPTER EIGHT

Casper checked over the assortment of supplies unloaded by him and Johns. He noted the number of crates and barrels that set on the train station platform. They were his responsibility until he reached the end of the journey by train. Johns waited with him as neither the train nor Mr. Heywood had arrived.

It was starting to snow when Julia stepped from the carriage with Molly in her arms. Perkins followed carrying a small trunk and Molly's valise. A fine day to be leaving everything she knew behind, Julia thought as she crossed to the train station. But she was not leaving everything behind. She was going with Annabel and her daughters, and there were Molly and Mr. Van Holland. The child in her arms turned so she could see her father. A smile was on her lips.

Casper returned Molly's smile. Reassuring his daughter, he knew she was alright. The station was cold, dirty, and crowded with waiting passengers. Perkins took out a white handkerchief and placed it over a chair seat so Miss Julia could sit while they waited.

"It will be alright Miss," he said. "Mr. Van Holland is a fine man and capable of taking care of you. You must depend on his judgment. Mr. Forbes did very well in choosing him." Julia wondered if Perkins was reassuring himself or her with his statement.

The Heywood freight wagon arrived, the driver talked with Casper and Johns before unloading began. The boxes and crates of supplies were added to Julia's and placed in Casper's care. The train pulled into the station with clangs and bellows of smoke and steam. Julia gripped her fingers together in hopes she would not faint.

54

"It is time Miss," Perkins said dolefully.

Julia with Molly in her arms stood and walked toward the train. Her heart was racing as she swallowed down panic and mounted the iron steps. Perkins carried her small trunk and Molly's valise. A porter showed them to her private compartment. The Porter closed the door then left to help others boarding the train. Perkins placed the luggage on one end of the bench seat.

"There isn't anything more to be said," he told Julia.

"Yes there is," Julia replied. "I love you like a dear uncle," she told the old servant. "You have always been there for me all the days of my young life." A sob rose in her throat. "And I will miss you more than I can express." She hugged Perkins unable to control her tears. Stepping back, she gave him a watery smile, "I will remember to trust Mr. Van Holland and seek his counsel," she promised.

"Very good Miss," Perkins said then coughed to clear his throat. "There will be letters. I expect to hear someday that a young man has stolen your heart. Just make sure he is a young man worthy of your love," the old servant ordered.

"Yes Sir," Julia replied. "Annabel has arrived," she said next. The arrival of her sister soothed her feelings of panic. She hugged Perkins again before he turned and departed. For a minute, Julia felt lost then she turned to the window and looked out. She saw Annabel and her two daughters standing near the loading platform.

Charles was all smiles as he shook Casper's hand. "See you arrived in plenty of time. Where is Julia, Miss Warren," he asked.

"She boarded the train a short time ago," Casper answered.

"I'll see to Annabel. Load this stuff like a good chap." He clasped Casper's arm before he strode to where his wife was fussing over baggage and two girls.

Casper oversaw the loading then climbed into the freight car. He waved to Johns as the man drew away from the loading dock. Over the next few hours there would be cities and towns where freight was loaded and unloaded. It was his responsibility to see none of Julia's freight went astray during these stops. As the wide door on the freight car closed, he sat down on a crate. His thoughts were on Molly, wondering how his daughter was doing.

Through the train window Julia saw her sister and brother-in-law board the train. She heard their footsteps as they came down the narrow passageway and past her compartment. Their voices muffled as they entered the compartment next to hers.

Molly wiggling on her lap drew her attention away from the window. With trembling fingers, she unfastened the child's coat and slipped it from her shoulders. The compartment was warm as snow continued to fall in the train yard. There was nothing of beauty beyond the window. Steel tracks and trains. Workmen scurried to and fro. She folded Molly's coat neatly and placed it on the padded bench seat beside them. She removed her coat and placed it over the child's. Julia swallowed hard as the train gave a lurch and began to move. "Oh Molly! Am I doing the right thing?" Julia closed her eyes shutting out the world beyond the train car.

Julia leaned back waiting to see what would happen next. As the minutes drug by and nothing happened she began to relax. "We're on our way Molly." The child sat on the seat beside her and watched with wide blue eyes. "I'm glad you're here," she admitted. "I'm not very brave after all," she confessed, taking Molly onto her lap finding her presence a comfort. They settled down for a long ride. Julia counted buildings as they passed. She rang the bell summoning the Porter and asked if a meal could be brought to her compartment.

The young man nodded his head before hurrying away to comply with her wishes. He had been given special instructions concerning the occupants of the two private compartments. They must be important for the order had come from the head office.

"One thing at a time," Julia counseled. "Don't take on problems before they happen."

The train was running smoothly, no starts and stops as the countryside opened up. She helped Molly with her meal, watched the passing scenery from the train window and managed to eat a little herself.

There was a knock on her door. Julia believed it would be the Porter calling for the dinner tray. "Yes," she said.

Casper stood framed in the door. "There won't be another stop for about forty five minutes. I've come to see Molly."

"Come in," she said. Turning to look out the window, her features were pale and drawn as she ignored Casper.

Casper lifted Molly onto his lap. "I see you're having a good time," he told his daughter, his voice soft and gentle.

56

Julia caught back a sob, not wanting him to see how distressed she was feeling. She sat stiffly erect, her eyes not moving from the window. "Have you had dinner," she asked at length.

"Not yet."

"There's food on the tray if you care to eat. It will allow you more time with Molly," Julia offered.

"Thank you," Casper answered in his most polite voice. He thought how young and afraid Miss Warren looked.

Casper left a sleeping Molly. Julia opened a book, one of several she had packed in her small trunk. But, she felt unsettled and unable to concentrate. Surely, her feeling of dread would soon pass? The longing to undo what had just been done and for peace once again to enter into her heart. A tear rolled down Julia's cheek. Was she going to cry again? She felt all alone and abandoned. Leaning back, she closed her eyes. She woke to Molly softly patting her arm. Attending to Molly and her needs diverted Julia's attention.

By the time Annabel knocked and entered her compartment Julia was smiling. "We're going to dine," her sister informed Julia looking at Molly in surprise. "Who is this," she asked.

"This is Molly and you only have to look at her to know she is Mr. Van Holland's daughter." Julia said.

"Right," Annabel said, smiling. "You did mention Mr. Van Holland had a family. I guess I wasn't paying much attention at the time. Where is Mrs. Van Holland," she asked, gathering the child into her motherly arms.

Charles looked from Annabel to the child she was holding. "Must we be inflicted with the hired help," he demanded irritably.

"Rubbish," Annabel replied good-heartedly. She walked past her husband not in the least putout by his comment.

Julia was glad she did not need to answer Annabel's question. Her sister would learn soon enough there was no Mrs. Van Holland. Julia hoped to be spared Charles' condemnation when he learned. A married Mr. Van Holland seemed more, well, more respectable. Julia wondered why she felt a need to deceive Annabel then realized it was Charles she hoped to deceive as long as possible.

Clara decided to be mother. Taking her roll seriously, she guarded Molly as furiously as any mother. Her childish voice telling Molly not to spill her milk and that she must eat her green beans as they were good for her. As they walked back to their compartments, Clara held onto Julia's hand. "Can I stay with you, Aunt Julia? I fear Molly needs me," Clara stated in just the right motherly tones.

Annabel had difficulty controlling her laughter. "Well, Aunt Julia," she said.

"Yes Clara, I'm sure Molly would love to have you play with her."

"Oh, I'm not going to play," Clara informed them importantly, "I'm going to take care of her."

"Perhaps you should stop by your compartment for a nightgown first," Julia suggested. "Molly might need your care all night. That is if your mother doesn't mind."

"Mother doesn't mind. Do you mother," Clara said, importantly.

"We'll get your nightgown," Annabel replied.

There was a knock on the compartment door. When Julia opened the door, Casper stood in the passage way. "I noticed your light is still on. I want to make sure Molly is alright," he said.

"Molly's sleeping," Julia whispered.

"May I come in the morning?" Casper noticed Miss Warren looked a lot more relaxed.

"Yes," Julia said before closing the door.

CHAPTER NINE

Julia, Clara and Molly were eating breakfast in the dining car when Annabel and her youngest daughter, Wilma, joined them. After giving her order, Annabel looked speculatively at her sister. "Now, tell me the truth," Annabel demanded in her big sister, I'm smarter tone of voice.

"The truth," Julia questioned.

"There is no Mrs. Van Holland," Annabel declared with finality.

"I never said there was a Mrs. Van Holland. I said he was bringing his family and Molly is family," Julia explained patiently.

"Your words implied a Mrs. came with the Mr.," Annabel insisted, "and I want to know why the ruse?"

Julia sighed pushing away her unfinished breakfast. "Charles, if you really want to know. I'm tired of bickering. No, his demands," Julia corrected. "First he wanted me to travel with you. Why should I when I have the means to travel independently. Uncle John investigated and says the price of goods is highly inflated at the forts along the route. With my wagon, we can take everything we need which will cut expenses. Plus my traveling independently, will give you and Charles as much privacy as can be expected. It is never wise to become burdensome even with family." Julia laid out what she hoped were reasonable explanations. She could not very well say she detested Charles.

"I see," Annabel said thoughtfully, before adding, "It will be worse once Charles finds out there is no Mrs. Van Holland."

"By then we'll be on our way," Julia replied. "That is unless you tell him first. Uncle John hired Mr. Van Holland to see me safely to Oregon Country. Perkins told me to trust him and listen to his counsel. I gave my word. I promised. If both Uncle John and

59

Perkins trust Mr. Van Holland then I'm to trust him also. Charles is not responsible for me. Uncle John placed the responsibility in Mr. Van Holland's capable hands." Annabel listened in silence puckering her lips and frowning. Charles was not going to like this revelation one little bit. "Its not that Uncle John doesn't trust Charles," Julia continued, wondering how true the statement was as she said it. "You and the girls are enough responsibility and Uncle John believes Charles shouldn't need to worry about me as well. He went to a lot of trouble to find just the right person to watch over me. And watching after Molly is a help. You know how hard it is for me to travel even as far as New York City. Caring for her is helping to control my fears. I have something else to think about." Annabel conceded the point. Julia did look less worried and haggard then she normally would have.

Julia knew it was no use talking further, Annabel would do what she thought best. She sat drinking coffee as her sister ate breakfast. Everything was so difficult at times. Julia wished once again she had never started on the venture.

As they were leaving the dining car, Annabel asked if she could join Julia saying Charles preferred to sleep late. They settled down in Julia's compartment, the three girls playing happily with a wooden Noah's ark complete with small three inch animals. It had been Molly's favorite toy so Miss Jordan wisely packed the Ark and animals among the child's clothes. Annabel flipped idly through a magazine reading gossip and viewing fashions while Julia read a novel. Turning the page, Julia wondered how many times she would read through the few books she brought with her before reaching her destination.

Casper knocked on the door waiting for Julia to answer. He wondered if he was too early, but later in the morning there were cities and towns where the train stopped and his presence was required in the freight car.

Annabel rose and opened the compartment door. Casper stepped back and quickly glanced to make sure he had the right compartment. "Excuse me. I've come to see Molly," he said. Hearing her father's voice, Molly ran into his arms. He lifted her holding the child to his chest.

"Come in," Julia invited, her voice devoid of warmth. If Annabel informed Charles of his visits, which seemed likely, Julia did not want her sister telling tales. It was better to let Annabel

60

know Mr. Van Holland was an employee and nothing more or Charles would make Julia's life miserable.

"You're busy," Casper began. He could see Molly was being given care which was his concern.

"Nonsense," Annabel interrupted in her most cordial voice. She wanted to know more about the man Uncle John and Perkins felt was trustworthy.

Casper looked from one sister to the other unsure of his welcome. "Your time is limited," Julia stated. "Please come in, we were just…" She did not finish her sentence but turned to look out the window. The scene was dreary. Endless fields either freshly plowed or waiting to be plowed, fence lines where tall trees grew, and white farm houses.

"What my sister means to say," Annabel picked up where Julia left off. "Charles likes to sleep late and two noisy children in a small compartment, disturbs his rest." Annabel had the gift of making people feel comfortable around her. She genuinely liked people, all sorts of people. Settling on the seat across from Casper, she started a conversation talking in general about her travels, asking him questions and giving her opinions freely.

Julia looked on occasionally and at other times gave her attention to the passing scenery outside the train window. Annabel was out going and friendly while Julia was quietly reserved keeping apart from the activity in the small compartment. At length she heard Annabel exclaim, "So you weren't born in the states?"

"My parents immigrated to America when I was a small child," Casper explained

"How fascinating," Annabel interjected sincerity into her words as she continued to tell about her travels in Europe.

Julia would have sworn Annabel was flirting with Mr. Van Holland if she did not know her sister better. Annabel was completely devoted to Charles. So she must be trying to find out what sort of man Casper was. At length Annabel leaned back content in her belief Casper was still grieving his wife's death as Julia insinuated. Still five months together held dangers, she was sure Julia had not considered.

As the speed of the train slowed, Casper stood and kissing his daughter good-bye left the compartment. He smiled on the way to the freight car. It was natural enough for Mrs. Heywood to be concerned about him. He was spending a lot of time with her younger sister. And he was just beginning to realize how close a

61

relationship theirs was likely to become. He had not given much thought to it before. He had focused on learning what Mr. Forbes had laid out for him to know. Since the journey had actually started, he wondered about the day in and day out aspect of what he had undertaken. He was sure once they started traveling by wagon he would see even more of Miss Warren. He was just starting to understand Mr. Forbes' worries about unforeseen entanglements. Were they likely to happen? Would his ethics be tested?

At noon the two families dined together. A meal Julia would gladly have forgone but to appease Annabel she joined them. Being as pleasant to Charles as she knew how, not once questioning his reasoning or taking offense. Julia being agreeable was a new experience. Charles was pleased to know all he needed to do was get Julia away from the influence of her stuffy family for her to see things his way. His hopes were renewed Julia would fall in line with all he had planned for her.

As they left the dining car, the train pulled into a station coming to a halt with many jolts and grinds. The Porter came down the aisle calling out the name of the town and how many minutes they would be stopped to take on water and coal.

Annabel said, "I see a man selling newspapers. I won't be but a minute."

"You're not thinking of leaving the train," Julia asked in alarm.

"Certainly," Annabel replied dismissively. "Don't be such a worrier. I'll be right back and the Porter just said we are stopping here for twenty minutes. That's more than enough time to buy a newspaper."

Julia stood at the window and watched Annabel descend from the train, talk to the man selling newspapers, and return. Charles placed his hand on Julia's arm escorting her to their compartments. He was in a congenial mood not even commenting on Molly's presence. He had accepted Julia's explanation that a freight car was no place for a child.

"I'm going to put Molly down for a nap," Julia said, stopping at her compartment.

"May I come too," Clara asked. She was seven with Charles' dark hair and Annabel's blue eyes.

"If it is alright with you parents," Julia replied, "And if you promise to let Molly sleep." Annabel joined them in the corridor and gave her permission.

It was late afternoon when Casper knocked on Julia's compartment door. Molly was just waking up from her nap. The girl smiled at her father as he lifted her from her bed. She laughed wiggling in his arms.

"What have you been doing today," he asked, sitting down placing the child on his lap.

Molly thought for a moment before telling him about Clara. How Clara had slept with her and the games they played. Then, she told him a big man had brought them cake, looking at Julia to see if she had said the word correctly. She leaned against her father watching him with trusting eyes. She ran her hand over his chin feeling the day's growth of fiscal hair. This was familiar to her, Casper coming to hold her on his lap at the end of the day. Molly curled against him; his hand fondled her golden hair. He settled back against the corner of the seat. Stretched out his long legs and relaxed. Molly crawled off his lap and sat beside him playing with her miniature animals.

Julia glanced at Casper, realizing he was sleeping with his arms folded across his broad chest. Molly looked at Julia and placed a finger against her lips. She was sure Molly was imitating someone else and wondered who had cared for the child while Mr. Van Holland had worked. His wife was dead. Surely there had been someone, a friend or neighbor perhaps.

Julia remembered the loneliness she had felt after her beloved father's death. What was it like to lose someone as close as a spouse? It must leave a very deep void and thought it explained the sadness she often saw in Casper's eyes.

He sighed and shifted position. Molly looked up at him to see if he was awake and continued playing. Content he was there with her.

The Porter bringing a supper tray disturbed him. Casper sat up with a start and looking at Miss Warren was embarrassed. She gave him a placid look.

The Porter stopped and glanced at Casper. "Sorry Sir," he said. He should have known a pretty young woman with a child would be traveling with her husband. He closed the door to the compartment shaking his head. The pretty ones were always taken.

Casper stood to leave. "Please stay and have supper with Molly," Julia invited. He hesitated looking at Molly and wanting to be with his daughter as long as possible. He settled back on the seat conscious of the fact he and Julia were spending a lot of time together. Julia took the tin covers off the dishes. "They seem to always bring a lot," she explained. "It's a waste. I guess when they are making up the trays they don't know whether it's for a man or a woman."

Julia filled a plate for herself, remembering Casper would need more to eat than she did. After all, he was working. He ate while watching Molly eat and visiting with the child. Molly was well behaved. Watching father and daughter together, Julia understood why. He was firm yet gentle and Molly responded to her father's love.

Casper did not address any of his comments to Julia. Yet it was not the strained, awkward silence between them that had existed earlier. Julia must live a quiet, simple life which would explain her calm reserve when around others. He did not force his attention upon her with idle talk.

Julia began to relax in Casper's company knowing it was Molly he came to see. She was there because it had to be that way. Before he could finish his meal the train began to slow. He finished in a hurry, told Molly good-bye, stood and left the compartment.

CHAPTER TEN

The air was bitterly cold when Julia stepped off the train in Saint Joseph Missouri. A thin layer of snow covered the ground. The train depot was crowded as passengers disembarked. Voices rose and fell as people were met and greeted. It was the end of the line. The train went no further. Ahead lay the endless Kansas prairie.

"I thought we left winter behind," Annabel complained. Stepping from the train, she held onto Clara's hand while Wilma pulled on her other hand. Her daughters wanted to go in two different directions. Annabel frowned as she gazed at the dismal looking town. Saint Joseph was not flashy as had been Chicago and countless other cities along the train route. It was a rude awaking as to what she should expect over the coming weeks.

"Mr. Heywood," a young man asked. He removed his wide brimmed hat respectfully. Charles turned to the stranger. "I'm Ray Riffe. My company built your Prairie Schooners. I was told to expect you today." While the two men talked, they walked to where two canvas top wagons stood. "Your man said I was to bring the wagons as you have supplies to load. I hear Mr. Horn's wagon train is camped across the river."

Charles stood with a cigar in one hand, his face ruddy with cold. He looked pompously superior and detached from the hustle around him. "Draft horses," he sneered. Four sturdy draft horses were hitched to each wagon.

Mr. Riffe had been warned and was prepared for Charles' condescending anger. "Your man brought the horses from Pennsylvania," he replied calmly.

"I wasn't told," Charles retorted. He clamped the cigar between strong teeth and walked over to the nearest Prairie Schooner.

"There's a saddle horse," Mr. Riffe stated. Indicating a splendid looking chestnut gelding teetered to one wagon. "Your man oversaw the purchase."

"That's more like it," Charles declared. He ran one hand over the chestnut horse's rump.

Julia hurried to stand beside the second wagon. It blocked the strong wind blowing across the prairie and around buildings. "You will be warmer waiting inside," Mr. Riffe suggested. He lowered the tailgate, taking Julie's elbow, helped her to climb inside the Prairie Schooner. The wind buffered the wagon and it rocked back and forth. Julia walked to the front and waited out of the wind. It was a bitterly cold April afternoon.

Casper carried the first barrel across the train yard and placed it on the wagon's open tailgate. "Can you bring my trunk," Julia asked politely. "Martha packed wool blankets. With this cold, I am going to need one," she explained.

"Right away," Casper replied.

Julia's small traveling trunk slid into the wagon along with Molly's valise. A few minutes later, Casper carrying her large trunk over his shoulder turned his back to the wagon and lowered the trunk onto the tailgate. "Is this the one you meant," Casper asked. When Julia said yes, he placed one hand on the tailgate and swung his feet onto the wagonbed. "Where do you want it," he asked.

"Up here," Julia replied. "The wind is cold today," she continued.

"You have the key, Miss," Casper asked, kneeling in front of the trunk.

"Julia set Molly on her feet and reached for a necklace she wore around her neck. "Perkins insisted," she explained, pulling the necklace over her head.

"Right," Casper replied, Perkins would insist. Julia handed him the key. He inserted the key in the lock and opened the trunk's lid.

"I can manage now," Julia said, taking the key when Casper offered it to her. She pulled out a wool blanket, closed the lid, sat down on the trunk with Molly on her lap, and the wool

66

blanket wrapped around her shoulders. All you could see of Molly was her eyes and the top of the child's head.

After seeing Julia and Molly were settled, Casper walked around the Prairie Schooner looking it over. He lay on his back and slid under the wagon to inspect the calking. There would be rivers to cross. A water tight wagon kept the supplies dry. He looked over the brake. The axels were well greased. A bucket of axel grease was in the box built onto the side of the wagon. There were extra lengths of harness, thread, needles and wax to do repairs, an assortment of tools along with a short handled shovel."

"Your man gave me a list of tools and supplies," Mr. Riffe explained, standing next to the wagon as Casper inspected his workmanship.

"Everything is in order," Casper replied after he completed his inspection. Johns had drilled him on what to look for and what he should find. Otherwise, Casper would have been clueless. His time in Johns' company was time well spent.

Julia watched as Casper loaded barrels and crates in her wagon. The additional weight tamed the wagon's rocking and the queasiness left her stomach.

"This is the last one," Casper said. A good thing too, there was little room left on the wagonbed. "Once we reach Mr. Horn's camp, I'll arrange the supplies so you can move around," he stated.

A few minutes later, Casper was back with a barrel. "Mr. Heywood's wagon is full," he explained. He put one hand on the open tailgate and jumped into the wagon. He stacked crates and moved barrels to allow room for the extra cargo.

"It is starting to snow," Casper said, standing at the back of the wagon and looking over the train yard. "I didn't count on it being so cold. Is Molly alright?" His voice was deep with concern.

'We are warm," Julia replied. "Will you ask Annabel if she packed wool blankets? If she didn't I have another."

"I'll ask," Casper replied. He was back a few minutes later with another barrel then several crates were loaded. "Mrs. Heywood says she has blankets," Casper called. Julia sat on her trunk with her feet propped on the crate in front of her. Casper could see the top of her head.

The wagon dipped to one side when Casper climbed aboard the driver's seat. He picked up the reins and shouted, "Haw." The wagon rolled away from the train depot. Julia could hear the sound of horses moving along the road and men's voices rose and fell away. She could not see and was glad. Saint Joseph was a community of mostly rough looking males making their way west. Julia wondered for the first time how many women would be on the wagon train.

Julia removed the wool blanket and sat Molly on the crate in front of her. She pulled off the child's gloves and felt Molly's fingers to make sure they were warm. Molly turned her head until she could see her father's back then smiled.

"I know how you feel," Julia said, wrapping Molly once more in a blanket. Seeing Casper driving the wagon was an unexpected comfort. Then, Julia admitted it was because he was familiar in a world as alien as if she had been dropped on some distant foreign soil. Nothing had prepared her for the strangeness of her surroundings. She had never traveled further than the coast during the summer months or a mountain lodge in the winter. All had been within a hundred miles of her home.

"Hello the camp," Julia heard Charles shout. On her hands and knees crawling over top of crates, she made her way precariously to the front of the wagon and placed her hands on the back of the wagon seat. She saw a group of a dozen or so covered wagons making a circle. A campfire was in the middle of the circle and men stood around the blaze.

"We're looking for the Horn wagon train," Charles shouted. He wrapped the reins around the brake handle and stepped to the ground. He shook a man's hand. Julia did not like the looks of the strangers. They were rough looking with beards and long hair about their shoulders.

"Mr. Horn is camped about a half mile further north. Hear they're fixing to pull out in a day or two," the tall rangy looking man said. "There's been trouble since a wild bunch joined up with them a short time back. I'd keep close watch on my Mrs.," he advised.

Charles thanked him for his advice.

The Horn camp looked much the same as the other. More than three dozen wagons were parked along a narrow stream. Women were preparing an evening meal. Children played in sight of their anxious mothers. Men gathered in small groups talking while others chopped brush or were busy with the endless chores around a campsite.

Mr. Horn, a weathered gaunt man with gray hair at his temples, separated from the group of men and greeted Charles.

68

Mr. Van Holland alighted from the wagon and joined them. "We will be here a couple of more days," Mr. Horn instructed. "Pull in behind O'Fallon and his Mrs. Make sure you have everything on the list before we move out," he handed each a paper. "What you don't have you can purchase in town. Mr. Olsen has the fairest prices, but I'd still be careful he ain't above taking advantage of greenhorns." He looked at Charles when he made this last statement. But apparently, Charles did not catch Mr. Horn's implied criticism.

"A hard bunch is around," Mr. Horn went on to say. "Caution your Mrs. to stay close to your wagon and don't go off without escort. We always get a few wild ones," he admitted. "This year we seem to have more than our share." This he said with regret. "I don't have to tell you our worst fear is fire so keep a close watch on your campfire. An out of control fire can burn a wagon train to ashes not to mention the prairie for miles."

Casper handed the list to Julia without comment. She read through the items. The quantities were listed per adult. There was also a list of items needed per wagon. These included things such as an extra wheel, axel grease, extra horse shoes and horse shoe nails. Julia was surprised at the detailed list not realizing most of the settlers were what Mr. Horn termed, 'greenhorns'. Ax, hammer and nails, two water barrels, the list went on. The food items listed were coffee, flour, salt, bacon, beans, rice, and oats the list seemed endless and apparently covered any need that might arise.

"This seems like a lot, especially the amounts," Julia said after looking over the list. "It says two hundred pounds of flour, ten pounds of coffee, and fifty pounds of bacon. Martha helped me decide what would be needed. We can go over the list after supper. I'd feel better if you help me check everything," she told Mr. Van Holland.

He waited until Charles had maneuvered his wagon into position giving the Heywood wagon the lead. Julia watched as he pulled his wagon in behind and reined in the team.

"If the weather holds, we'll do it tomorrow," he said. "I want to pack the wagon so we know where everything is. That way you will be able to find supplies as you need them."

Taking Molly from her, he helped Julia over the wagon wheel. The ground was damp with snow. The brown grass growing in clumps was knee high with green sprouts showing near the roots.

"Miss," Casper said drawing Julia away from the others. "Mr. Horn said to caution you about going off on your own. It's not like home, there are a few men," he stopped speaking, his eyes on her face.

"I understand," she told him. "Uncle John already cautioned me." Casper nodded his head. Relieved he did not need to say more.

Charles selected a campsite between the two wagons and off to one side. Mr. Van Holland cleared away the grass to bare ground. Julia climbed back into her wagon searching through the crates until she found the one she wanted, noting its position. She continued to search for a second crate. They were clearly labeled and the first to be needed. One contained pots and pans and other cooking utensils, the second crate was supplies for the first few meals.

"Miss," Mr. Van Holland said, appearing at the back of the wagon.

Julia climbed over the crates to sit on the tailgate dusting off her hands. "We need this crate tonight," she said, laying her hand on the one she wanted. "The one to the far right. I'll show you after you unload this one." Within a few minutes he had the first crate unloaded. The second was more of a challenge as a good deal of the crates had to be shifted.

"I'm sorry," Julia told him. "It was so cold when we arrived I forgot to tell you these two would be needed to set up camp."

"Not to worry," he answered. She gave him a faint smile, knowing Charles would have been in a roaring temper. Prying off the lid on the first crate, Casper waited for Mrs. Heywood and Julia to unpack what they needed. Then he nailed the lid back on and stood the crate on end so they could use it for a work table.

The second crate was packed with supplies. Each bag clearly marked and in a convenient size to allow for a variety of food to be packed in the same crate. Thought had gone into the selection of items and into the packing. A coffee grinder was packed next to a bag of coffee beans. There were dried white beans and rice, dried beef, salt and pepper, dried herbs and a tin of oats just to name a few items.

Mrs. Heywood selected what she wanted and began making stew. Julia, following her sister's directions, helped. It was

70

a friendly atmosphere. The girls were playing tag, Clara and Wilma letting Molly catch them amid squeals of laughter. Every one was glad to be free of the confines and motion of the train for a few days.

Casper unloaded a few of the smaller crates, situating them around the fire to use as benches. He relaxed on one crate filling his pipe then lit the pipe with a twig placed in the fire. Julia had never seen Casper smoke and gave him a surprised look.

Mr. Horn stopped by the camp on his tour of inspection. He did not leave new arrivals to themselves for long. Experience told him the first days were a critical time to see how they settled in and how much they knew. Mostly how much they knew, he had baby sit 'greenhorns' for so long he naturally expected them to be dumb over the least little thing like building a campfire and cooking over an open flame.

Julia filled a cup with coffee and handed it to him. He admitted the campsite was set up better than expected and the coffee the young wife handed him was good. Annabel invited Mr. Horn to stay for supper and he accepted. If the food was half as good as the coffee he was in for a real treat. The food was as good as expected and the company pleasant. He was quick to notice Mr. Heywood did not like the younger man and it was over the young woman he introduced as his sister-in-law. The two women were sisters; he knew this without being told. They resembled one another. And the young girl, Molly could only belong to Mr. Van Holland, same blond hair and pale blue eyes. The two older girls didn't look much like Mr. Heywood. They were the daughters of Mrs. Heywood so he assumed they were the man's daughters as well.

As Mr. Horn got up to leave, he said, "Meeting in the morning. Expect you men to attend."

"Yes Sir," Casper answered.

Mr. Horn thanked Annabel for the meal and tipped his hat respectfully to Julia. The young women were on his mind as he walked back through camp. Give me a plain looking wife anytime he thought, pretty women were the Devil's handiwork. Though, Mr. Van Holland looked as if he could handle himself if needed. And the two young women did not try to attract men. He would watch the situation.

By firelight, Julia read. Mr. Heywood strode through the gathering gloom, restless. Annabel was on his arm their heads

71

together talking, her soft laughter floating on the air. "It's getting cooler," Annabel said, coming closer to the fire. Charles removed his coat placing it about his wife's shoulders. Annabel called Clara and Wilma in from playing. Molly followed and came to stand in front of Julia, waiting patiently to be noticed. "Well little one," Julia said, closing her book. "It's time I saw to you."

"How you two managed to collect so much dirt in such a short time is beyond me," Annabel told her daughters, examining their hands and faces.

Julia picked up Molly and said, "Let's see if we can find Molly under all this grime." She washed the child's face and hands, and brushed her long hair before braiding it. "Good night," Julia called over her shoulder as she walked toward the wagon.

Mr. Van Holland followed her taking Molly so Julia could climb inside. She turned, pulled back the canvas flap, and reached for Molly. "Thank you," she said.

"Goodnight, Miss," Casper replied.

* * * * *

Julia woke to the rattle of chains. Mr. Van Holland was unhooking the team of horses from the wagonbed where he had chained the animals the night before. She rolled over to check on Molly who was asleep beside her. The interior of the wagon was dark. She struggled into clothes and with nimble fingers wrapped her one long braid on top of her head sliding in hair clips to secure the braid. Then, she dressed the sleepy child and they left the warmth of the blankets.

The grass was damp under foot and the air cold when she made her way to the campfire. Surprised to discover Mr. Van Holland had the fire blazing warming the air around it. Julia sat Molly on a crate near the fire and pulled her winter coat around the child's shoulders fastening the buttons down the front.

Molly looked about with wide blue eyes.

"Don't move," Julia ordered.

Since Annabel was not yet up, Julia started breakfast. After making coffee, she put the coffeepot on the fire to boil then sliced bacon placing the strips in an iron skillet.

Mr. Van Holland came back from watering the horses and staked the animals a short distance from the wagon to graze. He poured a cup of coffee and took a drink. "This is coffee," he asked.

72

"I know," Julia apologized. "It's worse than awful. I never can make coffee the way Annabel does."

"If it's all the same with you, I'll make the coffee from now on," he said sternly.

Julia glanced over her shoulder to see if Molly was still where she had placed the child. "I don't mind," she replied with a friendly smile.

Casper soon had the coffeepot back on the coals. "I need a better table," Julia declared. "Do you think you can come up with one that can be easily set up and taken down? Even with all the planning, there are things Martha and I didn't think about. Unless, Annabel remembered to bring a table. She and Charles often go hunting or fishing and is better equipped to know what is needed," she added thoughtfully.

"I'll see what I can do," he answered. Picking up Molly, he held the child on his lap.

Julia passed him a plate of oatmeal sweetened with honey. "No butter and no cream," she lamented.

"This is fine," he assured. He fed Molly from his plate as he ate. As the bacon cooked, Julia passed the slices to Casper. She ate oatmeal while she fried more bacon.

The gray light gradually brightened and streaks of violet, red and gold colored the eastern horizon heralding the coming sun. Removing the last slice of bacon from the skillet, Julia pulled the pan off the coals and onto the ground to cool. She stood arching her back. "I am never going to get use to cooking over a campfire," she complained.

"A far cry from home," Casper observed.

Julia did not answer. Gathering the tin plates, she walked over to the crate she used earlier to slice bacon. It was one of the larger ones and up ended so it was a fairly good height but provided little work space.

She placed a kettle of water on the fire to heat. "We should probably boil the children's drinking water. Who knows what's in the water." She shuddered at the mention of the dingy, muddy creek water. "Doctor Morris insisted all drinking water be boiled after Stanford came down with an illness when we were children. Doctor Morris said he believed there was something in the water making Stanford ill," Julia explained.

Casper had never heard of boiling drinking water. But, he was brought up in a ghetto where Doctors rarely visited the ill. "It's

73

not a bad idea," he said, looking at Julia, "There are several new canteens."

Annabel and her daughters soon joined them by the fire. "Coffee," she said pouring a cup. "Clara and Wilma were anxious to get up. I could have slept another hour." She sank onto a crate gratefully. "You didn't make this," she told Julia after taking a sip. "Mother despaired of ever getting Julia to learn to cook. Father was adamant that his girls be more than 'useless females'. His term for the endless troop of friends we brought home." This she said to Casper. "We had to earn our daily bread," Annabel continued. "Personally, I didn't appreciate it at the time. It was an embarrassment. My friends couldn't understand all those hours I spent cleaning and dusting, cooking and learning the proper way of keeping house. Or the fact I was required to help Miss Jordan make my day dresses." She laughed softly, "Remember Renee," Annabel asked Julia. "I thought she was going to have apoplexy the time I showed her the pink dress I made. I was so proud of it. She looked at me in horror declaring, 'When did your father loose all his money'." Annabel laughed again. "But father was right. It's better not to be a "useless female'."

"Mother wasn't a 'useless female'," Julia stated, "I think mother was about perfect."

"Well," Annabel said doubtfully. "She was perfect for Father."

"That's all that is important." Julia passed her sister a plate of crisp bacon slices and warm oatmeal with honey.

Clara and Wilma were eating slowly not sure about the new fare they were being asked to eat. "You might as well eat up," Annabel told her daughters. "This is the way it will be until this journey is over." Getting up and handing Julia her plate, Annabel said, "I need to get the horses watered and out to graze."

Casper looked at Julia, he was not sure if he was expected to help Annabel. With her back turned to him, Julia was pouring hot water into a metal pan. He stood sitting Molly on the crate. Annabel led a horse across the field heading for the creek. The big black was pulling hard against his lead rope. Casper led Annabel's other three horses to the creek.

"Thank you," Annabel said with color high on her cheeks.

"I'll stake the animals out to graze," he offered.

74

CHAPTER ELEVEN

Julia sat on the wagon's tailgate with the supply list in her hand. Casper had gone to caution the girls not to play too close to the horses. With long easy strides, he came back across the field with the sun shining on his blond hair. Julia watched him, feeling the same stirring of emotions she had felt when he had held her in his arms. She frowned, trying to understand these new wondrous feelings.

Casper started unloading the wagon. Julia checked the labels on each crate as he set it on the ground. Together, they decided if the crate would be needed during their journey west or used once they reach Oregon. The crates to be used now were placed to one side and those needed at journey's end were placed on the other side. At last the wagon was empty except for two long crates. Casper stood wiping sweat from his face with a clean handkerchief.

"What's in the larger crates," Julia asked, looking in the wagon. She did not remember seeing the crates before. She looked through her long list turning pages of handwritten notes.

"Farming implements," he answered. "In one of Jorge's letters he wrote how costly and nearly impossible it was to get good farming equipment. Mr. Forbes asked Mr. Bundy to purchase the equipment when he was here ordering the wagons." Julia had her head tilted to one side considering the large crates. "I know they might cause us to be a little crowded at first," Casper continued. "Perkins, Martha and I talked it over and they assured me there would be room. I plan to farm once I get to Oregon and the implements are important."

She turned looking up at him with a friendly smile on her lips. So, Mr. Van Holland planned to farm once he reached

Oregon. What he would do in Oregon was a subject Julia had never considered. She planned to teach school and had spent a year getting her credentials.

Nathan Webb pulled his team of mules to a halt behind the last wagon. Jumping down, he turned to help his wife, Sara, from the seat. Casper looked up and gave the new arrivals a nod. The man was about his age, medium height, broad shouldered and brown hair that tended to curl around the nap of the neck and over his broad forehead.

"Nathan Webb," the man greeted with a handshake.

"Casper Van Holland," Casper said, returning the greeting. He took out his handkerchief and wiped sweat from his face before tucking the handkerchief back in his hip pocket.

"You have a chore ahead of you," Mr. Webb said, looking over the many crates.

"Decided to repack and make it easier to find what is needed before we leave," Casper explained.

Mrs. Webb was stout, robust and somewhat muscular in appearance. "I'm Sara," she said, coming to stand next to Julia.

"Julia," she returned, a shy smile lifting up the corners of her lips.

A sharp cry interrupted their conversation. Julia immediately excused herself and hurried over to Molly lying face down on the ground. Picking up the child and setting her on her feet, she inspected the girl's knees and elbows for scrapes. She hugged Molly close gently wiping away her tears. Clara and Wilma stopped playing and came to watch.

"Molly's alright," she called, gazing at Casper. He nodded his head in acknowledgement.

"I'm traveling with my sister and brother-in-law," Julia said to Sara. "Come and meet Annabel."

Annabel's greeting was warm making Sara feel at ease immediately. "You've just arrived. We're getting ready to sit down for our noonday meal. Please join us," Annabel invited.

"I don't want to impose," Sara replied, glancing at her husband who was still talking with Casper.

"There's always plenty," Julia assured, adding her invitation to her sister's. "It takes time to set up camp."

Annabel called, "Clara it's time to wash up. Please help Molly."

"Yes mama," Clara answered.

76

Casper and Nathan Webb strode over to the women. "You will join us," Casper said, sure Annabel had already invited his wife.

Molly climbed up on her father's knee looking from him to Mr. Webb. "I'll take her," Julia offered. Casper looked up thanking her with his eyes. Annabel filled a plate handing it to Casper along with the pot of honey. Knowing, he enjoyed honey over his biscuits.

Hot or cold Julia's biscuits were the best Casper ever tasted. He poured honey over the biscuits on his plate then passed the honey pot to Mr. Webb. The coffee was hot and strong, the stew flavored with onions and spices. Its gravy was thick. They settled down to a peaceful meal and talked of the upcoming journey to Oregon Country.

When the meal was nearly over, Charles came from the wagon and joined the group around the campfire. A scowl on his handsome face, he stared at Casper. It was obvious to everyone he did not like the younger man. Charles was sharp with the children and rude to their guests. He gave Molly and Julia a dark look extending his dislike from the father to the child.

Sara was so surprised by the tension that filled the air, she gasped in surprise. Casper quickly finished his meal saying he had work to complete. Nathan followed suit, thanked Annabel for a delicious meal and went to his wagon. Sara felt she must stay and help with the clean up. She wondered how the arrival of one person could so change everyone. Sara returned to her wagon thinking she had never met a more odious man in her life. And one to be avoided, she declared remembering his flirtatious glances.

Julia placed her hands on her hips and stared at the scattered crates and barrels. "They all came out, so they must all go back in."

Casper fit crates in the front of the wagon. He noticed how carefully Martha and Perkins had made plans. Each large crate was the same size and the smaller ones half the size of the larger. They all fit together so they made a flat surface. He placed the crates that would not be needed until after Julia arrived in Oregon in front. Decided by adding layers of blankets over the crates, he could make a bed for Molly and Julia.

The crates containing food were more of a chore. Julia wanted to check the amounts against Mr. Horn's list to make sure

77

they had brought enough of each item. The crates needed to be opened since she had listed only the number of sacks of oatmeal, flour and other items and did not include the weight of each sack. Casper pried off the lids so Julia could check pounds and ounces. She then figured the number of sacks and the amount of pounds. Once this was done she checked the number against Mr. Horn's list.

Casper hammered the lids back on the crates and stretched aching muscles. "About ready for a break," he asked.

"We're nearly done," she replied, still busy with her figuring.

"Is that a yes or a no," he asked. Casper looked at the lowering sky. The distant rubble of thunder herald an approaching storm. "I guess we work on," he conceded, his muscles protesting as he lifted another crate onto the wagon's tailgate.

"We can wait a few minutes," Julia said, sitting on the end of the wagon.

Casper leaned his hip against the wagon. "It will likely rain before long."

Julia nodded her head in agreement. "I can sleep in Annabel's wagon so you can have this one."

He noticed the resignation in her voice. "It might not rain," he suggested. "It's the rainy season and there will be lots of storms before we reach Oregon Country. I have a ground cloth and plenty of blankets. The wagon above me will keep off the rain," he reminded.

"It is still freezing at night. I will feel better if you use the wagon," she paused, looking at him. "I mustn't let Charles' behavior put your health at risk," she declared. "I knew he would be difficult. This is why I insisted on having my own wagon. But, I really don't mind occasionally sharing Annabel's wagon."

"Only you really don't want to," Casper observed.

"Perhaps," Julia acknowledged. "I know there are times I need to put up with Charles," she admitted reluctantly.

Julia picked up Molly and held her as Casper loaded the last crate in the wagon. The sleepy child leaned heavily against her shoulder.

Casper watched the gathering rain clouds before reaching for Molly. He held his daughter against his chest. "I don't think I'll get much done this afternoon," he admitted. He had worked in a cold warehouse not out in the weather. He noticed Nathan Webb going about his campsite ignoring the approaching storm and realized he still had a lot to learn. He just hoped he was up to the task.

* * * * *

In a quick burst, heaven opened up sending a sheet of rain falling as the air cooled. Julia looked out the back of Annabel's wagon at the falling rain. She pulled up the front of her skirt to keep the hem from becoming damp as she dashed for her wagon and climbed over the wagon wheel, pushed back the flap covering the hole in the canvas, and crawled inside her wagon. Casper was sleeping. Sitting beside him, Molly played with the tiny animals that went with the Noah's ark. Wind was blowing, driving rain against the side of the wagon. Julia tied back one flap letting in light. Sitting with her back against the wagon seat, knees pulled up, her long skirt wrapped about her ankles, opened her book, and began to read.

"What are you doing here," Casper asked, suddenly sitting up.

"Charles came back. He's been drinking," Julia explained. "I'm afraid," she looked away lowering her eyes before continuing. "He was being obnoxious," she finished.

"You should have awakened me," Casper said, his voice gruff. He picked up his hat and coat preparing to leave.

"You can't go out in the rain," Julia exclaimed. "I'll go back to Annabel's wagon."

"Miss," he said softly. "I will be alright."

79

CHAPTER TWELVE

After watering the team of draft horses, Casper brought the animals in and harnessed them to the wagon. Julia fried bacon. Hot flaky biscuits were wrapped in a cloth to keep warm. She poured honey over oatmeal ready for his breakfast. Casper rubbed his hands together holding them over the flames to warm. Thanking Julia when she handed him his plate.

"Thought we'd get an early start. You are still planning a trip into town," he asked.

"It needs to be done," she replied before sighing. Julia ate oatmeal and turned bacon in the skillet between bites.

Giving his attention to feeding Molly, he heard strain in Julia's voice. They ate in companionable silence, Julia mentally going over her list and wondering what she was forgetting. This would be the last chance to purchase supplies until they reached Fort Kearney in Nebraska.

Saint Joseph was as loud and crowded as Julia remembered. The town mostly catered to pioneers heading west. On the outskirts of town, businesses were gambling houses, saloons and places Julia did not want to think about. The roads were muddy from recent rains and a boardwalk the length of each building was crowded with shoppers.

Julia handed Casper the supply list along with a sack of gold coins. "It will be better if you keep these," she said.

"It shouldn't take nearly this much," Casper replied, noticing how pale Julia looked.

"Please," she said, "Keep it." When Casper helped her off the wagon, she caught hold of his arm pressing close to his side.

"You will do fine," he said, reassuring her.

"After the letters are posted," Julia began. "We'll visit the mercantile." The day before Julia had written a letter to John Forbes and another to Perkins and Martha telling them she had arrived safely in Saint Joseph. Casper had found her crying and believed Julia really should not have come on the journey. She should have stayed home surrounded by people she loved and who love her. He asked her to write Jorge a letter informing his brother, he was coming with Molly.

The Mercantile was busy, men pushing and shoving against each other as they waited to be served. A tall rotund man took Casper's supply list and began stacking merchandise on the counter and writing each item in a ledger book along with the amount. He added the total together and Casper handed him a twenty dollar gold piece.

"Don't get many of these," the man said, looking Casper over with a glitter in his brown eyes. He told a youth to help load the goods in the wagon.

Once on the road back to the campsite, Casper reined in the team. He lifted his Winchester from under the seat and slid shells into the chamber. "If I'm not mistaken, we'll be having visitors real soon," he told Julia with a stern look on his face.

Julia peered at him nervously. She did not misunderstand what he was implying but was sure Casper had a clear idea of what was to happen. "Give me the reins," she offered, "That way your hands will be free."

"Can you drive a team of horses," Casper asked, doubtfully.

"Yes," she answered. "Johns taught me how to drive my first pony cart before I was any older than Clara."

"Alright," he conceded, handing her the reins. Holding the rifle in plain sight, he tucked a revolver in the front waistband of his trousers leaving his coat hanging open. The blue steel of the rifle gleamed in the sunlight. Casper counted on a show of strength to discourage any-would-be thieves.

Several riders passed by a few minutes later and reined in their mounts. They thought better of their plan and rode on. Casper was vigilant until they were in sight of Mr. Horn's camp. Julia slumped visibly when he took the reins. "You did fine," Casper praised. "I don't believe we were in any real danger once they realized we were ready for them. They were out for easy pickings."

The next day started when Julia woke to the sound of horses snorting and the rattle of chains. Casper was talking softly to the animals as he led them away to be watered and staked out to graze. Julia dressed in the semi-darkness before she woke Molly. The air was brisk and cold, and the glow of the campfire warm and inviting. The coffeepot sitting in the coals was now blackened from use. After sitting Molly on a crate, Julia poured a cup of coffee and shivering sipped the warm brew. She wondered if Casper ever really slept. He was the first one up in the mornings and as far as she knew was the last to bed at night. He was ever vigilant about the wagons, not only hers but Annabel's also. He was capable and ready at all times to do what needed to be done without complaint.

Julia mixed biscuits and rolled out the dough. Poured bacon grease into a pan then coated both sides of each biscuit. She placed the pan in the iron Dutch oven to bake. Even Charles never complained about Julia's biscuits. By the time Annabel joined her, she had breakfast cooking. Annabel was starting to have stomach trouble. Her sister said it was the food and nothing to worry about. But Julia could not help but worry.

"This might be the last day we'll have for some time. Charles says we will probably travel fourteen days or more without a rest," Annabel told her younger sister over breakfast. Julia had heard the same rumor and wondered if it was idle speculation or if they would travel so many days before stopping to rest.

"Anyhow, I think we should do the wash first thing. The girls can use their hair washed and a good bath." Annabel took up bacon as she talked. She saw Casper lead the Black draft horses to the creek. They were in high spirits tossing their heads and high stepping. Annabel was thankful she did not need to ask Casper to see to the horses. He had taken over the responsibility. Charles rarely rose before noon. Annabel would be glad when they left. Her husband was staying out late each night which meant one of two things. Both of which she preferred not to think about.

Casper returned for Julia's bay draft horses. They were gentle and he had no trouble leading them to water and then staking them out to graze. He was returning across the prairie when Charles made an appearance. For once he was in a reasonably good mood.

"There's a hunting party this morning," he told Annabel. "It's time for fresh meat." Regardless of his faults, Julia admitted

Charles was a good hunter. It was one accomplishment he fully enjoyed and the food he would provide a welcome addition to their daily meals.

Casper greeted Charles with respect ignoring the other man's caustic remarks. He filled a plate with ham and biscuits accepting a cup of coffee from Annabel.

"I was just telling Julia there's a hunt on today if you care to come along," Charles invited in a rare show of friendliness.

Casper looked thoughtful for a moment before turning to Julia. He asked, "What have you planned for today?"

It was Annabel who answered, "We thought it might be wise to get the washing done."

Casper declined Charles' offer with a simple, "I'm not a hunter."

Charles seemed pleased by this revelation. "A man should know what he is good at doing," he replied and put himself out to be congenial. He poured coffee and stood with his back to the fire. "Julia did not make this coffee," he acknowledged after his first drink.

Casper coughed clearing his throat and grinned at Julia. He did not feel a need to be competitive with Charles. Julia turned away and tilted up her chin. "If you don't like my coffee you can make it yourself," she told Charles.

Charles laughed and surrendered. "Not me," he told his sister-in-law. He winked at Annabel. "But your coffee generally tastes like muddy water warmed up."

"Perhaps, I didn't make the coffee this morning," she said with a hint of mystery in her voice.

"Well, it's not Annabel's coffee," Charles demanded.

Casper smiled, knowing Julia was not going to admit to anything in front of her brother-in-law who seemed to enjoy teasing her.

Charles broke open a biscuit filling it with ham. He bit into the sandwich. "Where is the chestnut horse," he asked Annabel.

She opened her mouth but no words came out. For a moment she looked as if she was about to panic. "I'll bring the chestnut in. He's staked out with the draft horses grazing," Casper said. He walked in long even strides to where he had staked the horses. Julia was not the only one keeping secrets from Charles, he thought as he brought in the chestnut saddle horse.

83

Charles unpacked his saddle. It was well worn as if it had seen lots of service, highly polished and ornamented with silver trim. He tossed his saddle over the chestnut's back. The high spirited gelding pulled on the reins and Charles cursed the horse.

Casper watched the horse's antics. Found, he held his breath as the horse reared his hooves pawing the air. Charles had a firm hold on the reins and brought the horse under control. In the saddle, Charles waited as the horse back stepped and reared again. Casper admired Charles' handling the high spirited animal. He was not sure he wanted the privilege. Johns had spent most of the time training him how to handle a team of horses. They had gone riding only once.

Annabel and Julia were not the only women making use of the day to do the wash. The camp was full of drying lines strung from wagons. Wash tubs where brought out and buckets of water hauled from the nearby creek by older boys or occasionally a husband.

Julia scrubbed while Annabel rinsed and hung out. Then they traded places. Annabel washed Charles' and her daughters' clothes and Julia rinsed and hung out. Casper was content to haul bucket after bucket of water from the creek. The three girls followed in his foot steps. Hanging onto him when he was not burdened with water buckets.

Many heads turned at the sound of childish laughter to watch the handsome young man with the three young girls slowing his footsteps. Or to see Molly with her golden head bobbing as she rode on Casper's shoulders her fingers tangled in his blond hair. His hat worn by one of the other girls as they held onto his hands. Once he came from the creek with Annabel's girls tucked under his arms as he carried water buckets.

The washing completed, Casper lifted the wash tub and dumped the water away from the campsite. Annabel watched as he came back. "Why don't you call me, Annabel," she requested. "We are going to spend a lot of time together."

"Alright, if you will call me Casper," He answered in a friendly voice.

"A deal," Annabel answered. "And Julia," she asked.

He glanced to where Julia was standing feeling clothes to see if they were dry. "I think it would be better if I continue to call her, Miss," he replied. Annabel saw the look in his blue eyes and was sure he was falling in love with her sister. Casper was

84

erecting a barrier between them? She could understand Julia's kindness and her sister's generous heart appealing to him. He must be lonely since his wife's death. Annabel liked Casper and believed he was good for Julia. Her sister needed the kind of man who would look after her and at times be overly protective.

Julia felt the last little girl's dress on the line. Stretched, rubbing her back with the palm of her hands. "If our friends could only see us now," she said laughing.

Annabel looked thoughtful, before asking "You're not sorry you came?"

"No, of coarse not," Julia was quick to answer. "Well, not most of the time," she claimed honestly. "It's my life's ambition to get up before dawn and smell of wood smoke. Haven't you heard it's the latest fashion," she teased.

"I don't know what I would do if you hadn't come," Annabel added with a note of seriousness.

"You would have made out just fine," Julia assured. "You were always more resourceful than I am."

"Resourceful? Maybe," Annabel sounded doubtful. "I wouldn't have had the foresight to bring Casper," she told Julia with honesty.

Julia laughed softly. "I told you I'm not resourceful. I brought him along to do my thinking for me," she teased.

Casper caught the last of Julia's statement and turned to her with a question in his blue eyes.

* * * * *

Charles insisted he and Annabel spend the evening getting to know their traveling companions. He was not one to be content with his own company or even the company of his wife and daughters. Charles was social and needed the admiration of others to fulfill a need that existed in him. Annabel would have gladly bypassed the outing but would under no circumstance tell Charles how she felt.

He had given up trying to persuade Julia to do anything she did not readily agree to do. His sister-in-law was stubborn and he was not yet prepared to force her into compliance. Besides, the idea of Julia watching his daughters while he and Annabel visited appealed to him. The girls tied Annabel down. Mr. Van Holland

85

was visiting the Webb's camp. The young man had developed the habit of visiting with the couple next to them.

When Charles and Annabel left, Julia settled down next to the fire. "I'm glad that's over," she said to no one.

"What's over," Wilma asked.

"The grown ups have gone," she told Wilma with laughter in her voice. "Now, what do you want to do," she asked the child before grabbing and tickling her.

Clara gave her a serious look. Her lips puckered into a pout before she yawned. "I want to go to bed," she stated.

Julia felt light hearted. "Alright," she agreed. After washing faces, hands and arms, she sat Clara in front of her to brush her long hair. "What shall I do with this," she asked, gathering the girl's hair in one hand.

"Braids. Oh please braids," Clara implored. Julia knew Charles thought braids too provincial for his daughters.

"Well," Julia paused.

"Oh please, Aunt Julia. Mommy won't mind its only father," Clara stated, showing wisdom beyond her years.

"Well," Julia said, seeming to consider the request but Clara heard the note of teasing in her voice.

"Oh! Thank you!" Clara shouted. "I promise to take the braids out first thing in the morning. It can be our secret."

"Alright," Julia answered. "Our secret. Only if your father asks you're not to tell a lie. You must always tell him the truth." She divided Clara's hair down the middle of her head. After brushing each side to make sure there were no tangles, she divided the hair into three strands and began to carefully braid the long tresses.

"Me too," Wilma said, looking at Clara with sad envious eyes, "I want a secret too."

Julia laughed, "You want a secret too then come here," she said and put her finger to the child's lips, "Alright dear." She braided the little girl's hair.

"Do Molly's hair," Wilma said, accepting the younger girl as one of them.

Julia looked at the sleepy Molly curled up on her father's lap. With Charles and Annabel away visiting, he elected to return to camp and keep Julia company.

86

"By all means," Casper said, handing his daughter to Julia. He watched while Molly's hair was brushed and a braid made on each side of the child's head.

"There," Julia said when she had finished. "Now, we have triplets, all scrubbed and ready for bed."

"Story," Wilma insisted.

"Please tell us a story Aunt Julia," Clara added her persuasion.

Julia gathered Molly onto her lap. "It's off to bed then I will tell you a story."

"Pussy cat," Wilma asked.

"Any story you like. But first to bed." Julia stood taking Molly into her arms. Annabel's girls followed her to the wagon. Casper lifted the girls up so they could crawl inside under the canvas top.

"Good night," he told them. "Good night Miss."

"Thank you," Julia said, giving him a shy look.

The following day, Charles did not return to the campsite until early afternoon. His eyes were red brimmed and he was surly. He went to his wagon and slept the remainder of the day.

News passed along the wagon train informing the travelers they were leaving the next morning at sun up. Casper greeted the news with both a sense of excitement and dread. He abhorred idleness. All his tasks had been completed and the sooner they got underway the better. Yet, he knew there would be hardships and challenges ahead of him and Julia.

Annabel too was relieved. Charles was spending too much time in Saint Joseph where there was entertainment for any who sought it. "Charles has already gone through half of the money we brought with us," she confided to her sister as they shared the tasks of cooking supper over the campfire. Annabel was much more experienced than Julia.

The information worried Julia but she assured Annabel everything would be fine. She wondered how much Charles had lost gambling. She also knew there was nothing she could do about Charles' bad habits. Annabel dearly loved him, perhaps too much.

CHAPTER THIRTEEN

It was a cold gray dawn. Julia woke to the sound of horses stomping and the rattle of chains as Casper unfastened the horses from the wagonbed. She hurried to dress and then woke Molly. The child was half asleep when Julia pulled a dress over her head. They descended from the wagon to a cold morning. The campfire was a welcome sight with the coffeepot boiling in hot coals. She buttoned Molly's coat and placed her on an upended crate telling her to stay seated.

Molly blinked several times then sat looking around but did not move. Julia was troubled as she hurried to cook breakfast. She would never get through all her chores if she did not calm down. Taking deep breaths, she sliced bacon laying the strips in the large iron skillet over the fire. This completed, she made biscuits shaping the dough into round balls which she flattened. She greased both sides before putting them in the Dutch oven to bake. She turned the bacon strips then stirred oatmeal setting the three legged kettle in the hot coals.

All is going well, she repeated to herself, just don't panic!

Julia wondered about Annabel and Charles. It was time her sister and brother-in-law made an appearance. Casper led her team of bay draft horses from the creek and staked them to graze while he came for breakfast. He would later hitch the horses to the wagon while she cleaned the campsite.

Annabel and her girls tumbled out of the back of their wagon. Annabel was red in the face with her normal composure gone. She was agitated and had a tight pinched look about her lips. She sent Clara and Wilma over to Julia and began to unchain the horses from the wagon.

The blacks were restless pulling on their leads, stomping and tossing their heads. Annabel tried again to bring the horses under control. She felt strong hands take hold of the lines. Casper stood next to her taking the blacks' reins in a firm grip. She could hear Charles' oaths as the noise disturbed his sleep. Annabel took a quick breath as her face burned with humiliation.

Casper led the black horses to water. He did not say a word. Annabel followed leading Charles' chestnut saddle horse.

Julia had the girls fed by the time they returned. The first call came down the line of wagons. Annabel held back tears while her face paled.

Casper quickly finished his breakfast and went to bring in the bay horses. He hitched the team to Julia's wagon before going for the blacks bringing them to Annabel's wagon. She hurried across to help him finish the task.

Julia had the dishes in the crate and supplies repacked by the time they were finished. Casper shoveled prairie sod over the fire extinguishing the flames. Mr. Cooperfield was scout for Mr. Horn's wagon train. He rode down the line of wagons verifying all fires were out. For the next few weeks nothing was left to chance as the 'greenhorns' learnt how to survive on the trail.

"Surely tomorrow will be better," Julia mumbled catching back a sob. She wrapped left over biscuits and bacon in a cloth to eat later. Casper lifted the crates onto the wagon's tailgate, slid the crates into the wagon, closed the tailgate and put in the pins to hold it shut.

Annabel had her girls on the wagon seat beside her. Casper gave the harness one last quick inspection before handing her the reins. He did not comment on Annabel driving the wagon. In long strides, he came to Julia and helped her onto the wagon then handed up Molly. The last call came as he was checking the harness on their team. He placed his boot on the wagon wheel spoke and swung his leg over the side of the wagon and sat down next to Julia taking the reins from her. Annabel pulled ahead of them. Casper called to his team and the bay horses stepped out eagerly.

With pent up emotions, Julia brushed away tears not wanting Casper to see her crying. At last she was on her way. She had spent months preparing for today. It was the start of a new beginning. She wondered how Annabel felt now they were on the wagon trail to Oregon Country and how she was managing the spirited black horses. More important, why was Charles still sleeping when there was work to be done?

Glancing at Casper's profile, Julia wondered if he was feeling the same emotions she was experiencing. There was a tight fear in her chest. He appeared calm and intent on keeping the proper distance between them and Annabel's wagon in front. He gave her a quick glance. His blue eyes were bright and Julia realized Casper was not as calm as he appeared.

"I want to thank you for helping Annabel." Another quick turning of his head, he gazed at her. He saw admiration in Julia's eyes before she lowered her chin.

"Will you pass me the canteen," he asked.

Julia had filled the canteens the night before with boiled water. They were beneath the wagon seat. Taking off the cap, she passed the canteen to Casper and watched as he tilted it up to drink.

"Me too," Molly implored. Mimicking her father's actions, she took a drink from the canteen. Julia smiled realizing what a great responsibility it was to be a good example. She had noticed Molly mimicking her father before.

"What do you want to do today," she asked Molly. "Would you rather play with your animals or do you want me to read to you?"

Molly crawled into the wagon and came back with her favorite story book. Julia lifted her over the back of the wagon seat and settled the child on her lap. She opened the book, "I've a feeling young lady we are going to be thoroughly tired of this story by the time we reach Oregon Country."

Molly settled against Julia's shoulder with her eyes on the open book. Julia began reading out loud. Stopping as she read to point to drawings on the brightly colored pages. Molly likewise would place her fingertips on the picture repeating the words spoken by Julia.

Casper divided his attention between the trail ahead and the soft voices of Julia and Molly. The interaction between the young woman, he at one time believed cold and unfeeling, and his young daughter warmed his heart. He was surprised when Molly tilted up her face, puckered her lips and Julia leaned over to kiss her.

"Again," Molly giggled, turning the pages back to the beginning.

90

His heart filled with wonder as he witnessed his daughter being cared for and loved by Julia in an intimate and endearing way. Julia was not just giving Molly care she was giving his daughter a mother's love.

"Again," Julia said, hugging Molly's little body to her and tickling the child with her fingertips. The book slipped off her lap, Casper reached and caught it. Julia looked at him in surprise. She had forgotten his presence.

By the middle of the morning, Molly was rubbing her eyes sleepily and Julia knew it was time to make her comfortable on their bed. There was no graceful way of crawling into the wagon. She held up her long skirt hoping Casper would not watch as she stepped over the wagon seat. She more or less tumbled onto the bed he had made for them.

Molly taking a nap, Julia placed her book on the wagon seat and gathered her full skirt about her ankles before stepping over the seat's back. She only hoped she could find a more dignified way in the future. She settled on the seat adjusting her skirts before opening her book.

Julia sat for a long moment taking in the scenes around her. Dark clouds were gathering in the southwest. Green sprouts added color to the tuffs of winter dried yellow grass. The wide sweep of prairie looked flat. The appearance was false as there were many washes, gullies and rolling slopes. The wind picked up blowing cold air from the west. Julia tucked a blanket securely around her shoulders and was thankful for the warmth. She opened the book that was lying on her lap and began to read.

Casper glanced at the young woman beside him. His attention momentarily strayed from the job at hand. "Would you mind reading aloud," he asked simply.

Julia looked up but Casper's gaze was on the trail ahead. "You might not find the story interesting," she replied.

"We've long monotonous hours ahead of us," Casper stated. He glanced at Julia a second time. She opened the book smoothing the pages with the palm of her right hand.

"I'm reading a French novel," she explained. "But I can read something else if you like. I've brought several novels with me."

""This book is fine," he answered. "You speak French," he asked.

91

"I speak French but will translate the story into English for you," Julia explained. "I'll start at the beginning." She turned several pages and began reading in a soft clear voice. Casper listened with an interest only those who cannot read give to the written word.

Julia read until she completed three chapters then closed the book. She stared at the dark clouds moving across the sky but her mind was on what she had just read.

"It won't rain for hours," Casper declared.

By the noonday stop, Julia was sore and stiff from the movement of the wagon. It had swayed and jolted over the uneven prairie. The dark rain clouds hung low and the wind blowing across the open land was cold.

Casper unhitched the horses, staking them a short distance from the wagon to graze. Annabel was clumsy as she unhooked the team of blacks from the wagon. Her shoulders ached from the unfamiliar strain of holding onto reins all morning and snapping the reins to keep the team plodding along. She was glad that Johns had taught her and Julia to drive first a pony cart and later a buggy.

Julia unloaded the supplies needed for the noonday meal. Her anger grew toward her brother-in-law and with determination she fought to control it. She must not make Annabel's life any harder than it was by showing her anger. With more vigor than was necessary, Julia set up camp and began cooking their meal. Annabel joined Julia and stood rubbing her stiff achy shoulders. Julia clamped tight her lips and gave her a welcoming smile. At the same time vowing she would never volunteer to drive Annabel's wagon. Let Charles take on the responsibility. After all, traveling to Oregon Country by wagon train was his brilliant idea!

Charles Heywood made his appearance at the end of the meal. After pouring a cup of coffee, he used his charm to tease and coerce Annabel into a cheerful and loving mood. That his words and actions fell short of there intended goal on Julia, he seemed not to notice. Sure his behavior would be forgiven if not for his sake then for Annabel's.

Annabel helped Julia repack provisions and Casper loaded the crates into Julia's wagon while Charles strode to where the black draft horses were teetered. Julia was sure it was not to check on their welfare since he had called the horses nags in the most disparaging tones. It was Charles' way of getting out of work.

Julia began to wonder why he had ever proposed the journey. He was not the type of man to give up his creature comforts for long and yet here they were suffering hardships and trials at his whim.

In the afternoon Julia brought out her embroidery and sewed while the wagon bucked and swayed over miles of seemingly endless prairie. Since, she sat in tight lipped silence spoke volumes about her mood. The one time Casper had ventured to speak to her, she had answered in a sharp clipped voice.

At length Molly woke from her afternoon nap and crawled to the front of the wagon. She patted Julia on the shoulder. Turning, Julia smiled at Molly then reached over the back of the seat and sat Molly between Casper and her tucking a blanket around the child as the air was quite cold. Soon the first drops of cold rain blew against Julia's face taking her breath away. Shivering, she gathered Molly onto her lap. Molly peeped from beneath the warm wool blanket. The late afternoon sky darkened ominously with streaks of lightning flashing and the low rumbles of thunder soon following.

"Are we going to stop," Julia asked as the storm drew nearer.

"Can't afford to," Casper answered. "We need to cross the prairie and reach Fort Kearney during the spring rainy season. Mr. Horn wants to reach Oregon Country before it snows in the mountains."

Julia nodded her head signaling she understood since the wind blew her words away.

"You're getting wet," Casper said glancing at Julia. "You need to get in back."

Julia remained where she was fascinated by the wind driven rain that obscured the world around them. Huddled in the blankets, she watched the tall grass bend beneath the torrential down pour. The canvas top of Annabel's wagon bellowed in the strong wind.

"Julia!" he shouted leaning towards her. She looked at him noticing the concern in his blue eyes. The rain was a hindrance as she helped Molly under the wagon flap. Standing, she placed a steadying hand on his shoulder. The wind blew the blanket wildly around her as she stepped over the wagon seat and crawled into the wagon.

Molly looked at her with wide frightened eyes. Julia's hair was wind blown and damp with rain. She gathered Molly to her breast as thunder grew louder. Wind drove against the canvas top causing it to bellow then collapse. She sat with her back against the wagon seat. She felt each time Casper shifted his weight on the seat.

The plodding of the horses slowed as they braced wind and rain. The air grew colder and hail began to pelt the canvas top. Casper stepped over the seat and hunkered down with the reins in his hands. Annabel's wagon had stopped. The team of bays shied then balked and would have runaway except for Casper's strong hands on the reins. The hail passed as quickly as it began. The silence was eerie after the noise made by falling hail. On the horizon, a twister whirled across the open prairie. Julia pulled back the canvas flap to watch. Her heart was thumping out of control. The sky was nearly as black as night. Black clouds rolled across the heaven. The dark swirling cloud reached the ground and rose back into the air and then came back down with a long funnel touching the ground. The wagon rocked back and forth driven by wind.

Julia leaned against Casper speaking into his ear. "Are we alright?" She could feel the tight cords of his shoulder muscles as he held the horses under control.

As the roar drew nearer, Julia could see grass and debris pulled into the black funnel cloud as it swirled. She wrapped her arms around Casper's waist pressing her cheek against his broad back. She held Molly in her arms. The child protested being pressed against her father.

Rain stopped and the air looked green and smelled sweet. Julia held her breath and clung to Casper as the roar intensified. The wagon rocked violently and she hid her eyes against Casper's shirt. The wind roared past and the frightened horses strained and jerked violently against their harness. Julia shut her eyes and tightened her grip on Casper.

"I don't ever remember being so afraid during a storm," she confided her breath fanning his cheek. "The wind is letting up," she continued. Aware for the first time she was still clinging to him.

The sky began to lighten, the air smelled fresh. The wind, which a short time before had beat against the wagon, slowed to a gentle breeze. There was water everywhere. The ground was

94

saturated and the tall prairie grass displayed beads of water on every stem and blade.

"You need to change out of those wet clothes," Julia advised practically. "Give me the reins." She stepped over the seat and sat down with her back to Casper. Her heart was doing strange flips and her breathing was not normal.

Casper handed over the reins. He had conflicting thoughts about Julia. He wanted her arms around his chest holding him as tight as she could. Taking several deep breaths, he reached for his valise and took out dry clothes. The confines of the wagon when fully packed gave little room for changing clothes. He was buttoning his shirt when he heard Julia talking to someone.

"Yes Sir," Julia said.

Mr. Cooperfield looked at Julia with admiration in his eyes. She was a beautiful, reserved young woman. "One of the wagons blew over during the storm," he said. "It will take a few minutes for Mr. Horn to get it righted. Is everyone in your wagon alright?"

"Yes Sir," Julia replied.

Casper slipped off the end of the wagon and lifted the tailgate moving the pins to hold it closed. "Does Mr. Horn need any help," he asked. The ground squished beneath his boots as he walked to the front of the wagon. Mr. Cooperfield looked him up and down noting he was in back of the wagon changing into dry clothes.

"The wagon should be righted by now," Mr. Cooperfield retorted. "There will be a delay is all." He rode to the Webb's wagon and repeated what he had told Julia.

Casper placed his boot on the wheel spoke and climbed onto the wagon seat taking the reins from Julia. "Our first day on the trail and already a disaster," she wailed before gulping in a deep breath.

"We made it through the storm," Casper reminded calmly.

"Why do you think Charles decided to travel by wagon train instead of going by train," Julia asked, surprising Casper.

Casper did not answer right away.

"I want your honest answer," Julia insisted.

"I can only give you my opinion based on what I know," Casper reminded. He waited a few seconds before continuing. "I believe Mr. Heywood has gone through Annabel's money. You bought her half of the house," he continued when Julia opened her

95

mouth to protest. "You bought the shares in the company she sold to finance their trip to Europe."

"What you are suggesting is Annabel is broke," Julia said. "How will traveling by wagon train change that," she asked.

"What will Annabel do when all of her money is gone," Casper asked, not wanting to put into words what he was thinking.

"She will come to me wanting money," Julia whispered.

"Will you give her the money she asks for," Casper asked.

Julia looked indignant. "Of course I will," she declared hotly.

"Then you answered the question of why Mr. Heywood is traveling by wagon train," Casper retorted.

"He wants my money and knows I will willingly give it to Annabel when she asks," Julia whispered sadly. "Poor Annabel, she loves Charles deeply and will do anything to make him happy."

"Blind love can be a curse," Casper stated.

"We don't know for sure," Julia declared rallying her pride.

"No we don't," Casper agreed. "You asked me what I thought and wanted an honest opinion."

"Thank you," Julia said. "You're right of course. I shouldn't be upset because you gave me your honest opinion. I'm not really. It's Charles I'm angry with. Father did not want Annabel and Charles to marry. Mother thought he had a weak character. I heard her say as much."

Julia thought for a long moment before confiding in Casper. "Annabel says Charles has spent half of the money they brought with them," she whispered distraught. "I believe this is what is worrying Annabel and the reason she has not been feeling well."

Casper knew Julia was thinking out loud and did not expect a reply. He kept his true opinion of Charles Heywood to himself. He considered Charles not only weak but a crook. With Annabel's money running out, he was scheming to get Julia's money. Casper then remembered Johns' warning about his concerns in regard to Charles Heywood.

The call came down the line of wagons and they were on the move again. Several times over the next hours the wagons stopped as one wagon after another needed assistance over a bad patch of ground. The gullies were running high with water and wagon wheels cut deep grooves in the soft prairie sod. Both were impeding travel. By nightfall Julia was ready for a rest. A cold rain once more was falling.

The rain soaked wood gave out more smoke than heat making fixing an evening meal troublesome. Charles was ill-tempered and disagreeable. He soon strode off in what Julia referred to as one of his moods. The girls were not allowed to play in the tall wet grass. They were restless with nothing to do and started bickering.

Julia laid her head in her hands and sobbed.

CHAPTER FOURTEEN

"Molly is sleeping. I think I'll walk awhile with Sara," Julia told Casper as they prepared to start on the trail after a noonday stop. It had rained off and on for several weeks. The sun was out drying the ground and Julia was tired of sitting all day on the wagon seat or lying on her bed trying to think and plan the future. Casper's words about Charles' reason for traveling by wagon train rather than the Union Pacific Railroad were worryisome. At the same time, she knew there was nothing she could do about her brother-in-law's bad behavior.

Casper said he would stop the wagon when Molly woke. Placing his foot on the wheel spoke he climbed onto the wagon seat and snapped the reins. The team was reluctant to start off again. Julia waited for the Webb wagon to pass then fell into step beside Sara.

"A fine day," Sara greeted.

"Yes," Julia agreed. She arched her back to stretch sore muscles.

"Saddle sores, so to speak," Sara asked.

Laughing, Julia nodded her head yes. "And you?"

Sara nodded her head smiling in agreement. They walked in companionable silence careful where they stepped in the tall grass.

"Is your sister feeling better today," Sara asked at length.

"A little, it's not like Annabel to be ill," Julia confided

"Probably something she ate," Sara replied.

"Mr. Van Holland suggested the same thing. He asked me what Annabel ate this morning?" Stepping over a tuff of tall grass, Julia missed the startled look Sara gave her.

Sara shrugged her shoulders dismissing what she did not understand. "The illness will probably pass in a day or so," Sara suggested, noticing how worried Julia looked. "Your wagon has stopped," Sara said a short time later.

"Molly is probably awake," Julia said before hurrying to her wagon. Casper reached down to help her up, changing the reins in his hands as she slipped across in front of him. Julia sat down and raised the hem on her long full skirt checking for crawling bugs on her petticoat and stockings. She shuddered as she tossed a tick over the side of the wagon. Then she brushed down her skirt and reached for the whimpering girl.

"Have a nice walk," Casper asked.

"Yes, if it wasn't for these infernal bugs," Julia retorted.

Casper smiled. Julia did hate bugs.

Molly curled against Julia, one chubby baby cheek resting against her breast. Rubbing her eyes, she watched her father. He gave his daughter a grin and a wink. His vision rested on Julia as she brushed back Molly's fine golden hair from his child's face. He turned his attention back to the plodding horses but in his mind he could see the soft glow on Julia's face. He had not expected Julia to love his daughter. And more importantly, he had not expected to fall in love with Julia. At times she was warm and friendly, unconscious of the social gap between them. At other times she was a cool, arrogant young woman. Casper dismissed his thoughts. Saying his love was a fool's errand. Julia Warren would never return his love.

It was early evening when the call came down the line and the wagons stopped for the night. On the wide prairie the wagons made a circle. Casper pulled the team of bay horses close to Annabel's wagon. He wrapped the reins around the brake handle and threw one leg over the side of the wagon placing his boot on the wagon wheel then the wheel spoke before stepping to the ground.

Julia handed him Molly before she pulled back her long skirt and placed one high top shoe on the wagon wheel. Holding onto the wagon, she gingerly moved her other foot to the wheel and stood balanced on top. She glanced over her shoulder to see Casper holding out his hands to help her. She leaned into his hands and the next second her feet touched ground. "There must be a better way to get off a wagon," she declared.

99

Casper's fingers tingled where they had touched Julia's waist. "I will get the fire going," Casper said. They had stopped at noon near a creek. Annabel and Julia along with other women and children had gathered and stored wood in a sling built under each wagon.

Annabel removed the pins from the tailgate and started pulling crates from the back of Julia's wagon. She looked pale and gaunt. "Why don't you watch the children while I cook supper," Julia suggested.

Annabel held one hand over her stomach. "I do believe I am getting worse not better," she admitted reluctantly.

Charles came and took the crates from the back of Julia's wagon and carried them to where Casper was starting a campfire. A couple of nights a week he would play the dutiful husband and help around the campsite. Teasing Annabel and flirting with Julia to see her turn bright red. The remaining nights, Charles went off with friends, playing cards and carousing.

As soon as supper was over Casper strolled to the Webbs for a visit. He sat where he could watch Molly. Not that he worried about his daughter. Julia took her role as guardian very seriously, keeping watch over the three girls.

Clare and Wilma were soon at the Webbs playing with Molly, Casper keeping watch on all three girls. Julia washed dishes and made ready the camp for the next morning before sitting down by Annabel. She was reluctant to leave her sister.

"Why don't you go lie down," Julia suggested. "I will come and read to you."

Annabel looked at Charles hoping he would suggest he would sit with her. He was staring into the night. "Did you say something," he asked a minute later.

"I offered to read to Annabel," Julia replied.

He took Annabel's hand in his. "You do look tired," he said with just the right amount of concern in his voice. "An early night will do you good. Mr. Horn said this morning we will be at Fort Kearney in another day. There isn't another long rest until we reach Fort Laramie . Once we reach Fort Hall along the Snake River, we will be in Oregon Country. Annabel and I are going all the way to the coast aren't we, Dear," he explained, giving Julia a smug look.

100

"Mr. Horn takes the wagon train to Oregon City," Julia replied, wanting Charles to know she knew the itinerary of the wagon train as well as he did.

"Let me help you," Charles said, taking Annabel's arm. He walked with Annabel to their wagon and helped her inside. Julia watched but decided not to follow. Charles was being obnoxious and she did not feel up to dealing with self inflicted wounds.

Days settled into a routine. Up early, Casper would stir the coals in the campfire and make coffee before watering the horses and staking the animals out to graze. He ate a quick breakfast by the fire with Molly on his lap sharing his plate of bacon, biscuits and oatmeal. Casper cherished these few minutes the most. Starting a new day with Julia and Molly before Annabel and her girls joined them at the campfire.

He would then bring in the draft horses and hitch each team to the wagons. Annabel and her girls would be flustered and eat as Julia packed skillet and kettle into one crate along with tin plates, cups, and utensils. In another she packed supplies. First call passed down the line of wagons signaling everyone to get ready. Then a few minutes later, the second and last call was shouted from wagon to wagon. Annabel waited until the wagon in front of her rolled before following.

Charles never appeared before ten o'clock, often not until after the noonday break. Seldom was a fire started at noon since the stop was to allow horses, or oxen, or mules to rest and graze. The meal usually consisted of cold biscuits and beans.

In the afternoon Molly always woke from her nap hungry. Julia kept a tin of sweet crackers and another of dried fruit handy. Molly shared her food with her father. Giggling, she would eat a cracker then place one in her father's mouth. Her favorite dried fruit was raisins and she took one at a time feeding Casper and then herself. Molly would do this until her father would say no more. He would firmly close his lips and shake his head. One look from him and she would turn placing the raisin in Julia's mouth. She would give Julia a hug saying "I love you." Which Julia would promptly reply, "I love you."

Casper's heart never failed to respond to Julia's words. He would take a few deep breaths to calm his thumping heart and glance at Julia as she returned Molly's hug and kiss.

Though he could have held the canteen himself, he let Julia hold it while he drank. The water often ran down his chin and moistened the front of his shirt. If Julia was aware of the growing intimacy between them, she did not show any signs of doing so. Casper gave up his struggles against loving her. Knowing it had gone beyond the point where he could do anything about his feelings. He was in love and there was no way of going back. His only hope was to keep his feelings to himself. Even in this he wondered if he was succeeding.

One morning, little more than two weeks from Fort Kearney, Annabel woke in pain. Doubled over, her face pale and hands clutching her stomach, she woke Charles. His response to his wife's illness was simply to roll over and go back to sleep. Julia looked at her brother-in-law in disgust, went and joined Casper.

"It's obvious she can't drive this morning," Julia told him. "So I'll drive my wagon and you take Annabel's."

"Charles," Casper asked, but Julia just shrugged her shoulders dismissively and turned from him.

"If you're going to drive the wagon," he told her, "I want you in front of me so I can keep an eye on you." Julia wondered what good it would do but did not question him. His eyes were dark and his jaws clenched tight as if he was trying to control what he said.

"Alright, I'll pull round. There's plenty of room. Clara can ride with me and watch Molly," Julia said, knowing Casper was doing all he could to help. It was Charles she was furious with.

Casper nodded his head not trusting himself to speak. It was late morning when Julia looked down to see Casper walking beside the wagon. She stopped and he climbed aboard taking the reins without saying a word. Julia slid over after one glance at his face which was as dark as a thunder cloud.

Two days later Annabel was ill again and could not drive her wagon. Without objection, Casper drove Annabel's wagon only to join her later in the morning. His emotions were under tight control but Julia knew Charles had said something he would not share with her.

It was Charles who brought the subject up of Casper driving his wagon. "You should be helping Annabel more," he scolded Julia as he stood next to the campfire drinking coffee.

"I am," Julia answered.

"You're driving your wagon," Charles declared, punctuating his remark with a string of curses.

"I can't handle the black horses," Julia told him. "They are much too spirited in the morning."

"Rubbish, Annabel manages," Charles sneered.

"I'm not Annabel," she clamped her lips firmly together so as not to alienate her brother-in-law further.

"All the same," he looked at her, saw the tilt of her firm chin and knew to say more would be useless. He knew Julia's look of stubbornness.

Charles was still cursing when Casper came back from staking out the horses. Julia stood rigid before her brother-in-law with her eyes angry and lips tightly pressed together. He checked an impulse to intervene. After all, Charles was family. If his behavior was less than proper, Charles had not yet crossed the line where Casper felt compelled to protect Julia. His presence seemed to stop Charles' onslaught of obscenities. The man simply turned and stalked angrily away.

Julia ran to her wagon and climbed inside.

Casper set about preparing a meal. He was hungry and he knew the girls needed fed. Whatever passed between Julia and Charles, she would confide to him later.

Julia cried herself to sleep. Casper sat Molly on the bed beside her and placed one finger over his lips. Smiling, Molly imitated her father by placing her finger against her lips. Casper studied Julia's hot tear streaked face and grew angry. She looked young and vulnerable. He reached to brush hair off her face. His touch sent shock waves through him. A sense of hopelessness invaded his heart.

Julia woke to the sound of a strong wind blowing against the canvas top. The sway of the wagon as it rolled over the prairie heading for Fort Kearney. She crawled to the front and looked out.

Casper heard her and glanced to see Julia leaning against the wagon seat. She smiled up at him. The resilience of youth he thought. Handing her a cloth wrapped around cold biscuits, he said, "My biscuits aren't as good as yours but they are filling."

Taking the cloth, Julia turned to lean her back against the wagon seat. The napkin contained several biscuits which she quickly devoured. She reached across the seat for the canteen kept on the floor beneath the wagon seat.

"Here let me," Casper said. Shifting the reins to his left hand, he reached for the canteen

Julia whispered softly and Casper leaned over to hear her and felt the touch of her lips against his cheek. "Thank you," she whispered once again.

He nodded his head and held his breath until the impulse to kiss Julia passed. Molly woke from her nap demanding Julia's attention. Julia reached for Molly and the tin of sweet crackers before climbing over the wagon seat and sitting Molly on her lap. She handed Molly a cracker before speaking her thoughts out loud. "Charles objects to your driving his wagon and I refuse to drive the black horses. They are too spirited for me to handle," she excused. "I am wondering if we might be able to find someone to take over driving the wagon in the mornings as Charles appears too lazy to do so. There are a number of families with older boys," she suggested, bitterness creeping into her voice.

"I'll have a talk with Mr. Horn," Casper replied. "He might know of someone." He wondered if Julia would shoulder another expense to allow her brother-in-law to keep his life style. Why didn't the man simply take on the responsibility of his family?

* * * * *

Daniel Wheeler was sixteen, nearly as tall as Casper and muscular built. Mr. Horn suggested he might be interested in driving Annabel's wagon during the morning.

Casper and Julia had talked it over and had decided to offer the boy fifty cents for the half day of work. Casper took along a twenty dollar gold piece to pay the lad. He knew Mr. Wheeler and was confident the father would see his son carried out his obligation if he accepted the job. Casper was prepared to pay Daniel for forty days of work. He shook hands with Mr. Wheeler going straight to business.

"I'd heard your sister-in-law is feeling poorly," Mr. Wheeler said after Casper made his request.

Casper looked at Mr. Wheeler surprised he considered Annabel his sister-in-law but decided not to correct the man. After all, his interest was in seeing if Daniel was willing to drive the Heywood wagon. Daniel agreed to the wages and said he would be over right after breakfast. Casper thanked him then paid the lad twenty dollars. He started back to his campsite, his mind still mulling over what Mr. Wheeler said. Did the man mean, he thought Julia was his wife? He had not considered the possibility earlier or would have corrected the mistake.

When he arrived at camp, Julia asked, "Were you able to find someone?"

104

"Daniel Wheeler agrees to drive Annabel's wagon, he will be here in the morning."

"What's wrong," she asked. Sure something was disturbing Casper then wondered how she knew.

"Nothing," Casper replied. After all, he was not sure Mr. Wheeler meant to imply he thought Casper and Julia were married. It could be the man believed he was related to Charles.

"It doesn't seem natural," Julia confided to Casper the following morning as she sat next to him on the wagon seat. "I've never known Annabel to be ill before." Julia traced the title of the book lying on her lap with one fingertip. Her deep frown told how concerned she was over Annabel's illness.

Casper kept his eyes on the trail ahead, his mind turning over what Julia said. He was also concerned but did not like what he was thinking. Annabel's symptoms were the same as a woman who lived in his tenement building had been. In the end, it was discovered her nephew was feeding her a small amount of poison each day. Everyone thought the woman's indigestion was from something she ate. It took her weeks to die. Her nephew wanted the small amount of money given her by her employer when she retired and did his aunt in.

"Does Charles have a profession," Casper asked.

"As far as I know, Charles doesn't have a profession unless you consider gambling and hunting. Those are his two passions. They live off Annabel's money which is never enough. You are aware Annabel has sold most of her shares in Warren Enterprises. The fact was discussed the evening before we left on the train."

"What about your money," Casper asked reluctantly.

"Uncle John over sees my money until I turn twenty five or marry. Uncle John does the investing, usually in properties as that is what my father preferred. The property is rented and any money over the cost of maintaining the property I receive as income."

"Where did your money come from? I remember you or Annabel saying your father was not a wealthy man. The reason Charles was upset about you giving your cousin Stanford a half share in your holding. Charles said the money had never been Warren money," Casper reminded. He was having a hard time sorting all the connections out.

"My grandfather, that is to say my mother's father. Annabel and I are the only grandchildren and his property was divided

105

between us when grandfather passed away. Father managed the properties while he was alive and added to the family wealth. Uncle John took over the responsibility after father died."

"How old are you," Casper asked.

She looked at him in surprise as if to say what did her age have to do with anything. "I'm eighteen," she answered.

He gave her a swift glance. She was staring at white clouds, tall and majestic, gathering on the horizon. Julia was a mere girl. It explained why at times she appeared so young and innocent and why at times she looked haunted and fearful.

"It's a queer deal," Casper continued his voice serious. He probed for words. "I'm not sure you trust me enough for what I'm about to say."

She looked at him as if trying to read his mind. His golden hair showed beneath his broad brimmed hat, his firm jaws were square, clean shaven and browned by sun and wind. His mouth was a straight line which rarely curved into a smile for anyone other than his daughter Molly.

He glanced at her, his pale blue eyes serious as he searched her features. She did not answer just looked at him with uncertainty. "Your brother-in-law Charles how well do you know him," he asked after a long interval.

Julia thought for a moment deciding how much or what to say. "I've known him more than half my life. He can be charming when he wants to be or cruel when he chooses," she paused. "Annabel loves him deeply."

"Would you marry him if Annabel, if Annabel wasn't here," he asked.

Julia was shocked by Casper's suggestion. "You don't think? You can't mean? I...I," she stopped unable to complete her thought. She could barely breathe. A heavy weight pressed against her chest.

"It's the only answer I'm able to come up with," Casper admitted reluctantly.

"You think Charles wants my money," Julia eventually was able to say. "More to the point you think Charles is behind Annabel's illness."

"I'm afraid I do," Casper admitted reluctantly.

"I can't accept this," Julia told him. "I need to think on it. I will admit I don't like Charles but to attribute what you are suggesting to him. I'm not sure I can." She paused, thinking on what he asked. "No," she answered. "I could never marry him. You think this whole venture was to get me away from Uncle John. From the people I know and trust." She leaned forward resting her face in her hands to hide her tears.

Casper waited silently as Julia cried.

"Charles knows all Annabel needs to do is ask and I will give her any amount of money she wants," she said, a few minutes later after sitting up and squaring her shoulders. "As much as I detest Charles, I can't believe he would harm Annabel." Julia crawled into the wagon and laid across the bed crying. Her tears told Casper more than her denial that Julia had doubts about what she said.

Hoping he was wrong, Casper let her cry. He liked and admired Annabel and knew how much Julia loved her sister.

CHAPTER FIFTEEN

Mr. Horn accepted the coffee cup Julia offered him. He sat silently sipping the strong hot brew. His task was not going to be an easy one. The young woman was quiet and shy with a soft look about the face. A real beauty he thought and gentle in her ways.

"You know, a wagon master has many duties," he said, addressing his words to Julia. Sitting erect with her hands folded together on her lap, she gave him her attention. "Not all of them are pleasant. I'm the law which often… Well, I won't go into that right now. I'm also confessor, minister and undertaker," he concluded.

Julia nodded her head waiting for Mr. Horn to disclose where his line of talk was taking them. And which of these duties had brought the wagon master to their campfire. Upon his arrival, he had said he wanted to speak to her and Mr. Van Holland alone. This was enough to make her curious.

Mr. Horn took a deep breath and plunged into what he had to say. "Folks on the wagon train are riled," he began, looking first at Casper then Julia. "Decent, God fearing folks going west for a better life for them and their families, and they have learned Sodom and Gomorrah have come to visit. It's been brought to the attention of the folks that you and Mr. Van Holland aren't…," here he stopped watching for Julia's reaction, "aren't husband and wife."

Julia drew back blinking in surprise. "We have never said we are," Julia reminded him softly as dark color stole into her cheeks.

"No. No you never said you were. I'll concede that," Mr. Horn admitted, shaking his head. "But the general belief is that you are. Of course there's the child."

"Molly? What does Molly have to do with Mr. Van Holland and me not being married," Julia asked, tilting up her chin. A cool look came into her blue eyes. Mr. Horn watched the change come over her in dismay. He had hoped to avoid a scene. "Oh," Julia said thoughtfully after a few seconds. "Mr. Horn, Molly is not my daughter." This surprised Mr. Horn. He had assumed Julia was Molly's mother. "It's true I love Molly but that doesn't make her my daughter," she said, her voice turning frosty.

"No. No your loving Molly doesn't mean she is your daughter but it does raise the question in the minds of folks. You understand a wagon train is like a small community. Everybody is interested in everybody else's business."

"What you are saying is Mr. Van Holland and I, are being gossiped about," Julia stated firmly. "And what is being said is disturbing." Julia wondered how much of Mr. Horn's statement about Sodom and Gomorrah included Charles. His gambling and whiskey drinking would disturb the decent women on the wagon train.

Mr. Horn found it difficult to talk to this new haughty young woman. Casper felt a wave of sympathy for the wagon master. His visit confirmed what Casper had begun to suspect. Folks on the wagon train believed they were married and had been told they were not. He had hoped he was wrong. This was a dilemma he was not sure how to handle. What was Julia thinking behind her mask of aloofness?

"Gossip can be an ugly thing," Mr. Horn continued only to have Julia interrupt him.

"Yes," Julia agreed. She had dealt with the opinions of others since young adulthood. Her mother often schooled her, slanderous gossip was hard to deal with and truth seldom worked. Gossips did not appreciate the truth when hearing it. "Well, there is only one thing to be done." she stated coldly. "You said you act as minister, does that include performing marriages? I want you to know before you answer, there has never been any impropriety between Mr. Van Holland and myself. My Uncle John hired him to take me to Oregon. Mr. Van Holland has always been respectful and trustworthy in his duties and in his behavior toward me. If I find it necessary to consent to this marriage it is not because of anything we have done. I simply find gossip distasteful and there is no other recourse open to either of us."

Casper studied Julia's cold face wishing there was another solution. But for Julia to simply move into Annabel's wagon would not stop malicious gossip. The only thing that would was for Mr. Horn to assure folks that he and Julia were husband and wife.

Mr. Horn listened to Julia's speech sure he was hearing the truth. He nodded his head signaling he understood what she was saying. "Would you like your sister and brother-in-law as witnesses," he asked.

"I would prefer Sara and Nathan Webb," she said coldly. She was pale beneath her soft tan and her blue eyes glowed with anger. She had come to the conclusion her trouble was due to Charles' meddling. What Charles hoped to accomplish, she had yet to determine.

"I'll invite them over," Mr. Horn said, glad for a few moments reprieve. Nothing was more nerve-racking than an angry woman.

Julia went to get the girls. She seated them on crates telling Clara to keep a close watch on Molly and to sit quietly.

Casper looked at the plain gold band on the palm of his hand having second thoughts about slipping it on Julia's finger. A wedding band was required. He thought of the flashy diamonds Annabel wore and wondered if Julia would later want diamonds. Somehow, they did not fit the Julia he had come to love. But, there was a lot about Julia he did not know.

When Sara arrived, Julia gave her friend a hug, whispering in her ear, she would explain everything later. Sara quickly nodded her head though her eyes revealed curiosity. She looked surprised when Mr. Horn directed her and Nathan to stand before him. Casper and Julia stood between them and Mr. Horn asked Casper and Julia to join hands.

The service was short, covering the sanctity of marriage and that it was God ordained. Then Casper was saying, "I will." And Julia was directed to answer the age old questions asked of brides and she too said, "I will."

The feather touch of Casper's lips upon hers was dream like. Julia had not realized Casper had slipped the circlet of gold on her finger until Mr. Horn shook her hand. The metal pressed into her flesh and she was startled to see a ring on her finger.

Mr. Horn brought out his journal and filled in the date. Then he wrote, on this day in June he joined Casper Hiram Van Holland and Julia Ernestine Warren in Holy Matrimony. Sara and Nathan

110

Webb signed their names as witnesses. He closed his journal and wished them happiness before leaving. Sara and Nathan Webb also left. Their heads together whispering, they walked through the gathering dusk to their campsite.

Casper was not sure what he expected and whether or not he expected Julia's tears. Julia leaned her face against his chest sobbing out her heart. "It will be alright," he said, which made Julia cry harder.

Wiping away tears and taking a deep breath, she said, "I need to get the girls ready for bed. I told Annabel I'd keep them tonight." Then what Julia said came slowly back to her. She looked at Casper with wide startled eyes, realizing she was married to him. And, this was her wedding night.

"It's alright," Casper said, trying to calm the panic he saw in Julia's eyes. "Our marriage is not a conventional marriage. I don't expect a normal wedding night. We will talk things out tomorrow," he assured her.

He watched Julia turn a bright fiery red and wished he could take back his words. "Yes, we need to sort things through tomorrow," she replied. "Come girls. It's time for bed."

Clara held Molly by the hand as they walked to the wagon. Casper lifted the girls inside. Since Annabel's illness, Julia kept the girls most nights. Casper had rearranged the crates making two beds, a bed on each side of the Prairie Schooner with walking space between. He set the lantern on the floor so Julia could see to undress the girls and help them wash before pulling nightgowns over their heads.

Julia laid on her bed with Molly next to her listening to Casper chain the horses to the wagon. He unrolled his bedroll under the wagon and sought his blankets. Was he lying awake as she was doing? Lying awake wondering what the future held. Panic roiled through her mind and she groaned out loud. There was nothing she could do to change the past. She must look to the future and find hope.

Julia woke to the rattle of chains and Casper talking to the horses as he unfastened the animals from the wagon. The familiar cool morning air greeted her as she pushed back the blanket and hurried into her clothes before waking the girls. She helped Molly to dress and Clara helped her younger sister, Wilma.

It was a gray dawn. Julia rushed to prepare breakfast. She sliced bacon laying strips in the big skillet before placing the skillet over the fire. Stirred the oatmeal, she had left soaking overnight and placed the three legged pot among the hot coals.

Casper watered the horses and staked the animals out to graze. Coming into camp, he poured a cup of coffee and sat on the ground stretching his legs out in front of him. He leaned his back against the crate Molly sat on.

"You will have to face Charles and Annabel today," Casper said casually not looking at Julia. He was not sure how Julia felt about marrying him. If she was angry this morning, he did not want to be on the receiving end of Julia's sharp tongue.

"I know," Julia answered softly, having tight control over her voice. Casper heard her nervousness.

"Have you planned what you will say," he asked.

"The truth," was her terse reply. She handed him a plate of bacon, hot biscuits, and oatmeal laced with honey.

He ate while helping Molly to eat. Refilling his coffee cup, he asked, "What is the truth?"

"How do I know," Julia shouted, anger in her voice.

"Are we having our first fight," he asked calmly.

Startled, she looked at him then laughed. "You are just convenient," she said, glancing at Clara and Wilma. Casper knew her real anger was toward Charles. He had come to the same conclusion Julia had. The person responsible for spreading gossip was her brother-in-law.

"You want me to talk with Charles," he asked.

"It will be better if I do," Julia replied. Casper had always let her handle the decision making when it came to Annabel and Charles. "If I need help, I will yell," she said with a reassuring frown puckering her brow. She was angry and ready to do battle.

Casper leaned close to Julia and whispered in one ear, "I can punch Charles in the nose if you like."

Julia turned a bright red. "I don't think it will be necessary even if the idea is intriguing," she whispered. Casper understood her resentment which was enough to assure her everything would workout in the end.

Casper did not say anything more as he finished eating breakfast then went to bring in the black draft horses to hitch to Annabel's wagon.

Clara sat eating while looking thoughtful. "Does this make you father and mother," she asked Julia in terms the child understood.

112

Julia took a deep breath. She supposed her marrying Casper did make them father and mother. "Yes," she answered. "You can call Mr. Van Holland, Uncle Casper," she said.

"We already call him Uncle Casper," Clara admitted. "I like the name Casper," she stated simply.

Julia turned the gold band on her finger thoughtfully. Was the ring she now wore, Molly's mother's wedding band? She felt no rivalry with the first Mrs. Van Holland. Only sorrow Molly's mother would not see her daughter grow into womanhood. Life was in one of those difficult stages, her mother often warned her about. Difficulties were to be worked through and responsibilities faced with resolve. Julia would face the problem of Charles with resolve.

Clara did not go close to the team of draft horses Casper was hitching to the Heywood wagon. "I love you Uncle Casper," Clara told him with a shy smile on her lips.

He picked the child up and hugged her. "I love you, too." She placed her arms around his neck and kissed his cheek.

"Me too," Wilma said. After Casper kissed her, the two girls hurried back to the campfire.

Annabel came from the wagon and stumbled. Casper hurried to place one hand under her arm. "Thank you," she said, giving him a wan smile. He escorted her to the campfire and helped her to sit down on one of the crates.

"Molly and I are sisters," Clara announced, looking at her mother.

"Oh, that's nice," Annabel replied absentmindedly.

"The big man came and made Molly and me sisters," Clara persisted. "Didn't he," she stated, looking at Casper hopefully.

"You and Molly are cousins," Julia corrected gently.

"Cousins? But, I want Molly to be my sister," Clara said stubbornly. She gave Casper the same look he often saw on Julia's face.

"Being cousins is as nice as being sisters," Julia assured. "Stanford is my cousin and I love him as much as I do Annabel."

"I love Stanford," Clara stated. She tilted her head to one side thinking. "Molly is my sister cousin," she declared not willing to give up the idea she and Molly were sisters.

"What's this about the big man and him making Molly and Clara sisters," Annabel asked after her girls went to play taking Molly with them.

113

Julia took a deep breath knowing it was time to confide in Annabel. "Clara means Mr. Horn," she said.

"I know Mr. Horn came by last evening wanting to talk to you and Casper," Annabel replied when Julia stopped speaking.

"Charles has been spreading rumors," Julia said, deciding not to gloss over Charles' part in what happened. She was tired of forgiving her brother-in-law his many faults and making excuses. "Mr. Horn said the women on the train were riled after hearing it suggested Casper and I are not married. He was here to discuss the matter. I'm sure it was only a matter of time before we were asked to leave the wagon train."

"What did you do," Annabel asked, sure she knew the answer before asking.

"Casper and I were married. It is the only solution. Mr. Horn will tell the folks we are married and all the vicious rumors will stop," Julia said.

Annabel was silent for a few minutes thinking over what Julia told her. "Casper is in love with you but I couldn't tell how you felt," she said.

Julia was surprised by Annabel's words. Then, she wondered if Annabel was trying to ease her conscious. She knew she looked haggard and weepy. "I'm not sure how I feel about Casper," Julia said, deciding not to comment on Annabel's statement as to Casper's feelings. True or false, it was up to Casper to tell her.

"Casper is a good man," Annabel assured. While they talked, Julia fixed her sister a plate of oatmeal. Annabel moved the food around on her plate taking small bites to please Julia.

Daniel Wheeler's arrival ended family talk. He finished hitching the black horses to the wagon while Casper went for Julia's bays. The first call came down the line and Annabel returned to her wagon. Julia called for the girls and Casper stored the crates in the wagon before shoveling dirt over the campfire.

The Prairie Schooner rocked when he stepped on the wheel spoke and mounted the seat. He took the reins in his hands and waited for the second call to pass from wagon to wagon before shouting, "Haw."

Another day on the trail began and Julia was not sure what to expect and even more uncertain how she was going to handle new difficulties. She only knew, she must face problems with resolve and not worry over matters she could not change.

114

CHAPTER SIXTEEN

Julia told Casper she wanted to walk with Sara. "Clara can watch Molly for awhile," he assured her. She nodded her head rather than answer. Walking to the back of the wagon, she waved to Nathan Webb before stepping over the tailgate and dropping to the ground. She waited until Sara was abreast before falling in step beside her. Julia had told the other woman she would explain about Mr. Horn's visit and what had taken place. Now, she was not sure how to open the subject. They walked in silence until Julia knew she must say something.

"I never realized," Julia began haltingly, "That folks on the wagon train believe Casper and I are...," she took a deep breath before finishing the sentence, "Married."

Sara's sharp intake of breath told Julia, she too had believed them husband and wife. "Why," Julia asked giving Sara a quick glance. Hiking up the front of her long skirt, she stepped over tuffs of grass and watched where she placed her feet. The ground was rough and full of dangers. Besides long crawling things to step on. She could twist an ankle.

"I guess," Sara began after thinking. "You just seem so right for each other." Adding to herself, a blind man could see Casper was deeply in love with Julia. "When you introduced yourself the first day, you said your name was Julia and I assumed you meant Julia Van Holland. Then there's Molly," she continued, more than a little embarrassed. Sara knew there were folks who lived together without the sanctity of marriage. She just never thought Julia would be one of them.

"I'm not Molly's mother," Julia stated. It was the same reasoning Mr. Horn had given her the night before.

This did surprise Sara. "I'm sorry. I didn't want to think it of you. Only you so obliviously love the child. It's natural to assume you're her mother."

They continued walking in silence, Julia thinking over what Sara said. "My Uncle John hired Casper to take me to Oregon." Julia began her explanation, "I didn't want to travel with Charles and Annabel in their wagon. Knowing Charles, you can understand why. And so, Uncle John looked for an honorable man to drive my wagon. Casper's wife died last winter during an influenza outbreak. He has a married brother living in Oregon and driving my wagon is a convenient way for him to take Molly to live with his family."

The explanation was simple. Sara realized if she had known, she would have understood. "I'm sorry," Sara said again, hoping she had not offended Julia. "Your brother-in-law is a difficult man to get along with."

Julia smiled, reached over and took the other woman's hand squeezing her fingers. "Difficult hardly describes Charles' behavior. I don't want to leave Molly alone too long," she said. "She's at the age where she gets into everything and Casper needs to concentrate on driving. I left her with Clara." Julia laughed softly before looking at Sara. "I guess I do sound like Molly's mother." Sara knew she was forgiven as she watched Julia walk to her wagon.

Julia called to Casper and he reined in the team slowing the animals to let her climb onto the wagon. She checked the hem of her skirt for crawling bugs. She detested them. Then looked to see what Molly was doing. The girls were sitting on one bed playing with the set of miniature animals. Finding the girls were content to play for awhile longer, she stepped over the wagon seat and sat down. "I never gave you any consideration when I informed Mr. Horn we would marry. Why didn't you object," Julia said before turning to look at Casper.

Having mixed emotions, Casper shrugged his shoulders. "When a lady's virtue is in question and she suggests marriage, it's usually not too healthy for the man to object," he stated.

"Oh!" Julia stared at him with wide startled eyes. "I'm sorry," she said. "This must be horrible for you. I'm doubly in your debt."

"Why doubly?"

"I'm sure Charles started the rumors. That's why I was so angry. I never considered how this would affect your plans," she admitted, looking worried.

"It wasn't your doing," he replied. "Whether you suggested marriage or not, I've a feeling we would be married this morning."

"I don't understand," Julia said, giving him a worried frown.

"Mr. Horn brought his Bible and also his record book. He came fully prepared to marry us if we told him we weren't married," Casper stated. Julia blushed, tears shining in her blue eyes. "Things can continue as they are between us. Only I can't go on calling you Miss and Mrs. Van Holland doesn't sound right either."

"Julia, will do," she told him as tears rolled down her cheeks.

"I'd prefer Julia and forget about the, will do," he teased gently.

She laid her forehead against his arm and cried in earnest. He let her cry. Passing Julia his handkerchief, she fought for control and started hiccupping as she caught back sobs. Julia wiped away her tears. "Marriage is forever," Julia whispered, not sure what to make of Casper willing to continue as they were.

"Yes," he said seriously. Glad Julia took her promise as serious as he did. They had the rest of their lives to make their marriage work. Casper was willing to give Julia time and patience.

Her storm past, Julia opened her book and began to read. If at times her voice trembled and she stopped reading to sigh deeply, Casper understood the emotions churning in her heart. His emotions were churning as well. He loved Julia. The thought of her being his wife set his blood rushing through his veins. Yet, he could not take advantage of the fact they were married. It would be unfair to her. She was not in love with him. More importantly, she had been forced into marriage. There would come a time when she would be ready to look upon him as her husband and he anticipated the future.

Julia closed her book, her eyes resting on the plain gold band on her finger. She turned it thoughtfully. "What is your wife's name," she asked.

Casper smiled at her question understanding what she meant.

"Mary," he answered simply.

117

"Molly is named for her. That's nice." There was sincerity in Julia's voice.

"The ring belonged to my mother," he told her. He did not add Mary had worn it. "I was saving it for Molly."

"I'll cherish it until Molly is ready to someday wear a ring," she told him, meaning every word.

"I don't think Charles believed you'd marry me. I don't believe he realized Mr. Horn would be so provincial as to force us to marry. I've noticed he takes delight in harassing you. I think that was all he intended. That and he knew it would be embarrassing for you."

Julia did not reply. Her mind was actively coming up with and discarding ideas. She wanted to be prepared for Charles' wrath and have her answers firmly fixed in her mind before she needed to confront her brother-in-law.

Julia was pulling the crate of cooking supplies from the back of the wagon when Charles stormed toward her. Annabel was close on his heels talking nervously and waving her hands excitedly. "Julia," Charles said in his most condescending voice. "What's this I hear about you marrying...," he could not bring himself to mention Casper's name. "I'm responsible for your well being. Now, answer me. What have you done?"

Julia turned and faced Charles. "More to the point," she said calmly, "What have you done. You spread the ugly rumor that Casper and I aren't married and yet we are traveling together. It might be acceptable among your friends but most folks object to a couple living in sin," Julia stated then took a deep breath. "Furthermore, I'm of age and can make my own decisions."

Charles was not prepared for Julia's accusations. His face turned purple with rage and he looked menacing. "I'll talk with Mr. Horn and undo the damage you have caused," he declared heatedly.

"You can't," Julia said calmly. "Casper and I were married last night. Not even your threats can undo what has been done. You should have thought about the consequences of your actions before you started those hateful rumors. I'm married to Casper and intend to stay married." Julia picked up the crate and started for the campfire.

Charles grabbed her arm. "You can't pretend you want to stay married to...to....him," Charles sneered.

118

"Yes I do," Julia said, tilting up her chin stubbornly. She was ready to do battle and belatedly, Charles realized he was using the wrong tactic. Once Julia became stubborn there was no reasoning with her.

"You will change your mind in a few days," Charles stated superiorly. "Why he's no more than a hired hand. A degenerate. You can't mean you want to actually remain married to him," he sneered. "I will do all I can to fix your ghastly mistake. After all, I am wiser." He turned and stalked away when Casper came across the field after staking out the horses to graze.

CHAPTER SEVENTEEN

Julia crawled over the wagon seat drawing her skirt and petticoats with her. Placing one hand on Casper's shoulder, she adjusted her undergarments tugging on a wayward petticoat. "There," she said at last. "I sometimes envy a man his freedom."

"Is that one of my shirts," Casper asked, looking at the shirt in Julia's hand.

"It is missing a button," she answered. "I'm replacing all the buttons since I don't have one to match." She placed his shirt on her lap and stared at the rolling prairie grass.

"What's troubling you," he asked. She tried to hide her unhappiness but he always seemed to know when she was troubled.

Julia did not answer right away. Her voice was thick with unshed tears, "Annabel asked me to take care of the girls if, well you know?"

"I knew she would ask you," Casper said, giving Julia a swift reassuring glance. Annabel believed she was dying and the future of her daughters weighed heavy on her heart.

"You like Annabel, don't you," Julia whispered, wondering why the thought disturbed her.

"Why should that surprise you?"

"I guess I never thought about it before." She leaned against his shoulder wrapping her hands about his arm. Hot bitter tears ran down her cheeks while she drew comfort from his presence and strength. He leaned over placing his cheek against the top of her head.

"Charles is...well...sometimes I wish I could swear," she declared breathlessly. Then dismissed the thought as not being her, she disliked vulgarity. Found it demeaning.

"I can have a talk with Charles if you like," Casper offered.

"No," she said holding on to his arm tighter. "I'm afraid your talking with Charles will only make matters worse," she admitted sadly. Casper let her cry knowing Annabel's request was unsettling.

After a good cry, Julia squared her shoulders and went back to sewing on buttons. Molly soon woke from her nap. Taking care of the child drove the unhappy thoughts from Julia's mind. Really, there was nothing she could do but wait and see how Annabel did in the coming days.

The sky was awash with brilliant colors when Casper staked the horses out to graze, returned to camp, and cleared a place to make a fire. Julia mixed biscuit dough then quickly sliced potatoes while lard heated in an iron skillet. The three girls were playing tag. They badly needed to run off some of their energy after the long day spent inside the wagon. Annabel did not appear for supper. Julia took her a plate of food hoping her sister could be coaxed into eating something.

Annabel lay twisting in pain, her face hot and flushed. Julia dampened a cloth and wiped her sister's face before she straightened the covers on the bed. "You must eat, Dear," Julia insisted. Annabel was rapidly loosing weight.

"I know," Annabel answered weakly. She took a few bites and laid back. "The girls?"

"Casper is watching them."

"And Charles?"

"I honestly don't know. He went off as soon as we stopped for the night."

"I heard you and Charles arguing earlier." Annabel tried to keep the accusation out of her voice but failed.

"Yes," Julia said. "Never mind Dear, I'm sorry if our arguing hurt you."

"You don't like Charles," Annabel said, tears rolling down her face.

"I don't dislike him," Julia assured, taking Annabel's hand and gently squeezing her sister's fingers.

Annabel settled down, "What were you arguing about?"

Julia did not want to distress her sister but in the end decided to be honest. "He doesn't approve of my marriage to Casper so you see our argument had nothing to do with anything that can be changed." Julia washed Annabel's face again wondering how much more pain her sister could endure.

Julia heard the distant roll of thunder and brushed Annabel's hair from her face. "It doesn't matter if Charles doesn't approve of my marriage," she told Annabel softly. "I know he is only concerned about my welfare," she lied, hoping she would be forgiven the lie. Charles' interest was for himself and the changes her marriage would have on him. She waited until Annabel was asleep before leaving her wagon.

The air was hot and muggy and she still had the girls to get ready for bed. The storm held off. Lightning flashed across the heaven and thunder rumbled. Julia felt the weight of the world on her shoulders and wondered if it was the weather or was she grieving over Annabel.

She put Clara and Wilma to bed in their wagon, careful not to wake Annabel. Molly was sleeping in her arms when she walked to her wagon. Thunder was moving closer and the feel of rain was in the air. "Casper," she said softly as he waited to take Molly from her arms. "You can sleep in the wagon tonight. Charles is gone and I don't want to leave Annabel alone."

"Do you think your staying in Annabel's wagon is wise? Charles might return during the night," Casper cautioned. "You were arguing earlier." Julia blushed but did not look at him. "Her girls are with her. If she needs you during the night, Clara can run over here," he suggested.

"Are you suggesting Charles might turn violent," she asked. The thought had not occurred to her.

"I don't know Charles well enough to know the answer," Casper replied.

Julia sat down on the side of one bed to think. Charles was unpredictable when he was drinking. She did not want to leave Annabel alone yet Casper was correct about Charles' moody behavior. Slowly, she came to the realization she might not be safe as Casper suggested. "You can still sleep in the wagon. You are an honorable man and normal conventions no longer apply. I can sleep with Molly and you in the other bed," Julia stated after deliberation.

"I'll live up to your expectations," Casper said. Lifting Molly into his arms, he kissed his daughter goodnight before laying her on the bed. The night air was damp with moisture. Not a star pierced through the dark canopy of clouds overhead. "Perhaps I should see to the horses while you undress and get ready for bed," he said and left.

Julia quickly undressed, slipped her nightgown over her head and slid beneath the blankets. Her heart was beating rapidly as she settled down beside Molly. Soon she felt the movement of the wagon as Casper chained the horses to the side and quickly rolled over facing the wall.

Casper undressed and laid on his bed pulling the blanket over him. He listened to Molly's soft breathing and felt the movement of Julia as she shifted her weight to settle more comfortably in bed. His bed was warm and dry and comfortable. Even with the strangeness of being inside the wagon with Julia, he soon drifted to sleep.

Charles passed Julia's wagon on the way to his wagon. When he started the rumor of Julia and Casper not being married, he never contemplated Julia feeling she should marry Casper. Too late, he realized he should have foreseen the possibility. Annabel said her younger sister was a prude. He could have pressed Julia to leave her wagon and join Annabel in hers. After Annabel's death and Julia grieving, she would have been more pliable to his wishes. Then there were the children. Clare and Wilma would need her care.

He cursed as he paced back and forth. Cursed not foreseeing Julia's reaction to the rumors and cursed her stubbornness. He cursed Casper feeling nothing had gone his way since the man came into Julia's life.

Charles thought of Julia, her youth and her sweetness. How much she reminded him of Annabel at her age. Except Annabel did not have Julia's stubborn streak. He had moved to swiftly and misjudged his sister-in-law. It was too late now. There had to be a way out, he owed Cohen money which the man wanted. Cohen was another blunder. The man was dangerous. Had proved it tonight when he admitted he did not have the money he owed. For the first time Charles was afraid. These westerners were a different breed of man.

He knew Julia had money with her. He had searched through her belongings aboard the train; both the freight car and her personal luggage. He had searched a second time without finding where her money was hidden. Pacing and trying to untangle the mess he was in, Charles came to the conclusion it

123

was all Julia's fault. If she had been more agreeable none of this would be happening now.

While he paced he heard Annabel's groan escaping between fevered lips. Annabel was the key to his solution. Julia would do anything for her sister. If Annabel asked Julia for money, she would give any amount. And his need for money was urgent. Later, he could coerce Julia into giving Annabel a generous allowance, enough to keep them in style. Julia was tenderhearted where Annabel was concerned.

He went to Annabel placing his hand upon her feverish brow. He dampened a cloth and washed his wife's face. Playing the devoted husband would be easy. It was not Julia he wanted but her wealth. He envied Julia's wealth.

Julia woke to the sound of rain on the wagon's canvas top. She waited for her eyes to adjust to the darkness. Casper was breathing deeply as he slept in the other bed. She made sure Molly was covered with the light weight blanket. Shutting her eyes, she listened to the sound of rain and viewed her changed future with its many complexities.

Dawn brought a gray rainy day. Mr. Horn had visited the evening before informing them they would reach Fort Laramie in another week. He also cautioned them the Fort was a rough place for pilgrims.

By noon the sun came out flooding the world with its brilliance. The grass was wet underfoot and gullies and washes full of water. The brown spring grass was now green and a blue sky seemed to go on forever. There was little to distract from the endless grass and sky overhead.

Julia looked at Casper with wondering eyes and blushed each time he looked at her. There was a growing intimacy between them, Julia was cautious to recognize. Her heart quickened each time her husband was near. His friendly smile did funny things to her stomach. The touch of his hand sent shivers down her spine. Each time they were together, she wanted to touch him. Julia was awaking to love and was not sure what to do about her wondrous feelings.

CHAPTER EIGHTEEN

As the days passed, a shaky Annabel joined Casper and Julia around the campfire. "I think I'm feeling a little better today," she assured a concerned Julia. Indeed over the next few days Annabel began to improve. And as the days continued to pass, Julia began to have hope Annabel was over her illness.

The wagon train arrived at Fort Laramie in the late afternoon. The Fort's walls were constructed of adobe bricks and set on a plot of land near the Laramie River. Indian Teepees stood in front of the Fort. Mr. Horn called everyone together, men as well as women, and cautioned the weary travelers of the dangers associated with both the Fort and the Indians. The wagon train would stay for one week, purchase needed supplies from the general store, and rest before continuing westward.

The next morning, Casper staked out the horses to graze. He carried buckets of water to Julia's wagon and filled both water barrels before going off with Nathan Webb and Mr. O'Fallon to the Fort.

Molly and Annabel's daughters ran back and forth beside the wagons playing tag while Annabel sat on a crate watching over them. As water heated to do the wash, Julia strung a line between the two wagons. She started washing Molly's and hers soiled clothing.

Behind Fort Laramie, mountain tops were visible. Mr. Horn called the tall peaks the Rocky Mountains. Julia stopped washing and stared at the mountains feeling overawed by their grandeur. "They are a sight," Annabel said after noticing Julia's interest.

"I was wondering how we're going to get over them," Julia replied.

125

"I'm sure Mr. Horn knows a trail. He has been bringing wagon trains to Oregon Country a good many years," Annabel replied.

"I'm sure you are right. How are you feeling today," she asked with concern deepening her voice.

"I'm feeling better," Annabel replied. "Just useless as you won't let me help."

"When I know you are well, you can do as much as you want," Julia replied. She picked up one of Molly's dresses and started washing the garment. "Molly is outgrowing her clothes," she said a moment later.

"Children have a way of growing," Annabel replied.

"I'm going to need to make Molly new dresses before long," Julia continued.

"Are you happy," Annabel asked. Julia believing Annabel's renewed interest in life a good sign. Her sister was listless being idle.

"I am happy," Julia affirmed.

"Do you know where Charles has gone off today," Annabel asked. Knowing Julia kept track of everyone's coming and going. She doubted Julia was even aware of her habit. Her sister was such a serious person.

"He went to the Fort with some of the men," Julia replied.

"Mr. Cohen and that bunch of thugs, you mean," Annabel replied.

Julia did not answer. She knew as well as Annabel did that the two hundred dollars Charles had asked Annabel to get from her was to pay a gambling debt he owed Mr. Cohen. Julia had given Annabel the money without questions. Though Charles' subtle hints, she make Annabel a generous allowance would not bare fruit. She was willing to give Annabel money when her sister needed but was not willing to make her sister an allowance for Charles to squander as he pleased.

"What does Charles plan to do once we reach Oregon Country," Julia asked. She wondered why she had not thought to ask before. Somehow, the future had always seemed far away.

"Do," Annabel asked as if the thought never occurred to her.

"You know," Julia said with a smile in her voice. "Casper is going to farm. Nathan Webb is going to start a dairy farm. The reason he has brought two heifers and a bull calf with them. Mrs.

126

O'Fallon has a flock of chickens and says back home she sold eggs and chickens. She plans to do the same out here. How she tells a pullet from a rooster is beyond me. I guess I don't know much about farming."

Annabel laughed for the first time in weeks. "I know what you mean," she said. "As for what we will do once we reach Oregon Country, I don't know."

"Surely, Charles has some idea what he wants to do," Julia said. "I have been trying to remember what occupation Charles did before you left for Europe."

"He's a lawyer," Annabel said.

"A lawyer," Julia replied thoughtfully. "Then he can open a law office. I'm sure with all the new people coming to Oregon Country there are land disputes as well as other cases that needs a lawyer."

"You've been worrying," Annabel declared.

"Well, yes," Julia admitted. "I came west to be with you and now I find we will be separating. Casper's brother lives in the south and I didn't know Charles' plans."

"Charles hasn't said where we plan to settle," Annabel admitted.

"I'm sure he will need to be in a city. Do they have cities in Oregon Country," Julia asked, frowning.

"You're asking me," Annabel replied with a soft chuckle. "I'm sure there are towns. I can't imagine a city like Boston or New York City. Towns," Annabel said once again.

Julia finished washing hers and Molly's clothes and hung them on the line stretched between the two wagons. She blushed darkly, before dunking Casper's shirts in the washtub. Annabel laughed softly which only made Julia turn a darker red. "You have lived a sheltered life," Annabel accused.

"Perhaps," Julia reasoned.

Even with the luxury of having a bath and doing the wash, Julia knew she would be glad when they left Fort Laramie. Two girls from the wagon train went missing and Mr. Horn and the men searched for three days without finding them. A young Captain from the Fort questioned the Indians and Teepees were searched without the girls being found. Mr. Horn spent long hours at the Fort helping to question the enlisted men. Julia and Annabel worried over their girls and stayed close to camp.

A day later, one of the girls returned and admitted she and her friend had been lured away from camp. She had managed to escape their captors. The Fort sent a troop out and the next day the other girl returned. Mr. Horn announced the wagon train would leave the following morning.

Julia was relieved to leave Fort Laramie behind. Each day of travel brought them closer to the mountains. Julia would look up at the distant towering granite sentinels and feel overwhelmed. She was weary of traveling, of marking off each day with seeming little change and little progress. She was restless wanting life to change. She was just not sure what change she wanted.

Then one day Annabel was very disturbed but refused to confide in Julia. Her eyes were red rimmed and her face pale beneath its golden tan. After prodding by Julia, Annabel admitted Charles had asked her to leave the wagon train with him and others when they reached the California Trail. Naturally, he told her they could not take the girls into the gold fields. They would be better off left with Julia. Annabel was upset at the news. She had left her daughters for a year in Julia's care while she and Charles toured Europe. Now, he was asking her to leave them again. Annabel was certain Charles would go with or without her and her heart was breaking over the decision she must make.

Julia put Molly to bed, came close to the fire and sat on one of the crates. Her face troubled as she stared into the flames without seeing them.

"What's wrong," Casper asked. He was spending a few quiet moments at the fire before he brought in the horses and chained the animals to the wagons.

Julia glanced at him and then looked away, "Annabel just told me Charles wants to leave the wagon train when we reach the California Trail. He doesn't want to take his daughters with them. Then, Annabel asked for more money," she admitted.

"I see," Casper said, looking thoughtful. He had heard rumors of the gambling debts Charles was accumulating.

Julia spread her skirt over her knees and ran one hand over the folds. "She said the money is for their trip to California but we don't reach The California Trail until Fort Hall and that won't be for weeks yet." After a long pause, Julia added, "Charles pretty much spends their income faster then it comes in."

"That's not unusual." Casper told her.

"I never spend my allowance," Julia confided studying Casper's face. Firelight reflected off his strong features. "I gave her all the money I have with me," she confessed a moment later. "But, Annabel said it wasn't enough. May I have what is left of the money you are holding for me?"

Casper was surprised by the way she asked. "The money is yours. You can do with it as you please," he replied

"Casper," she said gently. "It is no longer my money to use as I please. Perhaps, Charles is right and I should just have Uncle John give Annabel an allowance. That way she won't need to keep coming to me for money." She looked at him again and her eyes were troubled. "I don't want to give Annabel an allowance because I figure no matter how much money I give her, Charles will squander it and send Annabel to me asking for more."

"Have you given Annabel a lot of money over the years," Casper asked then waited as emotions raced across Julia's expressive face one after another. "If I say it's unwise to give Annabel money every time she asks for it what will you do," Casper asked.

"Uncle John tells me not to give Annabel money as Charles only gambles it away." Julia answered honestly.

"You have not listened to John Forbes," Casper pointed out logically.

"Uncle John is not my husband."

"And neither am I," Casper reminded her.

Julia thought for a moment trying to understand Casper's reasoning. "You are in name," Julia eventually said. "And by law, what I have is yours," she stopped speaking and took a deep breath. "I want to do what you think is best."

"I can't make the decision for you. Even if we were really husband and wife, I would not interfere when it comes to you and Annabel," Casper declared. "What are you going to do once you give Annabel the last of your money," he asked.

"Depend on my husband," Julia admitted as color rose in her cheeks. Casper's heart stopped beating then took off at a gallop. The look in Julia's eyes was mesmerizing.

"Does this mean what I think it means," Casper asked.

"It's time I stopped being a prude," Julia declared. "And admit I want to be your wife in more than name only. I know so little about men and life or even what I want. Except, we are

129

married and since you and I both agree marriage is forever. We should start being what Clara calls mother and father."

Casper took her hand and felt Julia trembling beneath his fingers. "That's only the first of my problems," Julia said, squeezing Casper's fingers. "We haven't talked about Clara and Wilma. What should I say to Annabel," she asked. She could not continue speaking. She could not see leaving Molly in another's care. Not even Annabel. Then, she realized Casper would never ask her to give up her children. He had struggled to keep Molly with him even through hardships.

She leaned toward Casper parting her lips invitingly. A gesture she had seen Annabel do on many occasions. She shut her eyes hoping she was not wrong about Casper wanting to love her. His kiss was gentle and she sighed deeply before stiffening when she felt Casper's hands on her ribs.

"I am a prude," she admitted with a soft laugh.

"You're just inexperienced," Casper corrected. He touched her cheek with his fingertips. "I'll get your money and you can take it to Annabel while I bring in the horses," he said. He kissed her parted lips gently once more before leaving.

Julia took the money Casper handed her and waited with her lips parted inviting him to kiss her again. Uncertain if she was doing the right thing where Charles was concerned. Believing as she did, the money was no longer hers to do with as she pleased regardless of what Casper said.

Annabel accepted the coins from Julia and counted them. "This is all you have," Annabel asked nervously. Knowing, the money was not enough to cover Charles' gambling debts.

"Annabel," Julia explained sounding frustrated. "I've spent a lot of money getting us here. The train tickets, the freight, the hotel bills and paying for the supplies. I needed to ask Casper for the money," she added. "It is all the expense money left. When we started out, I could not imagine needing so much money but Uncle John insisted I would and now it is not enough."

Annabel flushed a bright red at Julia telling her she had gone to Casper for the money. Realizing for the first time, her relationship with Julia was changing. Married, Casper was involved in her sister's finances. "Thanks," she said, hugging her. "I'm sorry if my asking has caused problems between you and Casper. You know I'd never knowingly hurt you."

130

"You haven't caused a problem," Julia assured her. "But this is all of the expense money I have. You must tell Charles."

"What will you do," Annabel asked. She held the coins in her hand not sure she should take the last of Julia's money.

"We have everything we need for now," Julia said, taking Annabel's hand and closing her fingers over the twenty dollar gold pieces. "Casper and I are going to homestead. The land is free if we make improvements. Uncle John will likely send one of his assistants out on the Union Pacific Railroad to check on me once we are settled," Julia said with a smile. "Whoever, Uncle John sends will have a satchel of gold coins with him and a letter from Uncle John scolding me."

Annabel smiled knowing her sister was telling the truth. "John Forbes is likely to show up at your door bringing Aunt Clara with him," Annabel warned. She kissed Julia on one cheek before going back to her wagon. Charles would have to be satisfied with what money Julia had given her.

CHAPTER NINETEEN

Casper was walking to the horses when Molly ran to her father. He scooped her up into his strong arms. "What have I told you about coming too close to the horses," he scolded.

"Sorry," Molly said, a tear rolled down one cheek. "Can Clara come with us," she asked shyly, not sure her request would be granted after her disobedience.

"You need to ask," he looked at Julia.

"Mommy," Molly stated.

Casper looked at his daughter in surprise. Julia could feel color rise in her cheeks. Realizing Molly was following her father, she had rushed across the field to stop her.

"Say yes, mommy," Molly pleaded.

"Mommy says yes," Julia said, kissing her.

"Mommy says yes, Mommy says yes," Molly chanted leaning toward Julia. Julia kissed Molly on the lips.

Casper wondered when Molly realized Julia was her mother. And when had the child started calling her mommy? For Julia was not surprised by Molly's term of endearment.

Casper placed Molly on his shoulders and held Clara's hand as they walked across the field. He sat Clara on the back of one of bay draft horse with Molly behind her. The girls' short legs hung over the horse's belly and Clara knotted her fingers in the horse's mane. Molly wrapped her arms around Clara's waist. Casper led the horses slowly to the wagon. He chained the animals while Julia took Clara to her wagon and came back. Sitting Molly on the wagonbed, he placed one arm around Julia's shoulders waiting for her response. She leaned her head against him and looked up. His kiss was gentle as he held himself in check. After a week of sharing his bed, Julia was still shy around him.

"I'll give you a few minutes to get ready," Casper said. He turned his back to Julia and sat on the tailgate. A moment later, Mr. Horn and several men came to Annabel's wagon. "I'll be back in a minute," Casper called before walking away.

Julia heard voices and wondered what was taking place. She came to the back of the wagon and looked through the canvas opening.

"Julia," Casper shouted, rushing to the wagon. "Annabel needs you." She heard strain in Casper's voice and reached her hand for him to take.

"What's wrong," she asked.

"Charles has been hurt," Casper declared, placing his hands around Julia's waist and lifting her to the ground. He looked in the wagon and saw Molly was sleeping.

Julia hurried to Annabel stopping when she saw her sister pacing back and forth at the side of the wagon. She ran to Annabel folding her sister in her arms. Tears streamed down Annabel's cheeks and her face was gray. "Dear, what's the matter," Julia asked. She could barely get the words out. Her throat was tight with fear.

"Charles," was all Annabel was able to say before she burst into great sobs as Julia held her.

Over Annabel's shoulder she saw Casper. Concern was etched across his features and his mouth formed the word, "later." Inside the wagon, Julia heard muffled voices. She wondered what could have possibly happened. Casper said he would tell her later, now Annabel needed her reassurance and her comforting arms.

Julia gently rubbed Annabel's back. Softly assuring her sister everything would be alright. Casper stirred the coals in the campfire and added wood. He filled a kettle with water placing the kettle over the fire then made coffee. Mr. Horn and another man, Julia did not know, emerged from the wagon. Mr. Horn washed his hands in the tin basin then tossed out the water. Casper handed each a cup of black coffee which they drank without comment.

Annabel waited tense and trembling with Julia's arm around her shoulders. "Well," Mr. Horn said addressing her. "A nasty business, knife wounds are always tricky. He's cut up. I can't say Mrs. Heywood. If Charles makes it through tonight and tomorrow there's a good chance he will live. As I said, knife wounds are tricky."

Julia was watching Casper's stern face. Their eyes met, it was as if he was transferring his strength to her. The feeling was tangible.

Annabel stood trembling. Her sobs stopped and a glazed look came into her eyes. Julia thought her sister was going to faint. In a tight controlled voice, Annabel thanked Mr. Horn and the other man. She walked to her wagon, climbed inside, and sat down beside Charles taking his hand in both of hers.

Her face pale and drawn, Julia stood at the tailgate watching. Casper came to stand beside her, placing his arm around her shoulders. Julia did not cry, she could not cry, not yet. She was not aware of Casper leading her back to the fire or him placing a cup of coffee in her hands. She did not feel the tin cup's warmth against her cold fingers.

"Julia," Casper's voice sounded far away. "Julia, look at me." She looked at him then. He was kneeling in front of her with his hands around hers holding the cup. "Take a drink."

She shook her head no, pulling away from him.

"Take a drink," he ordered. This time their hands moved bringing the cup up to her lips. She shivered as the warm liquid entered her mouth. She did not want to swallow but had no choice as Casper tilted up the cup. Then the sobs came, large soul racking sobs that shook her small frame. Casper gathered Julia to his breast. One large hand tangled in her hair pressing her face against his shoulder. His other hand was about her slim waist. She cried until she had no more tears then sat silently leaning against him. She could hear the strong beat of his heart.

"I'm alright," she said between hiccups, trying to pull away. He would not release her but continued to hold Julia close until warmth invaded her limbs and a soft glow crept into her cheeks. "Casper, I'm alright," she whispered.

He released her then leaning back on the heels of his boots, his blue eyes searching her face. "Yes," he said.

She wiped away tears with her fingertips. "Tell me," she hiccupped. "Tell me what happened?" He gave her a long searching look as if trying to decide just how much to confide. "Tell me, please. Not just what you think I need to know but all of it." Her voice was firm. The voice Julia used when she had come to a decision.

Casper nodded his head before complying. "It's not going to be pleasant," he warned. "I'll tell you what I know, not what I suspect."

"The truth Casper," she insisted, "And all of it."

"Alright, you already know Charles likes to play cards." Julia nodded her head up and down slowly. She knew where his discloser was going. She was aware of her brother-in-law's vices. "While we were in Saint Joseph, he fell in with a crowd whose main pastime is playing cards. This I don't know for sure but I suspect Charles had lost most of his money before we started for Oregon Country." Casper said.

"Annabel has confided as much to me. She says about half. And he continued playing cards after we left. The absences at night," Julia added.

"Yes," Casper said, surprised Julia knew about Charles' gambling. She seemed sheltered against life's trials. He was beginning to believe Julia knew more than she let on. He skipped what he was about to say. "Charles owes this man, Cohen a large sum of money. He kept promising to pay. Tonight he admitted he was broke and unable to pay the debt. There were words, threats and Charles shot Cohen with a gun he had concealed in his coat pocket. Cohen knifed Charles before he died."

"Died!" The word was a sob, a mere whisper between tightly shut lips. "And Charles?" When Casper did not answer, she asked again willing him to tell her the truth.

He shook his head. "I've seen a few knife wounds in my time and this is the worse I've encountered. Mr. Horn was being generous when he told Annabel of Charles' chances. I'd say they are nil barring a miracle."

"Oh." She looked at him not really seeing him. She was seeing her sister and thinking what Charles' death would mean to Annabel. "Why didn't he say how desperate he was to pay Mr. Cohen? Charles must have known I'd have moved heaven and earth for Annabel's sake."

"Don't blame yourself, Julia. You gave Annabel all the money you had. If we had come up with some way to pay Cohen, Charles would have continued gambling. Some men can't help what they are. Charles is self-indulgent. He would have taken everything you own and it still wouldn't have been enough."

"I know, only." She stopped and looked at Casper before dismissing her thought. She had promised Perkins to keep her store of gold coins a secret. She had promised and Julia made it a practice never to break a promise. "I'm a very wealthy woman," Julia said, knowing Casper already knew. "I'm sure I could have worked something out with Mr. Cohen."

"Julia, it would not have made a difference. Remember, it was Charles who shot Cohen first. He intended to kill him in order to get out of paying his debt. Charles would have come back to the wagon, saddled his chestnut horse, and rode away deserting Annabel. He could not have stayed with the wagon train after killing Cohen. He knew what he was doing. His mistake was in thinking Cohen would not exact revenge."

"I want to stay with Annabel," she said. In her heart, she knew Casper was right. Sooner or later Charles would have gambled away all of her money as well as Annabel's. The knowledge did not lessen her burden.

After climbing into the wagon, she was not sure Annabel was aware she was there. Her sister clung to Charles' hand silently willing her husband to live. Julia checked on Clara and Wilma pulling the covers up and straightening them around the sleeping girls. Would Charles be alive when they woke in the morning? "I must stay calm. I must help Annabel through this." She sat next to Annabel and smoothed her long skirt around her legs. She felt cold though the night was warm.

The rattle of chains, the snort of horses woke Julia. She lay stretching before opening her eyes and sitting up. Annabel was holding Charles' hand. Her sister's face was calm as she watched her husband's breathing.

Casper led the horses away from the wagons. Julia slipped off the wagon's tailgate and ran after him. He stopped when she slipped her hand under his arm. Her face was pale, streaked with grim and her hair was disheveled. Her clothes wrinkled and soiled.

"Julia," he asked.

"Charles is still alive," she answered. "Are the wagons going on today?"

"Mr. Horn called a rest stop. They're burying Mr. Cohen this morning."

In her concern over Charles, she had forgotten about the other man. "Does he have family," Julia asked then held her breath as she waited for his reply.

"I don't know."

"Will you find out for me? Ask Mr. Horn if there is anything we can do, please."

"I will."

Julia hurried back to the wagon. Only then did she realize how wrinkled her dress looked. She changed being careful not to wake Molly. Removed what few hair pins were remaining in her hair and applied the brush. The routine of brushing her hair and plaiting it soothed her frayed nerves. She left the single long braid free as most of her hairpins had disappeared. They were probably on Annabel's floor. She chose a dark green skirt and shirtwaist, thinking them suitable for the funeral of the unknown Mr. Cohen. When she looked out of the wagon, Casper was leading Annabel's team out to graze. Charles' death would add an additional burden on him, she thought.

Casper and Julia attended the funeral. They walked to the prepared gravesite with Sara and Nathan Webb. The young couple asked after Charles' health. The news had spread fast and Julia could feel questioning eyes on her as she stood with the others around the gravesite.

Mr. Cohen had not been married. This eased Julia's pain but added the burden of regret. A man should leave something behind, something more then a memory that would quickly fade away.

The few friends Annabel and Julia had made among the women on the wagon train came by with well wishes. Julia thanked each one graciously. Mr. Horn visited twice during the morning. Charles developed a fever, Julia and Annabel took turns bathing his hot forehead with cool water. Clara and Wilma were sent outside to play. Julia felt inadequate in answering Clara's questions. Casper took over the responsibility of watching over the girls. Charles' end came suddenly. He stopped breathing without ever gaining consciousness. Annabel sat holding Charles' hand. His face was calm and serene.

Julia, pale and shaken found Casper. He folded her in his arms. She was unable to cry.

Casper stood beside the grave of the man who had set into motion the events affecting his life. He did not stand in judgment of Charles Heywood. It was not his place to do so. As he watched the grave being closed, he reviewed the events of the past months. It had been Charles who decided to journey west. And it had been because of his taunts Julia had decided to go with

137

her sister. If these events had not taken place, he would not have met Julia. Nor would he be standing beside her as Julia's husband. It was strange how much one person influenced the lives of those around him.

The following morning Annabel was up before Julia. Silently, she prepared breakfast. Clara and Wilma needed her to stay strong so she could care for her girls. She must not close her heart for their sake. Her grief would pass. It must pass!

CHAPTER TWENTY

Daniel Wheeler arrived before breakfast was over. He accepted a cup of coffee from Annabel, looking at her with uncertainty darkening his youthful features. Casper had Annabel's horses hitched to her wagon and was just completing the task of readying Julia's team when the first call came down the line of wagons. Annabel dried the last dish packing it away in the crate. Casper came to load the supplies into the back of Julia's wagon.

Without speaking, Annabel led her daughters to their wagon and climbed inside. Her face was set in determined lines as she prepared for the day's journey. She looked out the back of the wagon fixing the view in her mind. This was where Charles rested. She would never visit his grave again. She squared her shoulders. Overwhelming panic rose inside her heart and tightened her throat as the wagon began to roll. She moved to the tailgate and gripped the top edge while sitting on the floor staring at the back trail. She did not cry.

Wilma was too young to understand about death. Annabel was not certain Clara knew what was happening. They played with their baby dolls and chatted happily. Her girls had Casper, strong and vital, who always showed them kindness and love to fill their need for a man's guidance. She turned from the view and gave her attention to her daughters. Clara was learning to read. It had been Julia's idea. Saying the long hours spent riding in the wagon was the perfect opportunity to teach Clara. Wilma was harder to distract during the long monotonous hours.

Casper snapped the reins over the backs of his team of bay draft horses and shouted, "Haw." Molly sat on the wagon seat beside him. She was telling Julia about the new dress Wilma's baby was wearing. Julia wondered if Molly was envious of Wilma having a baby and thought perhaps it was time to make Molly a baby of her own. Later, she would look through her fabric to see what she could use to make a baby doll.

Molly stood on the wagon seat holding onto the sleeve of Casper's shirt. Julia moved closer to the child to keep her from falling as the wagon swayed and bumped over the trail. Molly rubbed her hand over Casper's jaw feeling the short hairs growing on his chin. Julia studied what Molly was doing and reached out her hand to touch the side of Casper's face.

He turned startled eyes toward her with a question in their blue depths. "I was wondering why you looked different this morning," Julia said as a soft blush stole up her cheeks.

"I didn't have time to shave," he admitted. His eyes were a beautiful pale blue as they looked at her.

Julia brought Molly onto her lap. The child leaned against her. "What do you want to do this morning," Julia asked.

"Wilma," the child answered.

"What if we make you a baby," Julia asked.

Molly looked at her with wondering eyes. She nodded her head in agreement. Julia helped Molly climb into the back of the wagon then followed her. With many laughs and giggles, they set about making Molly a cloth doll out of muslin. Julia embroidered smiling lips on the face and wide blue eyes like Molly's.

"She needs hair," Julia told a very sleepy Molly. "What do you think," she asked, holding up the creation for Molly to inspect.

Molly rubbed her eyes taking the uncompleted doll in her arms and laid down on her bed. Julia brushed back the child's hair and leaning over kissed her cheek. Molly was already asleep with her new baby wrapped in her arms.

Julia joined Casper on the wagon seat and opened her book. For a short period of time she had forgotten her fears and worries. Now as she sat beside him, her mind returned to Annabel. Why had Charles not told her how dire his need for money was? She had given him all the expense money she had left but there was the money for necessities once they reached Oregon Country. The money, she promised Perkins she would not reveal to anyone. She would have broken her promise and given it to Charles to save his life.

She could not concentrate on what she was reading and soon closed the book. She rested her hands on top thinking. Then to her surprise, she leaned against Casper with her cheek resting against his shoulder. He glanced down to see if she was crying, but there were no tears on her cheeks, just a look of doubt clouding her blue eyes.

"Julia," he asked softly.

"I'm alright. Well, I suppose," Julia amended. "Poor Annabel! After all the heartache and trouble she's gone through with Charles." Julia stopped speaking, there were some things best left unsaid.

"Annabel is a strong woman," Casper replied.

"She has had to be," Julia exclaimed. "I didn't like Charles but I never wished him harm."

"Julia, whatever you are thinking Charles' death was not your fault," he insisted. It was like Julia to take responsibility for things she could not control.

"I suppose," Julia whispered.

"Charles would have kept taking and taking until you had no money left. You said yourself Annabel is nearly broke. She sold her home to you and her business shares so they could travel in style while in Europe. Whatever you are thinking, it would never have been enough," Casper insisted.

Julia remained silent gripping his arm as miles passed under the plodding horses. They had lost two days and Mr. Horn was attempting to make up lost time. They stopped for only a few minutes for dinner letting the horses rest and graze then they were on the trail once more.

The evening stop was at a waterhole. Casper took a bucket and refilled both water barrels on Julia's wagon before refilling Annabel's barrels as well. The girls followed along behind him or took turns helping him carry the water bucket. Julia was sure he could have accomplished the task in half the time without so much help. Admiring his patience with the girls, she boiled water and filled canteens with drinking water.

Silently, Annabel went about fixing supper then sat toying with her food while Julia saw to Clara and Wilma. The girls were too young to understand Annabel's distraction. Either too young or Charles spent so little time with his daughters they did not miss him. Julia found the thought depressing. She opened her mouth to say she would take the girls for the night then decided Annabel needed her daughters with her.

Wilma was rubbing her eyes and Clara blinking back sleep when Annabel rose and headed her sleepy daughters toward their wagon. Julia watched with a tight throat and glistening eyes.

Casper picked up Molly and placed one arm around Julia's shoulders. "It's time my girls went to bed," he said.

"I've things to do," Julia protested as Casper urged her toward the wagon.

"I'll see to the fire. Everything else can wait until morning. It's been a hard day," he added. Julia looked washed out. Her features were pale and her eyes overly bright. "I'll be a few minutes."

Julia was tucking a blanket around Molly when she heard Casper chain the horses to the side of the wagon. She undressed and put on her nightgown and still Casper did not come to bed. Sticking her head through the canvas opening, she saw her husband washing dishes. Her heart went out to him. He was doing her chores. "I'm very fortunate," she whispered before lying down. She was sleeping with tears on her cheeks when Casper came to bed.

There never seemed to be enough time to do all the chores before the first call come down the line of wagons. Casper brought in the horses, hitched them to the wagon, and they were moving on.

Having cold beans and biscuits for dinner was becoming tedious. Annabel's girls were often fussy eaters. Julia tried substituting cold oatmeal soaked in water with raisins or dried fruit. Molly ate whatever Julia gave her.

"One more day is completed," Julia said as the western sky colored with streaks of gold and bronze.

"We're more than halfway to Oregon Country," Casper replied.

"Halfway," Julia whispered, her voice sounding discouraged.

"We'll soon be at Fort Bridger along the Green River. Mr. Horn says we will rest four days before continuing on to Fort Hall," Casper stated. Julia was not the only traveler weary of the day to day grind of packing and unpacking a wagon. Of eating cold meals and doing without even rudimentary niceties.

"I'm not complaining," Julia retorted. "After all, it was my idea to come. I could have ignored Charles' barbs or even decided the Union Pacific Railroad was preferable. No, I had to agree to

142

live five months in a covered wagon and punish myself for my stupidity," she exclaimed.

Casper tried to hide his smile but was too late.

"Alright, laugh if you must," Julia conceded. "Mother said life is never easy. I'm just wondering why I didn't listen to her."

"Even after hearing Jorge's letters on the hardships he endured, I didn't realize how grueling travel would be. If I had known, I probably would not have brought Molly."

"Molly is flourishing," Julia replied glancing at the child seated between her and Casper. It was true. Molly was growing. Her blond hair was bleached by the sun, her skin a healthy tan, and she had developed sturdy arms and legs.

"You're worrying about Annabel," Casper replied with intuition. "Given time, she will do fine."

Casper wondered if part of Julia's problem was she had always lived having servants. He could do nothing to ease her burden when it came to work. There were meals to cook and chores to complete each day. As Julia had noted, she had chosen to come.

"Why don't you take Molly in back and lay down for a few minutes," Casper suggested.

"The sun is nearly down," Julia replied. "I might as well wait and go to bed early."

CHAPTER TWENTY ONE

In August the wagon train arrived at Fort Bridger along the Green River. Julia stared in disbelief at the poles stuck in the ground surrounding the Fort. Many log cabins both inside and outside the stockade. Twisting her fingers together on her lap, she took a deep breath. "Oh dear," she whispered.

Casper was finding the strangeness alarming as well. "We will be stopping for a few days," he said.

"If this is Fort Bridger what can we expect to find later on," Julia asked, dismayed over the crude structures making up the Fort.

"Jorge said he lived in a one room cabin his first years in Oregon Country," Casper explained.

"Don't think me a weakling if I say, I want to go home," Julia declared. Casper took her hand in his and gently squeezed her fingers. "I am not prepared for this," she moaned.

"This place makes the ghetto where I lived habitable," Casper admitted.

"Well, we are here so we might as well get off the wagon," Julia declared with resignation.

"It will be alright," Casper said, squeezing her fingers once more. He swung over the side of the wagon and reached up to help Julia down. She clung to his arms looking distressed.

"You won't need to worry about me wandering off," Julia said, letting go of Casper and straightening her shirtwaist. "The Fort doesn't look any better from down here," she admitted, taking another deep breath. "I guess I've lived a sheltered life but this place makes Miss Wayne's Orphanage look like a palace." Casper gripped her hand as if he thought she might fly away. Julia

144

admitted if she could fly, she would not stop until she reached the safety and comfort of home.

"I need to water the horses and stake them out to graze," Casper said, gently untangling his fingers from Julia's hands. The men around the Fort reminded him of Arlen. The man from Texas said he did not cotton to civilization. Casper doubted the men he saw coming in and out of the Fort would think much of civilization.

"Do you mind if I go with you," Julia asked, placing one hand on his arm. She did not feel comfortable away from Casper. Fort Bridger was a shock to her senses.

"I thought Saint Joseph was bad," Annabel said, coming to stand beside her sister. They both stared in dismay at the Fort.

"Well, we are here," Julia retorted, a few seconds later, "And can't do anything about the Fort's condition."

"Let's get supper started," Annabel suggested. "Maybe the Fort will look better after we have eaten." Julia gave her sister a dubious look.

The following morning, Mr. Horn organized a hunting party while women brought out washtubs. Everything that could not be washed was pulled from the wagons and aired. The girls played in the sunshine while their mothers worked. Lines stretched between wagons were soon full of drying clothes.

"And to think, Mr. Horn said this is a rest stop," Annabel said smiling.

"I've learnt," Julia began with her hands in a tub of hot soapy water, "That men rest while women work." She smiled at her sister. Annabel was back to being her old normal self. At least when she was around her. Past hardships and heartaches seemed in the distant past. Or, did it seem that way because each day was full of new challenges.

The men returned from hunting and meat was distributed among the travelers. Annabel boiled their portion in the three legged kettle while in a separate pot potatoes, carrots and onions boiled. Julia made cornbread to go with Annabel's stew.

The clothes dry, Julia took down the garments and folded them. Ironing was not worth the effort and clothes were worn with what wrinkles the wind did not blow away.

The following day was much the same. Casper joined the men as they went to the Fort. Many families bought supplies. Casper returned with a sack of peppermint sticks and gave one piece to each girl. He offered Julia the last peppermint stick.

145

The morning they were to leave Fort Bridger, after the horses were watered and staked out to graze, Casper filled the tin washbasin with hot water and carried it to the end of the wagon. Julia watched him speculatively, wondering what he was going to do. When the dishes were washed and put away, she wandered over to where he had disappeared. He had a small mirror hanging from the canvas and his face lathered with soap. He was shaving. Julia slipped onto the open tailgate and watched silently.

He glanced at her rapt face. A longing to kiss his wife assailed him and he turned away giving shaving his full attention

"I was wondering," Julia began, after he wiped soap from his face.

"What are you wondering," he asked his voice rough with desire.

"We have two wagons and..." She paused straightening the front of her skirt. A sure sign Julia was nervous. Casper wondered if his wife was aware of her nervous habit.

"We have two wagons," he prompted.

"I'm not sure Annabel is up to driving all afternoon every day. She seems well unless you know her," Julia explained.

"I've been thinking the same thing," Casper admitted, tipping up Julia's chin to study her face. "Are you up to driving your wagon?"

Julia looked at him without saying anything. Her heart was beating too fast at his touch. He was leaning over to kiss her when Molly and Annabel's girls ran up to them. Molly pulled on Julia's long skirt wanting attention. Casper smiled at the look in Julia's eyes. She had wanted him to kiss her.

Casper lifted his daughter standing Molly on the wagon beside Julia. The child showed Julia the wild flowers she had picked. Julia hugged her daughter close as Molly told her about picking the flowers. "Must have long stems," the child said, pulling out one flower and showing Julia. The stem was twisted and the flower head wilting.

"I think it needs a drink of water," Julia said. Molly frowned at her. "I'll show you," Julia said, slipping off the wagon. She took a cup and after filling it with water placed the flower in it.

"Drink," Molly said, bending over with her nose close to the cup. She handed Julia the remaining flowers and Julia arranged them in the cup.

"Pretty," Julia told her.

146

"Pretty," Molly answered.

Casper closed the tailgate. "We can talk this evening. Pull around Annabel's wagon. I want you ahead of me," he ordered. "I'll take Molly and Annabel can watch her."

Julia pulled her wagon out front. Her heart was in her mouth as it rocked over the rough trail and up a steep incline. She snapped the whip as the horses bogged down in the rough terrain. The wagon swayed, the right side dropping into a deep rut created by the wagons ahead of her. She looked down to see Casper beside her. He climbed onto the wagon seat and shouted, "Haw." The wagon rolled out of the rut onto level ground. Handing her back the reins, he swung over the side of the wagon and walked back to Annabel's wagon.

The wagon train soon left Fort Bridger far behind them.

By evening Julia was sore and her shoulders stiff. She stretched as she descended from the wagon, wondering if she would ever get confident enough to drive over the rough mountain trail. More then once she had been near tears as the horses balked and she had snapped the whip over their backs. She stood hanging onto the wagon wheel wondering if the world was going to right itself so she could let go.

Casper stopped un-harnessing the horses when he noticed the green tint to Julia face. "Julia," he asked.

"Go away!" she snapped. "I want to die in peace."

He put his arm around her shoulders helping her to the back of the wagon. He lowered the tailgate so she could sit down. She leaned forward resting her forehead against his broad chest. "Just as soon as the world stops spinning, I'll be fine."

Annabel stepped up to Julia. "Poor Dear," she said. "Julia has never been a good traveler. Let her rest a few minutes," she advised. "It's the only way she'll feel better. I'll start supper."

Casper helped Julia to lie down. She closed her eyes and moaned as the wagon moved when Casper unloaded the evening supplies. He placed his hand on her forehead, his thumb brushing against her cheek.

Later, Julia woke hungry. The weakness she had felt earlier gone. Annabel smiled when her sister joined them around the campfire. She handed Julia a plate of food. "I saved this for you," she said.

"I'm starved. Thanks," Julia answered. The girls were playing. Molly holding onto the doll Julia had made her.

147

Annabel took the girls to her wagon and disappeared inside. Julia sat at the campfire thinking. "We have another problem," Julia said softly "I can drive my wagon for a few days but I'm not experienced enough and the trail is treacherous. You need to come to my rescue which is slowing us down. Mr. Horn is patient but I wonder for how long," she added.

"Daniel Wheeler has been paid until the end of the month," Casper said, keeping his voice low also. He did not tell Julia he had paid the lad out of his own pocket.

"That's good, but what are we going to do about hiring a full time driver for Annabel's wagon," she asked. She started to speak then changed what she was going to say. An idea occurred to her and she wondered if Casper would think it was worth trying. "We have lots of supplies left while other families are paying high prices for necessities. Perhaps Mr. Wheeler or if not him, someone else might be persuaded to take supplies for wages."

"That's a good idea," Casper agreed. He wanted to keep what funds he had to start farming. They could survive a lean winter. He was told the country was full of wild game and recalled Jorge writing he had lived his first winter on the bounty of the land.

He looked at Julia wondering if she knew how appealing she looked before focusing on what they were discussing. "I'll speak to Mr. Wheeler, now." He tucked a stray strand of hair back inside Julia's lopsided crown of braids. "You look tired," he said. "Why don't you have an early night? We can talk tomorrow," he said and strode off in the direction of the Wheeler wagon.

Julia remained seated at the campfire. The night was hot with no breeze. The dark forms of the mountains rose dwarfing the canvas covered Prairie Schooners. Stars came out one by one until the velvet sky overhead was bright with shining lights.

She would sleep better if she knew what Mr. Wheeler said to Casper's suggestion. She was reluctant to go to bed until her husband returned. It would be a relief if the matter could be settled. Poor Casper, she thought yawning as she struggled against going to sleep. He not only had her to look after but Annabel and her daughters as well. He seemed to take it all in stride, shouldering more and more responsibilities without complaint.

Casper returned expecting to find Julia sound asleep. She was sitting by the campfire more asleep than awake. He carried her to their wagon and placed her on their bed.

Julia yawned and rolled over to face Casper. "What did Mr. Wheeler say," she asked sleepily.

"Mr. Wheeler said he could use extra coffee and flour. He's willing to drive the wagon for as long as he remains with the wagon train. But, they're leaving early," Casper said. He wondered if Julia heard as his wife was breathing evenly.

Julia woke to the sound of Casper harnessing the team to the wagon. She looked down at her feet and realized she was still wearing her shoes. Casper had simply carried her to their wagon and put her to bed. Longing for a wash, she changed into new clothes and brushed her hair and plaited a braid. Leaving the braid to hang down her back as most of her hair pins had disappeared. Would they ever reach Oregon Country and when they did would she have any left? A sense of depression descended and Julia struggled to keep from crying.

She crawled from the wagon and standing before Casper burst into tears. He wrapped comforting arms about her shoulders letting her cry. "I'm sorry," she said at last, pulling away from him. "I don't know what has come over me. I just wanted you to hold me." Casper smiled. "You probably think I'm a big baby," she declared.

"No. I think you've worried yourself into a state of exhaustion." She slipped her arms around his waist leaning against him.

"As much as I'd like to stand here all day with you in my arms this isn't getting my chores done," he stated after a few minutes. Putting his hands on Julia's shoulders he gently pushed her away.

"I'm hungry," she stated. She stood watching him complete the task he was doing. Standing close so when he turned he bumped into her.

"Julia," he finally said in exasperation. "We're going to still be setting here when everyone else has reached Fort Hall."

She did not understand the mood that suddenly came over her. A need to be near Casper, she wanted the feel of his arms about her again. She longed to ask him to hold her but did not know how to form the request. So, she just stood in his way.

He looked at her in frustration. "Alright, what do you want?" He sounded as if he was talking to Molly.

She wrapped her arms around his waist burying her face against his shirt. She stood there until he held her. Sighing, she

149

relaxed against him. He did not understand what she wanted. He held her as he would have held Molly. "Alright Julia," he said his lips against her temple. His lips found their way to just behind her ear. Warm and soft as silk, he kissed her.

"I," Julia started to say. She pulled away from him, her eyes looking startled. "I'm hungry,' she said again, rushing from his arms.

Annabel greeted her as she approached the fire. "Breakfast is ready."

"I overslept," Julia admitted.

Annabel gave her a curious look but did not voice her opinion. "Clara is being mommy this morning," Annabel stated. The girls finished breakfast, Clara helping Molly then she washed the younger girl's face and hands.

Mr. Wheeler arrived before the first call passed from wagon to wagon. He accepted coffee from Annabel. Casper greeted the older man before explaining to Annabel their new arrangements.

"I have five boys," Mr. Wheeler explained. "Each one eats his weight in food every day. The extra supplies will come in handy. I will be here tomorrow in time to take care of your horses," he continued. "I have admired the horses pulling your wagon. I haven't seen too many draft horses but understand they are strong animals."

Annabel went with Mr. Wheeler taking her girls with her.

Julia stood watching Annabel with her head cocked to one side. "Something wrong," Casper asked.

"Do you think it is possible Annabel is attracted to Mr. Wheeler," she asked doubtfully.

Casper glanced at Mr. Wheeler and Annabel. "Anything is possible," he replied. "That's the last call," he said, hurrying to load the crates of supplies and shovel dirt over the campfire. Annabel's wagon was rounding the curve in the trail ahead of them when Casper mounted the wagon seat and shouted, "Haw."

Julia crawled over the wagon seat and sat a respectable distance from Casper. Her leather bound book closed on her lap. She was downcast and feeling miserable. "I'm sorry for the way I behaved this morning. I don't know what came over me."

Casper glanced at her and saw tear tracks on her cheeks. "You did nothing wrong this morning," he said, trying to comfort her with his words. "It's not unusual for a wife to be playful with her husband."

"I," she paused, refusing to look at him.

"It's also not unusual for a husband to kiss his wife now and again. Even when others can see," he added gently. When she did not respond, he sat thoughtful for a moment. "It's probably my fault," he concluded. She glanced at him, a question clearly visible on her features. "I should kiss you more often. It is a husband's privilege you know." Believing he was teasing a slow blush rose in Julia's cheeks. Not replying, she opened her book and began reading where she had left off the day before.

Casper noticed she did not slide over close to him as she normally would have done. He wondered if his kiss had done more harm than he realized. Julia was a very proper young woman when it came to it. And being openly kissed was not something she would take lightly.

When the noon stop was called, Annabel joined Julia in preparing a quick meal. The girls played tag nearby; running off some of their exuberance after being confined to the wagon all morning.

"Mr. Wheeler is a widower with five boys," Annabel explained while helping Julia fix bowls of cold beans and biscuits with honey. The noonday stop was short and a campfire was not lit. "Daniel is his youngest son. Mrs. Wheeler was one of the first to succumb to the rigors of the journey. Mr. Wheeler says his wife was never a strong woman. I believe, he agrees to drive my wagon because he's lonesome for a woman's company," Annabel finished sympathetically.

Casper unhitched the teams staking the horses to graze. He caught Molly in his arms as he walked past her, lifting his daughter to sit on his shoulders. She curled her fingers in his blond hair. Clara took his hat placing it on her head where it wobbled being much too large. Wilma raised her arms wanting him to carry her also. He lifted Wilma holding her under one arm. The child squealed in delight, kicking her feet and flailing her arms. In resent days, it was not unusual to see Casper with all three girls hanging onto him.

Annabel stopped and looked at them as they walked toward camp. "Casper makes a wonderful father," she told Julia.

Julia looked up, a smile forming on her lips. "Yes," she said thoughtfully.

"You know you're very fortunate." Annabel continued. "I love Charles with all my heart but it doesn't stop me from knowing the kind of man he was," she paused, having doubts about what she was about to say. "For a long time I've known how it would end. I kept telling myself to expect it," she gulped back a sob and Julia did not say anything. She looked at Annabel trying to understand. "It didn't matter," Annabel continued. "The drinking, the gambling, and the womanizing," she stopped and refused to look at Julia, "Charles was not faithful," Annabel admitted.

"Oh Annabel, I am sorry," Julia exclaimed.

"It didn't matter," Annabel reasoned before Julia could say more.

Julia looked at Casper and wondered if she would be as accepting? And knew she would not. She would not be able to accept him wrapping his strong arms around another woman or sharing his kisses with someone else.

Annabel did not say anything more. Telling Julia seemed to ease some of her pain. She knew she had loved Charles too much and had allowed too many transgressions. Yet, she had not known how to stop Charles from destroying himself and their marriage.

When the second call came down, Annabel joined Mr. Wheeler on the wagon seat. Julia watched for a moment, as he helped her sister climb over the wagon wheel. Two lonely people, Julia thought. Perhaps they could help ease each other's pain. She had not liked Charles but had rarely allowed herself the privilege of admitting it, even to herself. The new revelation that he had been unfaithful to Annabel disturbed her more then she liked to acknowledge.

Casper helped Julia onto the wagon and handed her Molly before taking his place beside her. She loved him, Julia acknowledged for the first time. Was this the reason for her mood swings lately?

CHAPTER TWENTY TWO

Mr. Horn's trail went through mountain passes and over rough grades. The miles traveled each day grew fewer and the going harder.

"We're staying over today," Casper said coming into camp. "Mr. Horn has called a meeting of the men. He says we will rest here for a few days. Mr. Wheeler and I are going to check Annabel's supplies." Annabel looked up from the stew she was stirring. "Do you have records," he asked.

She shook her head, no. "I had a list," she said. "I'm not even sure where it came from. I just took it to the grocer and they delivered the supplies already crated," She said, looking bewildered.

"Oh," Julia said. "I think I have your list." She wiped wet hands on her apron before hurrying toward her wagon.

Casper was always amazed at the differences in the sisters. Julia had her lists and would check and double check every item and every detail. Annabel disregarded any form of order and never listed anything.

Julia soon returned with forms. Her name and address was across the top and listed below were items purchased, amounts in pounds and prices. She sat down next to Casper and went over the long list, item by item knowing Casper had a phenomenal memory. It was similar to the list Julia had used the day they arrived at the wagon train except for a few changes to suit the Heywood's eating habits.

"This gives us a place to start," Julia said. Casper unloaded Annabel's wagon. "The crates aren't marked so we don't know what is inside each one," Julia said, discouraged by the assortment of crates and barrels in Annabel's wagon.

153

"After we open a few we might be able to tell what's inside," Casper said. With hammer and crowbar he pried off the lid on the first crate. The first couple of crates were household items packed in excelsior. The next crate contained sacks of flour and the next was again household items.

Julia looked over the crates deciding all the crates looked identical. Lids came off the next two crates and they were filled with supplies. She thought Casper was noticing a difference. When he set aside a crate without opening it, she was sure. She stood hands on hips studying the unopened crate trying to detect what he saw that she was missing.

He walked over to the unopened crate and placed his hand on one of the boards making up the lid. Picking up the lid of a supply crate he placed his hand over one of the boards. She followed suit, her hand covered the board on the household crate but on the supply crate the board was wider then her hand.

"How did you notice," Julia asked. She would never have seen such a slight difference.

"Remember, I worked in the warehouse district," he replied, leaving Julia more mystified than ever. Casper stood wiping sweat from his forehead with a handkerchief. She counted the crates. "There should be three more," she told him.

"Does it list any barrels?"

"No," she answered after reading through the entire list again.

"In Saint Joseph, I loaded some of Annabel's supplies onto your wagon," Casper reminded. "The other three crates are probably in your wagon.

Casper had waited to move the barrels until last as they were heavier and more cumbersome to handle. "If they're not on the list, I'll just leave them where they are," he informed Julia. "Do you know what's in them by chance?"

"No," Julia answered. "And I'm not sure Annabel can give us an answer."

"It doesn't matter. We'll just leave the barrels." He told Mr. Wheeler, relief sounding in his voice.

Mr. Wheeler was in Annabel's wagon moving the crates to the tailgate for Casper to unload. "And to think all these supplies were just setting here untouched," Mr. Wheeler shook his head in amazement. He wiped his forehead with a handkerchief.

"It wasn't going to be for much longer," Casper stated. "The supplies in Julia's wagon are quickly being depleted."

"Well," Mr. Wheeler began, "I'll send my sons over this evening," he paused, stuffing his handkerchief into his hip pocket. "Coffee and flour is what I agreed to take but if you think it will be fair, I'd like some oatmeal as well. I can take less flour. I don't want to cause you folks to run short on anything."

"We agreed on two hundred pounds of flour. How much oatmeal would you like instead," Casper asked.

"A sack of oatmeal if you can spare it," Mr. Wheeler replied. Oatmeal was sacked in fifty pound sacks.

"You probably know what supplies we have down to the last bean," Casper said, turning to Julia.

"I do not," she snapped and heard Casper's soft chuckle realizing he was teasing. He had a pleasant laugh and Julia wished he would laugh more often. "Well, I do have an idea of how much flour and oatmeal we have," she admitted, only to hear him laugh again.

"I'll expect your sons after supper," Casper said, shaking the older man's hand.

Julia leaned against the tailgate and slid back until her legs hung over the edge. She had her list in her hand and her notes as to what was in each crate after it was opened. "There is plenty of coffee," She informed Casper. "Ten pounds of coffee beans goes to Mr. Wheeler. And there are plenty of dried beans," Julia continued. She looked up at Casper. He could tell she was thinking. "Does Mr. Wheeler smoke? There is a supply of cigars. I wouldn't want you to take up smoking just to get rid of them."

Casper checked his laughter. Julia was being normal to the point of being lovable. "I won't take up smoking cigars just to get rid of them. I do know who enjoys a good cigar." Julia waited for him to tell her when he remained silent, she asked.

"Mr. Horn," Casper answered. He was standing in front of her. His blue eyes were as bright as blue jewels. "Julia," he began, "What are your plans when we get to Oregon City."

"Whatever you say," Julia answered, color slowly rising in her cheeks. "I thought we were going to your brother's home."

Casper did not answer, his throat was too tight.

"Coffee, flour and oatmeal goes to Mr. Wheeler," Casper said, returning to their original discussion. "Cigars go to Mr. Horn." He set aside what was intended for Mr. Wheeler and then sorted

155

the remaining supplies between the two wagons. He reloaded Annabel's wagon.

Julia climbed into the wagon and helped slide the crates in place. Casper used the crates to make two beds for Annabel and the girls. The extra crates, he moved to the front of the wagon and stacked.

Once Annabel's wagon was arranged, Casper carried the remaining crates to Julia's wagon. She followed him to the back of the wagon and watched as he placed the crates inside. The last one loaded, Casper picked up his towel. "I'm going to the stream to cool off," he said.

Julia watched him leave with envy. It would be nice to submerge in a cool stream. Instead, she drug out the large wash tub and placed it in back of the wagon then poured in buckets of cool water. When finished, she curled her legs until she fit inside the tub. Julia felt refreshed after washing her hair and rinsing off sweat. Again, she wondered what she would find once they reached Oregon City. Dwelling on the crudeness found at Fort Bridger. Admitting once again, she was not prepared for the rough conditions she was finding.

Julia and Annabel had supper ready by the time Casper returned from the stream. He noticed Julia's wet hair and leaning over he whispered in her ear, "You could have come with me." He laughed as color stole into Julia's hot cheeks.

The man was impossible, Julia thought. Still she did envy his freedom. Casper refilled the water barrels as Julia cleared away supper dishes and put oatmeal in water to soak overnight.

The sun was setting behind the mountains casting long shadows. Casper came back to camp and chained the horses to Annabel's wagon. He then went for Julia's bays.

"Annabel has agreed to look after Molly tonight," he said. "We haven't talked over our future," he explained, adding another log to the fire.

Curling against him, Julia felt at peace. The shadows lengthened as the sun dipped below the mountains. The call of night birds filled the air and the scent of pine and spruce drifted on the breeze. "You were going to live with Jorge," she said after watching the campfire flames for a few seconds.

"I still plan to go to Jorge. I never intended to live with him for long. I want a place of my own. A place close enough, we can visit often and share work when necessary," Casper explained.

"We can build Annabel a house on the property," he said, thinking this was what was bothering Julia.

"I think Annabel will probably want to return east," Julia replied with a catch in her voice. "We haven't talked. It's more of a feeling I have."

"And you," Casper asked, holding his breath while waiting for Julia to answer.

"My place is with you. I have no plans to return east," she whispered.

"I hear the Union Pacific Railroad makes traveling easy," Casper replied. "Someday, we can return east for a visit. You don't need to be separated from Annabel forever," he said.

"Perhaps, Annabel will stay with us for a year or two," Julia replied wistfully. But in her heart, she doubted Annabel would. They sat holding hands as the flames burned low. Casper content to wait until Julia was ready for bed. Loving her the way he did, his heart was full of hope for their future. Julia was his wife and without realizing it she had pledged her heart to him again tonight.

The sound of chains rattling and the snort of horses told Julia it was time to get up. She quickly dressed. It was strange not having Molly to dress. Taking care of Molly had become part of her life. Casper helped Julia from the wagon stopping long enough to kiss her.

"Neither of us is going to get our work done," she reminded him after one kiss turned into cuddling.

"But think what fun we're having," he said before lowering his head to kiss her again.

She laughed and blushed at the look in his eyes. "We'll still be standing here when everyone has left if you don't let go of me." But Julia did not pull away from him.

"One more kiss," he insisted.

Mr. Wheeler came to the fire and poured a cup of coffee. Annabel's greeting was friendly. She was a handsome woman, the look of sadness in her eyes giving her a deeper beauty. She talked with him of the coming day.

The sun peeked over the mountains and vapor rose off the stream. The musty smell of the forest floor rose under the horses' hooves. Julia leaned her cheek against Casper's arm as their wagon rolled away from the campsite.

CHAPTER TWENTY THREE

The waterhole was nearly dry. Mr. Horn placed a guard with instructions no one was to get water until he could work out a system so each wagon got a share. It was not the first waterhole to have a limited supply of water. The much needed and expected late summer rains had not materialized. Heat soared and tempers were short. Worst still, the stagnant water caused some of the travelers to come down with an illness. It affected the children more than the adults.

Julia was thankful she had continued to boil their drinking water. At times it seemed a wasted effort while at other times it was inconvenient. Now, the three girls ran about the campsite busy at play while other little ones were suffering from the dreaded illness. Julia did what she could to help mothers. The work was tasking and the misery of the young victims tugged at her heart. But through it all they had journeyed on, pulling together for the good of all. There were days, Julia and Annabel drove their wagons so the men could help elsewhere. Nights, Julia lay in Casper's arms and prayed for rain.

Two weeks after the first illness, Casper grim and silent returned from a meeting of the men. Julia waited for him to confide in her. His back was to her and she knew he did not want to speak. But Julia felt she wanted to know and to share in this new hardship. After all, she was sharing her life and love with him. She waited before placing one hand on his shoulder. "Casper," she said softly. He turned his head and kissed her hand.

"Mr. Horn has decided to water the teams and push on before first light," Casper said. "The teams are the life of the train. If they," he did not finish his sentence. He stood and took Julia into his arms. "We'll make out fine," he infused confidence into his words.

"I know we will," Julia replied. She looked up and down the line of wagons realizing she did not see a fire.

"There's to be no fires until it rains," Casper explained. "We're fortunate to have plenty of oatmeal and dried fruit," he added.

"No fires," Julia asked.

"Mr. Horn says as dry as it is a spark could cause the entire countryside to catch fire not to mention the wagon train. It's better to be cautious," Casper stated.

"We have a cured ham left," Julia suggested, "Though all that salt tends to make me thirty."

"I don't mind eating oatmeal," Casper replied. "I'm for an early night since there's to be no campfire. I stand watch starting at one o'clock."

No children were playing as many of the families were bedding down early for the night. Molly was fussy and hot. She was listless when Julia sat on the edge of her bed and told her favorite story. There was no lantern to read by. Inside the dark wagon Julia undressed and lay on top of the blankets. Casper had rolled the sides of the canvas up to let in the evening breeze.

* * * * *

Eating sweet crackers, Casper harnessed the draft horses to the wagon. "You can't survive on that," Julia scolded.

"I might have to survive on less before we find water," he replied, drawing her into his arms. "As long as I don't need to survive without your sweet love," he teased, making light of her concerns.

Julia climbed on the wagon and waited for Casper to join her. She might as well stay up now she was dressed. The first call came down the line of wagons and Casper climbed onto the seat beside her. The second and final call came soon after and Casper shouted, "Haw". The wagon train rolled down the trail.

At day's end, supper was cold and unappetizing. Julia tried to get Molly to eat by opening a tin of raisins and another of sweet crackers. The three girls sit together sharing the bounty. Annabel sat next to Julia saying she would never have thought to offer the girls raisins or crackers.

The following day was little different. Julia wondered how Casper kept going. He was always cheerful in the face of hardship. Another day brought them to the end of the valley they had traveled through for four days. The trail climbed higher over the mountainous terrain. Julia looked beyond the mountain's crest back over their day's journey. The terrain was rocky and treacherous. The next day they came to a lake that seemed to stretch on forever.

Mr. Horn said the lake was lower then normal but water was plentiful for the weary travelers. Barrels were filled to the brim. Julia boiled drinking water and filled all the canteens. The women brought out washtubs and started washing clothes. When the clothes were on the lines drying, the tubs were used to scrub children.

Julia lifted a tub into the back of her wagon and filled it with cool water. She washed her hair leaning over the edge of the tub. Then, she undressed and sat with her legs crossed in the soapy water. Heaven she thought while relaxing in the tub. Molly was in the wagon with her and washed her baby in Julia's bath water.

"Are you descent," Casper asked from beyond the curtain Julia had hung over the back of the wagon.

"No," Julia answered. "Go away."

Casper laughed and Julia felt his weight on the tailgate. "You wouldn't," she scolded.

"No, I'll wait out here." Molly hearing her father's voice, lifted up the curtain, and crawled under. She was wet from head to toe. Her smile was broad as she held her clean baby for her father to inspect.

"I can see you are having fun," he told Molly.

Julia soon appeared. She was dressed in a cotton skirt and shirtwaist. Her brown hair hung loose and dripped water. She smelled of soap, looked young, and pretty. Having an abundance of water, their days of hardship were soon forgotten. "A real meal tonight," Julia said as she sat on the wagon's tailgate combing her hair.

Casper ran his fingers through her hair. "I know it would be easier if you cut it as many of the women have done. But I'm glad you didn't." He sat and watched as she combed out tangles then plaited her hair leaving the braid hanging down her back.

"Mr. Horn says we can't stay more than a day. It's getting late in the year. Once we reach Fort Hall we will be in Oregon

Country. The California Trail heads south from Fort Hall and some of the wagons are leaving," Casper explained.

"The ruffians, Charles gambled with are among them," Julia retorted angrily. She would be glad when the wagons of rough looking men left the wagon train heading for the gold fields in California.

"I can't sit here all day," Julia said a moment later. "Annabel is starting supper." Casper reached for her hand and squeezed her fingers before letting go. He would have Julia to himself once the day's work was over and Molly was sleeping in her bed.

The next morning, Annabel sat sipping a cup of coffee and watching Casper as he harnessed the team of bay horses to Julia's wagon. After Charles' death, he had shouldered the responsibility of caring for her and her two daughters. As deeply as she loved Charles, she had never felt as secure or protected as she did now. Casper took very serious his role as provider. From the beginning of their journey, it had not been unusual to see him with all three girls. If it was not for the fact Molly looked like her father, no one on the wagon train could tell which of the girls was his daughter? He gave each love sharing his time equally between them.

Annabel reviewed her thoughts as she watched Casper. She had something she needed to tell him. She knew he would not greet her news with anger. Charles would have. Charles from the first had treated her as a valuable possession. One he could pick up or put down at his whim. He had not wanted to be encumbered with responsibilities.

With resolve, Annabel placed her cup on the make shift worktable and headed to where Casper was fastening harness to the wagon. "I don't want you to feel it is an added burden," she began.

Casper straightened from hooking leads to the singletree and turned to give Annabel his full attention.

"Like I said," Annabel began again, "I don't want my news to be a burden." Casper could tell Annabel was nervous. She gazed at him with appeal in her eyes and uncertainty on her face.

"I'm having a baby," she said bluntly.

Annabel watched as Casper's eyes lit up with joy and a broad smile crossed his lips. "A new life is never a burden," he said. There was awe and wonder in his voice as he spoke.

161

"I wanted you to know as soon as I was sure," she continued. "I..." she stopped and looked at him with a mixture of happiness and sadness.

Casper gathered her into his arms in a brotherly way. "Don't worry," he told her. "It's a gift from Charles, a blessing to be cherished."

Annabel felt in her heart that Casper had just given her a precious gift. A child should be loved and he was prepared to love her unborn child even though it was not his. Just as he loved Clara and Wilma, she thought. Just as he had taken her daughters into his heart, he was taking this unseen baby into his heart also. She wiped away tears, wondering if Julia realized or understood what a great warm hearted husband she had.

"Thank you," she told him, pulling away. Her concern was gone and peace settled around her heart.

Julia did not witness the exchange between Casper and Annabel. She was struggling with wooziness and churning in her stomach as she sliced bacon. The smell seemed strong and overpowering. She knew it would pass soon. It had each day over the past week. Picking up a cold biscuit she nibbled on it slowly. It seemed to help. The churning slowed and she wondered if she was just hungry though she did not feel hungry.

The skillet full of bacon slices, she placed it over the fire. When she turned back to slice more bacon, Annabel was getting the next batch ready to cook. Thankful, Julia moved on to the next chore to be completed. What is wrong with me, she wondered nibbling the biscuit as a new wave of wooziness washed over her. Perhaps, she was just tired and sick of traveling. Sick of the endless days on the go, the sway of the wagon, summer heat, and being up before daylight rushing and hurrying so they could travel all day again.

Julia continued each morning to combat her illness. Not wanting to add to Casper's worries, she tried to keep how she felt from Casper and Annabel. The rough mountain terrain made travel difficult. It was hard on the team of bay horses. It was hard on Casper and Mr. Wheeler. It was hard on Julia. She felt tired and dispirited by the end of each day.

At times, she found Casper studying her with worry in his blue eyes and concern plainly written on his features. As soon as he realized she noticed, he turned away. But she did notice and this added to her burden.

162

Casper was first up in the morning and had a fire going and coffee brewing by the time Julia was dressed. The smell of coffee welcomed her to another round of chores. The lack of water grew to be a great concern as supplies diminished once again. The mountain streams were drying up. Mr. Horn posted guards at the waterholes and allowed each wagon a limited supply.

The teams of oxen, mules or horses were watered and cared for. They were the life of the wagon train. If the animals faltered or failed the wagon train would be doomed. Mr. Horn, more then anyone else knew this. No water was used except for drinking.

Rain clouds did not appear. Julia was sorry she complained about the prairie storms. She would gladly welcome the flash of lightning and the roll of thunder overhead.

One evening, Julia sat watching Annabel sew. The garment was small, dainty with green ribbons stitched onto white flannel. "What are you making," she asked after deciding she was not going to figure it out on her own. Annabel held up the small garment with a happy smile on her lips.

"What do you think," Annabel asked. Taking the garment, Julia felt the softness of the cloth and the prettiness of the stitches. It did not take Julia long to recognize what she was holding and to know the significance. With wondering eyes, she considered her sister's happy face.

"You are having a baby," Julia exclaimed.

Annabel looked at her in surprise. "Haven't you been listening to me," she asked, knowing she had told Julia, "I told you weeks ago."

Her sister had told her? Surely, she would have remembered if she had heard. "Are you sure you told me," Julia asked.

"Yes I am sure. I've discussed it with Casper. I didn't want him to worry. He does take his responsibilities seriously. And now," she paused, "well with Charles not here. I knew he would feel it is his duty to look after me and the coming baby."

Yes, Casper would feel the baby was his responsibility, Julia agreed. He had shouldered the burden of Annabel and her daughters. He never complained and he wouldn't. He just added their welfare to his daily duties.

Then Julia looked at the small garment. Her thoughts no longer on Annabel but on herself as she counted back days and weeks. She looked at her sister with troubled eyes. "Oh, dear," she said not sure she liked what she was thinking. Then, again she was filled with overpowering joy. "I've been feeling ill lately. Now I understand why." She leaned her head into her hands and began to cry.

"Julia," Annabel said her voice soft and full of concern. She placed one hand on Julia's shoulder leaning over her sister trying to stop Julia's flow of tears. "Why are you upset," she said, in her tell mother all about it voice.

Julia sat up and wiped tears from her cheeks with the backs of her hands. Her sister gave her a handkerchief waiting for Julia to mop up. "I've been feeling ill lately, especially in the mornings. The smell of food makes my stomach roil and…" she paused. "And, and I've missed. You know."

Annabel studied Julia, she did know. Her little sister was telling her she was having a baby as well. "Are you telling me," she began only to be interrupted.

"Yes. Oh, I don't know how to tell Casper." She twisted her fingers around the small garment she was holding. "He does so much already."

"Casper will think your news is wonderful," Annabel said, sure of her words.

"I don't know," Julia said. She often made things more difficult than necessary. It was a part of Julia's temperament Annabel had long ago accepted.

"Don't be silly," Annabel said laughing. "You've always been such a prude. Casper will be delighted."

"Do you think so," Julia asked doubtfully. After all, their marriage was one of convenience. If Charles had not started those ugly rumors, she and Casper would not have married.

"Maybe, your having a baby is just what Casper needs to keep him going," Annabel said at last. Julia gave her a dark frown. So Annabel decided not to try and convince her.

"Promise you won't say anything until after I do. I will tell him as soon as I decide how," Julia pleaded.

"I won't mention the baby to him," Annabel promised.

"I will tell him," Julia said once more.

The passing days were hotter and drier. Until one day, the weary travelers awoke to the rumble of distant thunder and a lowering of the sky. Yet, rain held off. But a cool breeze was refreshing and Julia leaned her cheek against Casper's arm and prayed rain was finally coming.

By late afternoon they came to a nearly dry streambed. Mr. Horn had the wagon train forge across even though it was getting late. In the middle of the night, Casper woke to the roar of water. By morning the stream was breaching its banks. Run off from rain higher in the mountains. The swiftly running water was a hazard to man or beast.

Julia stood beside Casper watching in horror as the water roared downstream. It was muddy and churning as it swept along. How could they possibly use such water for drinking or for any other purpose? Yet the wagon train was in dire need of water. The water barrels were empty on most of the wagons. And the teams of animals had been watered sparingly the night before in the nearly dry streambed.

Casper warned Julia and Annabel to keep a close watch over the girls. They had the habit of following him as he went about camp. He stood on the riverbank with the other men talking over the best way of drawing water. Rushing downstream, the foamy water carried uprooted trees, brush, and the carcasses of dead animals.

Julia got out a square of muslin and strained the water before putting the kettle over the fire to boil. Even with straining, the water was not clear. Annabel used it to make coffee. Julia boiled the last of the water in the barrels and filled the canteens.

By early afternoon the sky opened and rain fell. Casper took off the lids to the water barrels and set out the tubs to catch rain. Julia stood in the rain and let it wash away the strain of the past weeks. She caught Molly in her arms and swirled her around in delight. The first flash of lightning sent her and Molly scurrying to the wagon. Thunder boomed and echoed off the mountains. The lightning lit up the heavens and the thunder shook the earth. Julia and Molly covered their ears with their hands.

The horses neighed and thrashed about. The wagon swayed as they pulled against their chains in fright. She heard Casper trying to calm the horses and wished he would come and calm her. She held Molly close shaking in fear as the thunder rolled, echoed and reverberated. At long last from sheer exhaustion Julia slept. Molly curled up beside her, their heads under the covers to keep out the terrible flashes of lightning.

165

Casper found them huddled together sleeping. He brushed hair from Julia's face. His eyes alight with love. He listened to the sound of rain on the wagon's canvas top. The worst of the storm had passed with only an occasional flash of lightning lighting up the night sky. The horses were calm. After changing into dry clothes, he laid on the bed watching Julia sleep. Lying on his back, his hands behind his head, he closed his eyes, and was soon asleep.

The torrent of rain saturated the ground leaving the wagons standing in water. Julia leaned over the wagon seat and watched men as they walked about in ankle deep water. Many of the wagons were bogged down in mud. Casper unhitched the team of bays from the wagon and led them away.

"I'm happy about the rain but I do believe I can do without this mud," Casper said, hooking the bay horses in front of one of the O'Fallon sons' team of oxen. Nathan Webb and Mr. O'Fallon added their muscle to push against the mired wagon wheels. Slowly the O'Fallon wagon rolled onto higher ground.

"My wagon is next," Mr. O'Fallon said. Mrs. O'Fallon sat on the wagon seat with a ball of yarn and a crochet hook in her hands. She was a pleasant older woman with grown sons. The family was moving to Oregon Country along with friends.

Casper hooked the bay draft horses in front of the mules and stood next to the lead horse. "Come on Brighty," he said. The horse's muscles quivered as he strained into the harness.

"Hold on Pa," a young man shouted as he and his brothers hurried to put their shoulders against the Prairie Schooner.

Mr. O'Fallon was glad to step back. He pulled a handkerchief from his hip pocket and mopped his face. "This work is for the young," he admitted. He would never see sixty again. When he and Mrs. O'Fallon started out, they wondered if they were getting too old to leave the comforts of home. But, their sons were going to Oregon Country so they packed up to go along.

The ruts were getting deeper and the trail oozed with mud. The O'Fallon wagon rolled over the crest in the land and started down the other side. The wagon train moved slowly across a valley. O'Fallon women driving wagons as their husbands helped their father.

Mr. Cooperfield rode to where Casper and one of the O'Fallon sons were unhooking the team of bays. He watched for a long moment before riding over the hill and down the slippery

166

grade. He stopped at the Webb wagon. "Hook your mules to the wagon in front of you," Mr. Cooperfield ordered.

Casper had Annabel's wagon over the crest by the time Nathan Webb had his mules harnessed to Julia's wagon. Casper brought the black draft horses and hooked them in front of the mules.

"Drive the wagon. Once over the hill follow Annabel's wagon," he called to Julia. She moved to the wagon seat. Casper walked beside the horses and the men put their shoulders to the task. Julia waited wondering when the wagon was going to move. After what seemed an eternity, the wagon reached the top of the hill and started rolling down the other side. At the bottom Nathan Webb unhooked his mules and started back up the slippery trail. Casper hooked Annabel's black draft horses to the wagon.

"Think you can handle them," Casper called.

"The horses look worn out," Julia replied and heard Casper's chuckle. Annabel's black horses were more spirited than the bays Julia usually drove.

"Take it easy. I want to help Nathan get his wagon up the hill then I'll catch up to you," Casper shouted.

Nathan had his mules hitched to his wagon. Oxen from the wagon behind his were hooked in front of the mules. Men stood talking until the task was completed then they put their shoulders to the Webb wagon rolling it through the mud. Nathan was on the wagon seat. Casper again held onto the lead ox urging him to pull. Mr. Wheeler, the O'Fallon sons and Mr. Davidson put their backs to pushing the stuck wagon. The oxen and mules pulled the wagon onto higher ground and down the far side of the hill.

Mr. Davidson's wagon was behind Nathan Webb's.

After the Davidson wagon was pulled free, Casper climbed on the wagon seat next to Nathan. The mules soon caught up to Julia's wagon and Casper jumped down. "Julia," he shouted to get his wife's attention. She stopped the wagon and moved over on the wagon seat. She looked at Casper's muddy clothes and wondered how she was ever going to get all of the grime washed out. She laughed out loud at her thought.

"Something funny," Casper asked.

"I was thinking how wifely my thoughts were when I saw all the mud you're wearing," she said, laughing again.

"I do look a sight," Casper admitted, smiling. "Hopefully, the wagons won't get stuck again."

167

The wagons circled for the night. Annabel made coffee and brought Casper a hot cup. "You need to come over to the fire and dry," Annabel advised.

"If this mud dries I won't be able to move," Casper warned. He had spent the day helping to haul one stuck wagon after another out of the mud. He was exhausted and feared if he sat down for even a minute, he would fall asleep.

Annabel joined Casper grooming the horses and rubbing the animals down. The horses had grown lean over the past months. With luck the drought was over. This meant not only water for the weary travelers but more grass for the horses.

CHAPTER TWENTY FOUR

Casper and Julia stood on the ridge looking at the valley ahead of them. His arm was around her waist holding her close. The evening sun was behind the mountains, coloring the western sky with shades of lavender, red, and purple, and the soft glow of blues and yellows. Julia leaned her head against his shoulder, her eyes taking in the splendor and glory of sunset.

"In less then a month we'll be in Oregon City," Casper said, knowing it was what Julia longed to hear. He had found her vomiting after supper which reminded him she was not a traveler.

"A month," Julia whispered. "Casper. I have something I want to tell you," she said hesitantly, as color darkened her cheeks. She turned facing him. A warm smile softened her lips and her eyes glowed with happiness. "I am having a baby," she whispered.

Casper lowered his head to hear her soft spoken words. "I thought so," he said. "I wondered if you weren't telling me because you are upset about having my baby."

Julia's eyes grew wide with shock. "You knew. Annabel promised she wouldn't tell you," she said indignantly.

"Annabel didn't tell me. Remember, I have a daughter," Casper replied, waiting for Julia's reaction to his words.

Julia frowned darkly before smiling as she understood what Casper was saying. "And here I thought I was sparing you worries," she said with soft laughter. "You do so much," she added, placing her head against his shoulder. "I didn't want you worrying over me. I never realized you could tell."

Casper settled Julia close to his heart and kissed her forehead. She was not worldly wise which was all the more reason to cherish her. Forgotten was his anguish Julia might not want his baby. She had thought to spare him one more burden.

"I love you," Casper said. The look in Julia's eyes when she tilted back her head sent blood rushing through Casper's veins. His kiss was possessive. "I would like a son," he whispered against her lips.

"I don't have a say in the matter," Julia replied. She heard Casper's soft chuckle before he kissed her again.

"I was just stating my desire," he whispered. "I promise to love our baby whether it's a son or daughter," he vowed. Julia sighed and pressed against him. His words settled inside her heart bringing contentment to her soul.

Casper stood holding Julia in his arms as color faded from the sky. "Jorge wrote it will take another three weeks to reach Medford, where he lives, once we leave Oregon City," Casper said, going back to the subject they were discussing before Julia's revelation.

"When we get there, I'll be tempted to take an ax to the wagon and have a nice bonfire." Julia quipped, leaning back against Casper's hands and looking up at him.

"Oh, I don't know. I'm kinda sentimental over the old wagon." The look in Casper's eyes made Julia blush.

Hand in hand they strode back to their campfire. Mr. Wheeler was sitting beside Annabel having coffee and watching her daughters play. Mr. Wheeler was leaving the wagon train before they reached Oregon City. Casper believed the man was working up to asking Annabel to go with him and wondered if he should mention the possibility to Julia.

The night air was cool. Julia called Molly in from play. Tired, she made her excuses and went with Molly to the wagon and bed.

Morning came too soon. Julia woke to the sound of Casper harnessing the team to the wagon. Then, she remembered what Casper had said the night before. In less then a month the wagon train would reach Oregon City. The thought prodded Julia out of bed. She decided to count the days. A month! One more month with the wagon train!

In the distance, Julia heard the rumble of thunder and wondered if they were in for another thunderstorm. As much as she dreaded rain the water was needed. All day, the storm held off. When they stopped for the night, the air was heavy and the sky turned black blotting out the normally gorgeous sunset. Julia wrapped a shawl about her shoulders and called Molly in from play early. Molly had out grown all of her clothes. Julia was sewing new dresses and making matching dresses for Molly's baby doll. She would start on a warm jacket the following day as her winter coat was too heavy for the warmer temperature.

When morning arrived the sky was dark with a fine mist falling. Casper came to the fire to warm his hands after harnessing the team to the wagon. Julia and Molly waited in the wagon as he covered the fire with several shovels of soil.

"It is getting cold," Julia said, opening her trunk and looking for something she could make into a warm jacket. Molly was wrapped in a blanket. Finding nothing suitable, she opened a second trunk and pulled out a wool skirt. "I can survive with one less skirt and it will make a jacket for you to wear until it gets warmer," she said, holding up the blue wool skirt for Molly to inspect. "What do you think," she asked.

Molly bobbed her head up and down. "Baby," she said, holding up her doll.

"You want me to make your baby a jacket also," Julia asked.

"Yeah," Molly replied. She sat playing mama with her doll while Julia cut out and sewed her new jacket. Then, Julia started a jacket for Molly's baby.

By afternoon the mist turned into a steady rain. The rain and wind were cold. Casper put on two shirts and pulled his wide brimmed hat low over his forehead as he drove the wagon. Julia was glad she did not need to be out in the storm driving a team of horses over slippery mountain trails. That was one chore she gladly left to Casper.

Sunrise the following morning was spectacular. The sun crested the eastern mountain peak sending out colors that delighted the eyes. Seated beside Casper on the wagon seat, Julia viewed the sky full of orange, tangerine, yellow, and gold streaks. She breathed deeply the fresh air. Grabbing Casper's arm, she shouted, "It's moving." Julia pointed to the top of the canyon wall just ahead of them.

Casper glanced at her then to where Julia was pointing. The top of the canyon began to slide. He hauled back on the reins, tossed the reins to Julia, and left the wagon running toward Annabel's wagon, shouting as he ran.

171

Mr. Wheeler pulled up the wagon and began to back up.

Breathless, Julia stood to see if she could catch a glimpse of Casper. She heard him shouting. The slide was picking up momentum. A low rumble turned to a roar. Julia's heart pounded in her breast as fear gripped her. Then, she saw the lead mules on Mr. O'Fallon's team coming her way. Casper held onto the harness as he headed the team toward her. How he managed to turn the mules in the confines of the narrow mountain pass, only God knew.

Julia climbed down and ran across the distance separating her and her husband. She wrapped her arms around his waist leaning against his chest. She believed she was going to faint. Still pale and shaken, Casper dropped an arm about Julia's shoulders to comfort her.

Mr. O'Fallon climbed off the wagon and stood looking in horror as dirt and rocks dropped onto the pass' floor. "Did you see what happened to my son's wagon," he asked, his voice trembled. He shook his head and wiped his face with a large bandana. "My Mrs. about fainted. Says she ain't got the strength to stand up. We'd sure be goners if you hadn't hauled my team around." He looked at the pass once more worrying about his son's wagon traveling in front of him.

"I was too late," Casper said, placing one hand on the old man's shoulder. "I heard your son shouting. Maybe, he made it through the pass alright."

The old man's face was gray. "You did all you could," Mr. O'Fallon admitted. They stood watching the pass fill up with soil and boulders. Dust was thick on the air.

Mr. Wheeler joined them. "We must check," he said, speaking of the O'Fallon family in the wagon ahead of Mr. O'Fallon's.

Casper turned to Julia, kissed her lightly on the forehead. "I want you to stay here," he ordered. She nodded her head unable to speak and he brushed his lips lightly across hers.

Annabel slipped her arm around Julia. Her sister was still visibly shaking.

Men rushed past to survey the damage. They turned back to get shovels, pick axes and to unhook horses and mules from their wagons. The larger boulders would require the animals' strength to move. The men's faces were grim as they dwelt on the

172

work ahead of them. The mountain pass was blocked and it was a sure bet one or more wagons lay buried under tons of rubble.

Mrs. O'Fallon carefully climbed over the wagon wheel and stood next to Julia. She was puffing out her cheeks as she breathed through her mouth. "Only, the good Lord can save my son and his family," she said holding back tears. "I won't cry until I know for sure."

"What we need is a strong pot of coffee. I admit when I saw Casper run by shouting, I felt more than a little weak," Annabel said, putting one arm around Mrs. O'Fallon's shoulders leading the women away from the chaotic scene. Julia started a fire while Annabel made coffee.

Sara Webb brought a crate from the back of Julia's wagon and insisted Mrs. O'Fallon sit down. "I'll pray with you," Sara said, taking the woman's hands in hers.

Annabel brought out her largest cooking pot and started cutting up potatoes. "The men will need something substantial to eat after digging. Besides, when I'm nervous I like to cook. It keeps my hands and mind occupied."

Julia went to check on Molly, saying all the noise might have awakened her. She returned with a sleepy little girl and sat holding Molly on her lap. All along the wagon train women started fires and were cooking pots of stew or beans to have ready and waiting when the men returned. There were two dozen wagons remaining on this side of the landslide.

Julia was pale and held onto Molly for comfort. They could hear an occasional shout as boulders were unearthed and rolled out of the way. No one mentioned the landslide or the families likely buried under the rubble. They talked of their hopes and dreams in a new country as they sat around the campfire. Each woman took a turn holding Mrs. O'Fallon's hands and saying a few words of comfort.

Through it all, Mrs. O'Fallon sat quietly waiting.

173

CHAPTER TWENTY FIVE

As the day wore on, word came that one of the young men had climbed over the blockage and talked with Mr. Horn. All but one wagon had made it through the pass and was buried under the landslide. Mrs. O'Fallon did not say a word. She stood and walked to her wagon and went inside.

"I'll go," Annabel said, glancing at the women gathered around their campfire. "I understand the heartache Mrs. O'Fallon is feeling." Annabel did not say anything more. Julia watched her sister go inside the wagon before calling the girls to the campfire. She asked Clara to read out loud. She listened while making biscuits then put the pan into the Dutch oven to bake.

The men returned and grouped around the fire discussing the problems they faced. Women hurried to fill plates and pour cups of coffee to carry to fathers, brothers and husbands. It was decided the men would divide into two teams of workmen and men were picked to form the teams. Each team would work two hours and rest two hours as the labor was grueling.

Julia handed Casper a cup of hot strong coffee and filled a plate with stew. Wearily, he ate listening to the other men talking. While men ate, wives stood back out of the way waiting to be told what needed to be done next. Before Casper went back to work, he pulled Julia aside and held her for a long moment.

When evening came, Julia pressed Annabel to rest. Her sister looked pale and drawn. "Don't fuss," Annabel admonished before taking the girls and going to her wagon. Molly went with them.

Casper came to camp and sat leaning against a wagon wheel. He was too tired to lift his spoon to his mouth. Julia sat on the ground beside him. Her husband was barely recognizable covered in dirt and grime. It was the first time Julia saw Casper exhausted.

"Give me a minute," he said, leaning back and closing his eyes. Julia reached out and dusted gravel out of his blond hair. He smiled at the feel of her fingertips touching him.

"Casper," she implored, "you must eat before you fall asleep."

He roused himself and ate the plate of stew. The night air was cool in the canyon. "Bring me a blanket. I'll roll into it here under the wagon." Julia hurried to comply with his wishes finding him asleep when she returned. She let him sleep spreading the blanket over him.

By lantern light, the men worked through the night. In two hour stretches, they worked and rested. By morning word came across that the O'Fallon wagon was found. The women repacked their wagons and kissed their husbands good-bye. The women and children were to walk the half mile through the pass. Casper went with Julia helping her over the rocky trail.

"I'll meet you on this side," he promised before pressing her close.

"I'll be waiting," Julia replied. She watched Casper and other husbands walk through the pass to their wagons. She bit her lower lip to keep back a sob.

Mr. Wheeler was in the lead wagon. Driving slowly, he brought his team up the embankment caused by the landslide. The ground was loose and the dirt moved under the wagon wheels. Julia gripped Annabel's hand but would not look away. He brought the wagon down the slope. The wagon rolled and slid to the left, then straightened and continued until it reached the trail. Annabel was pale gripping Julia's fingers. She breathed a sigh of relief when her wagon pulled to a stop without incident. Mr. Wheeler's smile was encouraging as he climbed down and took Annabel's hand in his.

Casper started the wagon up and over the landslide. The top of the mountain began to rumble as loose dirt slid down. Julia caught her breath and held it praying for Casper's safety. She was weak and shaky as he pulled their wagon to a stop beside her. He took her in his arms holding her close as tears ran down her cheeks.

"I'm alright," he said.

"I know," she replied, unable to stop the tears from falling.

With the Heywood and Van Holland wagons out of the way, Mr. O'Fallon's wagon swung around and started across. The loose gravel gave way as the wagon started to descend and it toppled over and slid the remaining yards. Mr. O'Fallon managed to jump clear of the wagon as it rolled. The men soon righted the Prairie Schooner and Mr. O'Fallon's son drove it past.

With the next wagon more dirt was loosened and descended down the mountainside. Finally, the last wagon was across. Julia stood exhausted. Afraid to take her eyes from the scene before her, Casper stood by her side holding onto her hand.

The wagon train started out the next morning leaving seven graves alongside the trail.

Julia occupied her time by sewing Casper a new shirt. The wear and tear of travel was hard on clothing and she wanted him to look nice when they reached Oregon City.

Sara came and rode inside Julia's wagon. She had her quilt block with her and was embroidering as they talked. "We'll be leaving the wagon train in the morning," she told Julia and Annabel. "We're not going all the way to Oregon City."

Julia wrote Casper's brother's name and address on a slip of paper and handed it to Sara. "You make sure and write," Julia told her.

"I will," Sara assured. "It's nice one of us has folks where we can write. We will be able to keep in touch." They were silent for awhile. "It's like leaving family behind," Sara confided.

"I feel the same way," Julia answered struggling against tears. Over the weeks and months of hardships, Sara had become more than a good friend. "When do you think you'll be settled," Julia asked.

"Might be weeks before we find the land we want. I sure am tired of living in a wagon," Sara said, knowing Julia and Annabel felt the same way.

Julia smiled, "Jorge has a house already built. It will be nice to have a roof over my head even if it's not my own. Casper is planning to settle in Medford so we have a destination in mind."

Sara stood and waved to Nathan before she dropped off the end of the tailgate. Julia watched as Sara climbed on her wagon and sat beside her husband. She wondered if Sara would write or was she to lose another friend. Over the past year, she had lost too many friends.

Julia woke to the sound of Casper harnessing the bay horses to the wagon. Fearing she had overslept, she hurried into her clothes and pulled back the canvas flap to discover the gray dawn before sunrise. The air was heavy with the scent of pines and spruce.

Annabel was mixing cornmeal and water for Johnny cakes. Julia started slicing bacon laying the strips in neat rows inside the blackened iron skillet. Casper was whistling.

"You know I find it amazing how obtuse you can be sometimes to things going on around you," Annabel said to her younger sister.

"Obtuse," Julia said, turning to Annabel. "I don't know what you mean," she insisted, placing the skillet over the fire.

"I mean obtuse. Blind, unaware, not knowing, Obtuse," Annabel said in her forthright way.

"How am I being obtuse," Julia asked. She heard Annabel's soft laughter. "I suspected Casper was attracted to you the first time I saw you together."

"But that was," Julia began. She stopped turning bacon and looked at Annabel in disbelief.

"When, I thought he was a married man. You might say it gave me misgivings. But I knew you had more sense then to get involved with a married man. Still, it caused me to have second thoughts about Uncle John's judgment."

"What are you getting at," Julia asked sure Annabel was making a point.

"Alright," Annabel replied. "I'm talking about Mr. Wheeler. He has asked me to marry him."

"Oh," Julia said with misgivings. "Casper said he thought Mr. Wheeler would ask you. Have you decided what you will do?"

Annabel smiled at her younger sister. "So Casper told you to expect Mr. Wheeler to ask me," she declared. "I can see you would never have thought of it yourself. Obtuse," Annabel said, using the word again.

"Alright, I wouldn't have thought of it," Julia admitted. "I do want you to be happy."

Casper coming over to the fire put an end to their conversation. But Julia was thoughtful as she completed breakfast.

Mr. Wheeler arrived before the first call came down the line of wagons. He helped pack and load the crates into the back of

177

Julia's wagon. Then he lifted Clara and Wilma into Annabel's wagon and helped Annabel.

Julia stood watching. She was obtuse as Annabel suggested. Mr. Wheeler was a good man. Reliable and trustworthy, someone who would care for Annabel and love her the way she needed to be loved. A man of principles. Julia decided she could trust him with her sister's heart.

"Why are you smiling," Casper asked as Julia settled on the wagon seat next to him. Molly sat between them holding her baby doll in her arms.

"Annabel says Mr. Wheeler has asked her to marry him," Julia replied. "Annabel declares I'm obtuse," she said, her smile widening. "She believes you were attracted to me the first time she saw us together." Color stole up Casper's face as heat fused his cheeks. "Well, were you," Julia demanded.

"I was," Casper admitted. "I had qualms about spending so much time in your company."

"I am obtuse," Julia declared before sighing deeply. "I felt safe with you. I should have known my feelings were more than sisterly affection. Mr. Horn did us a great favor. You would have never asked me to marry you and I would have continued on blindly, not realizing my feelings."

"You do love me," Casper asked.

"Not with blind devotion," Julia replied. "But with a healthy love." Casper knew it was important for Julia not to love blindly after the disastrous love affair between Annabel and Charles.

"I don't want blind devotion," Casper assured his wife.

"And to think, I traveled all this way to be with Annabel and we will be separating as soon as Mr. Wheeler leaves the wagon train." Deep in thought, Julia gripped her fingers together on her lap.

"The Oregon and California Railroad reaches Oregon City. In a few more years travel all across the northwest will be easier. You and Annabel can visit back and forth," Casper encouraged.

"I wonder why Charles insisted we come by wagon train," Julia continued thoughtfully. She did not expect Casper to answer and he did not.

Casper knew Julia would never accept his suggesting Charles intended to kill Annabel and marry her. But, Casper was convinced this was the reason behind traveling by wagon train. Annabel's health improved as soon as he and Julia were married.

178

He did not believe it was coincidence. Charles needed Annabel to keep Julia's money flowing his way.

After supper, Julia sat watching as the sun set behind the western mountains. The sky was glorious with streaks of red, gold, and bright blue. Molly was playing with Clara and Wilma, and several other children had joined them.

"Julia," Annabel said, sitting down on the crate next to her sister. "Mr. Wheeler is leaving the wagon train and heading north tomorrow. I've decided to go with him," She said, waiting expectantly for her sister's reaction.

"I knew he would," Julia stated calmly, giving her sister a smile. She knew she would cry buckets of tears but not until after Annabel left. This was the right thing for her sister to do and she did not want Annabel hesitating to follow her heart. "I was only waiting for you to tell me."

"I'll miss you," Annabel stated fondly. "You came all this way to be with me and now we're separating."

"I came because you needed me." Julia stated, knowing Annabel understood what she meant without explaining. Julia had not trusted Charles to look after her sister properly. Suspected, he would leave Annabel as soon as her money ran out. "And now you don't. Besides, I have Casper and a new family. And you have Mr. Wheeler and a new family," Julia explained.

Annabel wiped tears from her cheeks. "A woman has never had a better sister. There's so much I want to say but I don't know how to even begin."

Julia smiled at Annabel concealing her heartache. They sat together near the fire talking over the past. Sharing stories of family, friends, and events that had shaped their lives, they laughed and wept a few tears.

"In the morning," Annabel said. "Mr. Horn will marry Mr. Wheeler and me. You and Casper will be our witnesses. Then, we will head north. I know this is the right thing for me to do. I'm not sure if I love Mr. Wheeler and he knows it. But I am attracted to him." She paused and sought the right words to assure Julia she was happy with her decision. "I've learned love is not enough. A man's character is also important. I think I started realizing it even before Charles' death. When...when he asked me to leave the wagon train with him and give you the girls." Annabel hid her face in her hands. "I want a man who is honorable and trustworthy.

179

Who loves my girls as much as I do. I believe I've found him in Mr. Wheeler."

Julia hugged Annabel. Not sure what more to say. "We will say good-bye tomorrow," Julia said before turning to go to her wagon where Casper was waiting for her.

Casper stood beside Mr. Wheeler. Four months earlier he had stood before Mr. Horn listening to the same words and pledged his love to Julia. He glanced at his wife wondering what Julia was thinking. Julia smiled at him through her tears. She reached for his hand and squeezed his fingers before hugging Annabel.

Julia watched Mr. Wheeler drive away with Annabel on the seat beside him. Her throat was too tight to speak and she waved one last time before walking with Casper to their wagon. She waved at Clara and Wilma looking over the wagon's tailgate and caught back a sob. "I'm alright," she whispered.

Casper took Julia's hand in his. "Another week and we leave the wagon train," he said.

Julia placed her high top shoe on the wheel spoke and gripped the top of the wheel. Casper's hands were around her waist as she placed one leg over the edge of the wagon. She sat down on the seat and waited for Casper to hand her Molly.

Molly looked up at her and said, "Clara."

Julia took the girl's hands in hers. "Let's read your favorite story," she said.

"Clara," Molly said once more. Julia looked at Casper not sure how to answer Molly's concerns.

"Whatever you say, Molly won't understand," Casper stated. "Why don't you sit on my lap and help me hold the reins," he suggested to his daughter.

CHAPTER TWENTY SIX

The camp was quiet. Molly sat with her father, his strong arms holding her close. As Julia cooked the evening meal, she handed Casper a strong cup of tea saying, "I've never learnt to make good coffee."

"I prefer tea," Casper said.

He noticed the droop of his wife's shoulders and the tightness around her mouth. She was unsuccessful in concealing her heartache from him. A short time later, she took Molly to the wagon. After undressing and washing the child, she put Molly to bed. Julia undressed and washed. There was no longer any need to conserve water. Two more days and they would be at Oregon City where the Oregon Trail ended. She brushed her hair and was plaiting the long strands when Casper pulled back the canvas flap. He sat down beside Julia and took her hand in his.

"It is alright to cry," he said soothingly. Julia burst into tears and buried her face against his shoulder. Casper gently patted her back before placing his fingers beneath her chin and tilting up her face. His kiss brought a rush of feelings and Julia forgot about her heartache wrapping her arms about his neck pressing against him. Being loved by Casper was too new and turbulent for Julia to think about anything else.

Julia heard Casper unchain the horses from the side of the wagon. She lay in bed wondering what Jorge and Darcy would be like. Casper had told her very little about his brother. He had joked once about Jorge being younger and wondered why Casper found this funny. Julia drifted back to sleep and woke when Casper climbed onto the wagon seat.

"I overslept," she cried.

181

Casper shouted, "Haw," and the wagon rolled down the Oregon Trail. "You needed your rest," Casper called over his shoulder.

"I didn't mean to oversleep," Julia wailed. She sat on the edge of the bed trying to scramble into her clothes. "Did you eat breakfast?"

"I had oatmeal and coffee," he declared, giving Julia a quick glance over his shoulder.

"A fine wife I am, sleeping while you fend for yourself," Julia grouched. She placed one hand on Casper's shoulder and stepped over the wagon seat and sat down.

"You know, I was thinking," Casper began after Julia was settled next to him. "As soon as we're settled on our land, you should write Martha and Perkins and have them select several orphans to send out to us. With the Union Pacific Railroad going all the way to California and the Oregon and California Railroad coming to Oregon City it won't be hard traveling."

"Orphans," Julia said not sure she understood Casper's meaning.

"They will be a help around the farm while learning a trade," Casper elaborated on his idea. Julia had lived her entire life with servants. With the ease of travel, he did not see why they could not have a few young orphans working on the farm and helping with the housekeeping. Julia certainly had the money to pay their expenses out. "It would be nice if you took a few of Miss Wayne's orphans off her hands," he continued.

Julia smiled for the first time since her sister left the wagon train. "It's a grand idea. I'm glad you thought of it. I'll write Uncle John and we can post the letter in Oregon City," Julia stated. "How many orphans are we talking about," she asked excitedly.

Casper laughed out loud. His Julia was back making plans and lists. "Two to work on the farm," he suggested. "How many do you want in the house?"

"I haven't decided," Julia replied.

"I'll need to know how many rooms to build," Casper said, smiling broadly.

"Rooms," Julia said thoughtfully, giving Casper a frown. "You don't plan to live in a one room cabin?"

"Medford is a lumber mill town," Casper explained. "Jorge wrote he works for the Sawmill in the winter cutting trees. He has built him and Darcy a big house. Did I mention Jorge said in his last letter, Darcy is having a baby?" He looked at Julia with his eyes glowing. Julia was having his baby.

"No, you didn't," Julia replied. "I'm hungry," she declared before Casper could say anything more about his brother Jorge. "I wonder what is in these barrels. We've eaten all the sweet crackers and there's only one tin left of dried fruit."

"Drive the wagon and I'll open one," Casper replied, handing Julia the reins. He stepped over the seat and pried off the lid on one of the barrels. "Well, I'll be," he said in surprise. "I should have taken the lids off the barrels sooner. This one is full of apples." He rubbed an apple over his shirtsleeve before biting off a chunk.

"Apples," Julia declared. "I remember Martha saying she packed apples. We can plant apple trees," she said before laughing.

"Apple trees growing on own land. Now, there's an idea," Casper said. He picked up an apple and stepped over the wagon seat and took the reins. Julia sighed contentedly before biting into her apple.

Oregon City was a larger settlement then Julia had expected. There were a good many stores and shops along Main Street. She could see Willamette Falls and the river flowing along the Westside of town.

They arrived the evening before and circled the wagons outside of town. Julia cooked supper and cleared away. Casper went to a meeting called by Mr. Horn. The Wagon Master had brought them across the Great Plains and through the Rocky Mountains to a land ripe for settling.

Casper tugged on Julia's hand leading her along Main Street. They stopped at a hotel and he urged her inside for a meal she had not cooked over a campfire. She laughed softly and blushed. The meal was all they expected after months on the trail. Molly looked around wide-eyed trying to see everything at once.

Casper leaned over and whispered in Julia's ear. "You will wear your neck out if you don't quit turning your head this way and that way." He laughed when Julia turned a dark red.

Next they visited the mercantile. Julia saying they did not need to purchase supplies as they had more than enough for a month. After walking around the store, Casper acknowledged he was relieved. The prices were higher than they expected and they

183

left without making a purchase. They visited the Post Office sending Mr. Forbes a letter stating they had arrived safely.

In the evening's gloom they walked back to camp. "I had a nice day," Julia said as she lay beside Casper with his arm around her. "I'm ready to head south to your brother Jorge as soon as you are," she whispered.

Mr. O'Fallon came to their camp early the next morning when Casper was starting the campfire. "Understand you folks are planning to head south," he stated after shaking Casper's hand.

"We're leaving right after breakfast," Casper replied.

"Thought you might want to know there's a meeting this morning for anyone interested in forming a wagon train. My sons and I are going," he stated, "It's safer traveling in a group."

"I can wait another day and see what is being said," Casper agreed. He went off with Mr. O'Fallon and his sons.

The morning air was cold when they left the following morning. Tree leaves were shades of red and gold against a clear blue sky. Nine wagons formed the wagon train heading south. Four of the wagons belonged to the O'Fallon family.

The wagon train passed through small towns and stagecoach stations along the wagon road. The air was sweet with the scent of pine and spruce. A stream ran alongside the trail and the water was cold. They stopped to rest a week later. The women washed clothes and hung them to dry on lines strung from wagon to wagon. Mr. O'Fallon and his sons went hunting and brought back a deer to divide between the families.

Julia hung damp clothes while she watched Molly play with several other children near the wagons. Being the youngest, Molly was having a hard time keeping up with the older children. She stopped to look at the other children clearly not understanding being left out. Clara and Wilma had always made sure she was included when they played. With tears filling her eyes, she walked to Julia.

Julia sat on a crate and cuddled Molly understanding the girl's sadness. "As soon as I'm done with the washing; you can help me bake an apple pie for daddy," she told the child. "And we'll make crackers out of the left over dough and eat them with jam."

Molly's little head bobbed up and down in agreement.

Casper was surprised to come back to the wagon and find Julia had baked an apple pie. "How long does it take an apple tree to grow before it bears fruit," he asked, washing up for supper.

"You're asking me. I thought you were the farmer," Julia teased.

"I grew up in a ghetto. I didn't see a tree until I started working in the warehouse district," Casper replied.

"I don't believe you," Julia scolded, only to hear Casper's laughter.

"Alright," Casper replied. "The tenement I grew up in was several blocks from Mrs. Wayne's Orphanage. There were trees in the orphanage yard."

"You did," Julia declared in surprise. Maybe, this accounted for Casper suggesting they bring orphans out to help on the farm.

"I'm ready for an early night of it," Casper said yawning and stretching. He took the plate Julia handed him and ate supper. Later, he helped clean the campsite and carried the crates to the wagon. He chained the draft horses to the wagon.

"We leave at first light," he said sitting down on the edge of the bed. Julia was sitting on Molly's bed reading her a story. Molly snuggled under the covers and blinked in an effort to stay awake.

Casper removed his boots and set them at the end of the bed. He was looking forward to not driving a wagon each day. And was making plans for spring, hoping Julia would not mind spending her first winter in Oregon living with his brother.

"Come to bed," Casper requested reaching for Julia. She came into his arms with a contented sigh.

Julia rolled over in bed. The sounds of the horses being led away woke her. She had breakfast cooking when Casper brought the horses back from the stream.

"I made coffee," he called, staking out the horses to graze.

Casper warmed his hands over the fire before pouring a cup of coffee. He accepted the plate of oatmeal and bacon from Julia. Molly watched him as he sat on the crate next to her. The days were shorter and autumn winds were blowing. He wondered how many more days of fine weather they would have before snow set in. Jorge had written snow could get deep in the mountain passes. That at times they were cut off from the outside world for months. It was now close to the end of October.

Another day on the trail and they would turn off the stage road. Two more days would put them in Medford. The end was near and Julia felt like shouting hallelujah.

Julia had not gone out of her way to befriend the women on the wagon train south. They would be together so few days and departing could be to heart wrenching. Mrs. O'Fallon she knew from the time they left Missouri. It was another tear filled good-bye and a promise to write from the older woman.

Then Casper turned onto the road cutting through a mountain pass. They were on their own. It seemed strange not to have a wagon ahead of them. Their noonday camp was a silent one. Molly gathered pebbles on the bank of a nearby stream, Julia closely watching to make sure she did not venture into the water. It was a leisurely time. Casper was in no hurry to push on. He let Molly play as he rested. In the end, they did not break camp. Casper spent the afternoon fishing in the stream and they had their first pan fried fish in the new land.

The following morning Casper broke camp. Julia sat in the wagon resting as Molly played mama. They traveled all day through a valley of tall pines and majestic spruce and large deciduous trees shedding fall foliage. Night came quickly as the sun slipped behind the mountains and long purple shadows covered the valley floor. It was early when Casper unhitched the horses and staked them out to graze.

Julia drank strong tea and nibbled on a biscuit as she fried potatoes. A pot of beans boiled over the fire. The night was dark with few stars and a cold wind blew off the mountains. Casper wrapped his arms around Molly. The little girl looked up at him with trusting eyes and rubbed her hand against his jaw. Feeling the day's growth of hair on his chin, she giggled as his whiskers tickled her fingers.

Tomorrow, Julia thought as she dished up their last meal on the trail. She handed Casper a plate and brushed her hand through his hair. All the things they missed during their days of travel were waiting for them at the end of tomorrow's journey. Jorge had a house with a roof over it, a table and chairs where they could sit and eat a meal, and a comfortable bed to sleep in.

Julia lay in Casper's arms unable to sleep, she was thinking about tomorrow. Wondering what Jorge would be like and whether she would like Darcy. Casper's brother was not expecting her. The letter she had mailed in Missouri was before she and Casper were married.

She turned on her side knowing she should get some sleep. But there were too many unanswered questions in her mind. Casper stirred in his sleep pulling her closer to him. Her heart skipped a beat at the feel of his warmth. She loved him more now then when she had first realized what those stirrings of emotions meant. It was strange to think there had been a time she had not loved him. She had depended on him and found he was more then capable of dealing with any problem they faced. Yet, she had not loved him. It had developed slowly over the days and weeks they were together.

Once again, Casper did not seem in a hurry as they lingered over breakfast. He hitched the team to the wagon and they started off on their final day of travel. The town of Medford was one long street and many intersecting roads. A single mercantile, a livery stable with a corral for horses attached at one end, a school house at the edge of town with children in the yard playing. There was a bank across from the barbershop and even a hotel with a dining room. A cluster of small frame houses was on the out skirts and a few log cabins. A sawmill dominated the town with large structures and a long barrack to house workers.

Casper stopped the wagon in front of the mercantile and jumped down. A sense of well being invaded his soul as he looked over the town. He entered the large well supplied mercantile. The man behind the counter was short and spry. He had dark eyes and a friendly smile on his lips.

"Can you point me in the direction of the Van Holland farm," Casper asked, stopping in front of the long service counter. The man looked at Casper as if he was not sure he heard right. "The Van Holland Farm," Casper asked again.

The man noticed the covered wagon parked in front of the store. Jorge had mentioned his brother from back east was over due. He scratched his head thoughtfully. "Sure," he told Casper coming around the counter and walking out to the boardwalk in front of his store. "Just follow the road out of town for about two miles. Jorge Van Holland lives in the big white house on the left. You can't miss it."

Casper shook the man's hand thanking him.

The man stood scratching his head as he watched the wagon roll out of town. Finally, he shook his head and went back

187

inside the store. If he had not seen it with his own eyes he never would believe it.

The house was just as he was told, a large three story frame house painted white. A white fence ran the length of the front yard. A barn and outbuildings were in the back. Casper pulled the wagon into the yard as a small dark haired woman came out to greet them.

She opened her mouth but no words came out. Then she laughed, "You can only be Casper," Darcy declared.

"Darcy?" Casper jumped down from the wagon to look at his sister-in-law. She was small and attractive with brown eyes and very pregnant with child. He looked at her as all men do when confronted with a very pregnant woman wondering how to hug her.

She laughed and placed her arms around his waist leaning her cheek against his broad chest. "I won't break," she assured, blushing a soft rosy red.

"Miss Warren," Darcy greeted.

"Mrs. Van Holland," Casper corrected.

Darcy nodded her head, not surprised by the revelation that Casper and Julia were married. In fact, she would have been surprised if they were not. She had told Jorge to expect Casper to bring a wife once she had received Julia's letter.

Julia made it as far as the front door before collapsing. Casper carried her up the front stairs to the spacious bedroom Darcy had waiting for them. Darcy went back to attend to Molly as Casper made his wife comfortable. Julia opened her eyes once to look at him then sank down into the soft mattress and drifted into a deep sleep.

CHAPTER TWENTY SEVEN

Julia turned over in bed. A faint light was streaming in through the window curtains. She remembered Casper carrying her up a flight of stairs and laying her on a bed. Looking concerned, he helped her undress. The last she remembered was Casper pulling up the covers.

She looked about the room. The wallpaper had a light yellow background covered with pink cabbage roses. The bed was large and stood well off the floor and the mattress soft as down. There was a highboy, a bureau dresser with mirror, a washstand with a ceramic bowl and matching water pitcher. A wardrobe of fine dark wood stood across the room. Under the windows was a built-in window seat with cushions arranged over polished boards. A stone fireplace was built on the interior wall, a wide mantel across the top and flat stones on the floor for a hearth. In all, it was a beautiful room and one that could easily be found in one of the finest neighborhoods back east.

Julia rested a moment longer enjoying the luxury of lying on a real bed. She was hungry and remembered she had not eaten. Was it morning or evening she wondered. Then noticed the bed beside her had been slept in. The pillow was dented from Casper's head laying on it. It must be morning she reasoned. Morning and she had slept since yesterday afternoon.

Her trunk was on the floor at the foot of the bed. She opened it selecting a dark green skirt and cream colored blouse. The water in the pitcher was cool as she poured it into the bowl and washed her face. In the mirror, she studied her reflection. Her skin was a light golden brown. Her tan would not be considered fashionable back east but the look gave her a healthy glow. She turned sideways. In her white nightgown she could not discern a

189

difference in her silhouette until she ran her hand over the small mound that was her growing baby.

The pains of hunger made Julia turn away from the mirror and quickly dress and brush her hair before braiding the strands. Opening the door, she walked into a long hallway. All the doors were closed. Julia descended the stairs and stopped to peek into the parlor. The sound of metal striking metal led her to the back of the house.

Casper stood in front of the cook stove pouring a cup of coffee. She walked to him placing her arms around his waist giving him a hug before ducking under his arm to rest her cheek against his shoulder. She felt him stiffen and looked up to see what was wrong. Her eyes met a pair of startled green eyes.

"Oh!" Julia exclaimed before hastily stepping away. The man looked like Casper. He looked exactly like Casper except for having green eyes.

"You must be Julia," he said with a wide grin on his lips.

She nodded shyly, her eyes wide with disbelief. She stood with her hands locked together behind her back.

"I'm Jorge," he said with a twinkle in his green eyes.

They heard the backdoor open and Darcy came in followed by Casper and Molly. He was carrying a basket of fresh eggs which he set on the counter before going over to Julia. He could tell she was upset by the way she was standing.

"I'm sorry," Casper said, taking hold of Julia's hands. "I just realized I never mentioned Jorge and I are twins." He placed his arm around her shoulders bringing her close to his side. She looked at him with uncertainty shining in her eyes.

"We're like looking into a mirror," Jorge said after he stopped laughing. He was shaking his head at his brother. Imagine Casper not telling his wife they were twins and identical twins at that.

"I mistook him for you," Julia confessed as the color darkening her cheeks intensified. Her eyes were bright with embarrassment. Casper leaned over kissing Julia lightly on the forehead. Casper was the older twin. That was why he laughed when he called Jorge his younger brother. She leaned her cheek against his shoulder.

Jorge managed another laugh. "Don't let Jorge's laughter embarrass you. He flirts with all the young ladies," Casper told his wife.

"I use to flirt with all the young ladies," Jorge corrected, giving Darcy a playful wink. Though the brothers were identical in looks, Julia believed they were very different in temperament. Regardless of what Jorge said, he was still a tease and his green eyes revealed how funny he thought it was she had not known he and Casper were twins.

Jorge finished pouring coffee and strolled to the kitchen table. Molly also was having trouble adjusting to the man with her father's face. She made a wide circle around him and ran over to Casper wrapping her arms around his leg. She stared at Jorge with wide eyes and a deep frown puckering her features.

Casper picked up his daughter. "My girls are a little on the shy side," he told Jorge. "And slow to make new friends," he added as Julia stood close to him.

Julia sighed deeply and looked at Jorge. She had been wondering what her new brother-in-law would be like. She studied him still finding it hard to believe he looked so much like Casper. Then she remembered what Darcy had said the day before. "You can only be Casper."

Casper walked over to the table and took the chair next to Jorge. Molly turned her face to her father pressing against his chest. Jorge tried to make friends with his niece but Molly was having none of it. He ruffled her wavy blond hair and spoke softly to the child but she ignored him.

Julia asked Darcy what she could do to help. The kitchen was spacious with work counters along one wall and cabinets above. The iron cook stove had seen years of service and was polished until it shone. The kitchen table was well constructed and she wondered if Jorge had made it. The whole kitchen had the look of being especially made for Darcy.

Darcy took biscuits from the oven. A skillet of eggs were cooking, she gave the eggs a good scrambling before emptying the biscuits in a cloth lined basket. "There's jam and butter in the cabinet at the end of the counter," she instructed.

The jam had been placed in a dish. Julia carried it and the dish of butter to the table. She poured two glasses of milk and gave one to Molly. Darcy brought platters of eggs and ham to the table while Julia brought the basket of biscuits.

Casper's eyes rested on Julia across the table from him. She smiled shyly back. Their long hard journey was over. Jorge had a comfortable home with plenty of room. His hope was that Julia would like Jorge and Darcy and feel at ease around them.

"If you need work," Jorge said as he buttered a biscuit. "There's work at the Sawmill."

Julia opened her mouth to tell Casper about the money she had stored for when she reached Oregon. Before, she could say anything Casper answered. "Mr. Forbes paid me handsomely to accompany Julia to Oregon. The last three weeks in the east, I spent in Miss Warren's home and Molly's and my expenses were paid. I had very little opportunity to spend my wages. I should be able to make a fair start."

Jorge nodded his head as his brother talked. "I know the people who own one of the banks in town if you find yourself short on money," he told Casper.

His wife smiled shaking her head. "Don't let him tease you," Darcy declared. "Jorge is half owner of the bank he is talking about. My father owns the other half."

This was news to Casper. Jorge was making a good life for himself in this new country. "Some four years ago," Jorge explained. "Mr. Russell was talking about the need for another bank. One interested in developing farming in the area. No one seemed interested in undertaking the venture. So him and I pooled what funds we had at the time and started the bank. The problem we're facing is not enough ready capital. The area is short on real money. It's something the whole area is facing. Folks in town think we should print our own money but I'm against it. Though some of the towns around are doing just that."

Darcy cleared the table as the two brothers continued to talk. Julia helped Molly wash her face and hands. The girl noticed the orange tabby cat curled up in the corner of the kitchen sleeping. She leaned down and gently brushed her hand over the cat's back. Then, she sat on the floor next to it.

Casper and Jorge went out to look over the farm and do the morning chores. Julia helped Darcy wash dishes. "It's going to be a real problem for folks around town to know which brother is which." Darcy predicted. "They don't sound alike when they speak."

"They might start sounding more alike if they spend a lot of time together," Julia replied. She was watching Casper through the kitchen window. "Casper has blue eyes."

192

Darcy looked at Julia and smiled. "Jorge has green eyes," she finally said, realizing what Julia meant.

"That was what I noticed about him this morning. His green eyes and I knew he wasn't Casper." Julia placed the dishes back inside the cabinet. Molly came across the room carrying the cat in her arms with the tabby's tail dragging along the floor.

"You've found a new playmate," Julia said, kneeling down and rubbing her hand over the cat's head. "What's her name," she asked Darcy.

"Herschel," Darcy answered with a smile on her lips. "I figured she was going to have to do battle against a whole regiment of mice and she would need a nice military name."

Julia laughed.

Darcy's baby was past due. Though babies arrived when they were ready and not before. Jorge was taking the waiting hard. With Casper to divert his attention maybe he would stop being so anxious. She tugged down the front of her blouse, commenting on how uncomfortable the last weeks had been. Darcy was small and she was carrying her baby out front which made it difficult for her to do almost anything.

"I have trouble sitting down and then I have trouble getting up. I have trouble sleeping because I can't find a comfortable way to lie down," she said with a dismissive laugh. "Don't let my grousing make it sound like I'm not excited about the baby," Darcy added. "Jorge and I have been married more then four years and I was getting concerned because I wasn't having a baby yet." They were sitting at the kitchen table talking and drinking a hot cup of tea having completed the day's housekeeping chores.

The men came back to the house for dinner and planned a trip into town. Jorge telling Casper the bank had a list of properties in the area. The County Seat was Jacksonville a town about ten miles away. Once Casper had an idea which property he was interested in, they would travel to the County Seat to register the claim.

Julia reminded Casper she would like to make Molly a warm winter coat before it got any colder. He promised to get what she needed while in town.

"If I remember correctly," Darcy said after the men departed. "The thing I enjoyed most when my folks got settled was a nice hot bath. No more hurrying to wash in the back of the wagon while afraid one of my brothers or some other man would choose then to need something from the wagon."

Julia laughed nodding her head. She could name about a dozen more things she was enjoying now they were settled.

"When the men get back, I'll ask Jorge to carry the bathtub upstairs to your bedroom and heat water so you can have a real soak." Darcy leaned back in her chair. "Tomorrow we can get the washing done."

"Tomorrow I'll do the washing," Julia said. "I don't want us to be a burden. It will be a pleasure not needing to wait until we reach water." It was Darcy's turn to agree. It had not been so many years since she came west with her parents that she could not remember the hardships.

Casper had told of the many hardships on the trail the first night they arrived. Darcy and Jorge had not faced a shortage of water. The year each came west there had been an abundance of rain. Darcy's folks had settled in Medford several years before Jorge. But each remembered the wearing travel, the rush each day to move on. The days of rain with little protection, the thunderstorms that boomed and raged, and the sweltering heat during the long summer days. The lack of privacy was the hardest on Darcy.

The galvanized bathtub was long and deep and Casper carried up buckets of hot water to fill it. He told Julia his turn was next. Swimming in cold streams could never compare to a real hot bath. Julia would have been happy to be able to swim in a cold stream and she told him so which caused him to smile. He seemed relaxed and in good spirits.

Julia set before the open fire drying her hair. Casper lay on the braided rug on the floor watching her. "There is a nice piece of land about twenty minutes north of here." He said. "What do you think?"

She stopped drying her hair and glanced at him. "It will be nice to be close to family." The words were what Casper hoped she would say.

"I can cut trees this winter and have the Sawmill cut the logs into lumber. We can start building the house as soon as the weather warms in the spring." He studied Julia's face for her reaction to his proposal. "Jorge says the County Seat is in Jacksonville which is around ten miles from here. We will go in the morning. I want to register my claim before it snows."

194

"Whatever you decide is alright with me." It was the words she had said to him once before. He cupped his hand around the back of her head drawing her to him. His mind no longer on the journey to Jacksonville or the land he wished to file a claim on.

CHAPTER TWENTY EIGHT

Darcy rose from the table pausing as she stood and Julia noticed the tightness around her mouth. After a few seconds, Darcy refilled her tea cup. It was not the first time Julia noticed Darcy stopping to wait a minute before continuing on with her work. "Darcy," she asked, "Are you in labor?"

Darcy sat down on her chair. "I was waiting to say something," she admitted.

"Do you want me to find Jorge for you?"

"Not yet. He has been anxious. I might as well let him have as much peace as I can. It takes a while for a baby to come. He will go for my mother when the time comes."

Julia did not believe she would be as calm as Darcy. She suddenly found herself anxious about the baby she was carrying. She laughed as she admitted as much to Darcy.

It was late afternoon when Julia went to find Jorge and asked him to go for Mrs. Russell.

Jorge sat at the kitchen table moving his supper around on his plate. Casper was living on his land cutting trees to build a house and Molly was missing her father. She looked at Jorge as she ate. Then, she crawled off her chair and onto Jorge's lap laying her head against his chest. Jorge was surprised when Molly rubbed her hand over his jaw giggling at the feel of his rough facial hair against her fingers.

"So you've decided to make up to me," Jorge asked.

Molly's sudden acceptance of Jorge kept him occupied as he played with his niece. Before dark, he went to do the evening chores and Julia wondered if she should go along to make sure he did them properly. He was distracted. After Jorge left, Molly turned her attention to Herschel the cat.

Julia looked in on Darcy bringing her a cup of strong tea. She asked if Mrs. Russell needed anything. Mrs. Russell washed her daughter's face before straightening the covers on the bed. She asked after Jorge, before saying, "I do believe it is harder on a new father." Darcy's look was one of disbelief but she smiled as Julia told of Jorge's distraction and her wondering if the chores would be properly done.

It was nearly midnight when the whimper of a baby's cry reached the kitchen. Jorge was pacing back and forth at times muttering to himself. Stopping, he looked at Julia with what she could only describe as relief and fear. His muscles were taut and his green eye glowed.

"I'll go see," Julia said, not waiting for Jorge to ask.

She closed the bedroom door to find Jorge standing anxiously in the hall. "Darcy is fine," she said, assuring him Darcy was alright. "She wants to tell you," Julia said when Jorge asked if he had a son or daughter.

Jorge reached for the doorknob. "Mrs. Russell says Darcy's not ready to see you yet," Julia replied, placing one hand on Jorge's arm.

Jorge anxiously waited another ten minutes while wearing a grove in the carpeted hall floor. He raked his fingers through his hair so many times it stood on end. Julia understood his nervousness and knew nothing she could say would relieve his pent-up emotions.

At last, Mrs. Russell opened the door saying Jorge could see his wife. "I need a strong cup of tea," Mrs. Russell declared. She collapsed onto a kitchen chair and Julia poured her a cup of strong tea. "Twins," she announced, "Two healthy boys."

"Casper says there are twins born in each generation of his family for as far back as records go," Julia replied. "He wondered if Darcy was having twins," she explained.

"I guess it was to be expected," Mrs. Russell replied before picking up her cup of tea and drinking.

* * * * *

Julia fluffed Darcy's pillow and placed it behind her head. Then, she walked to the cradle and picked up a tiny baby boy carrying him to his mother. He was whimpering softly ready for his

197

mother to feed him. She turned to leave mother and son alone together.

"Please stay," Darcy requested.

Julia sat on the chair next to the bed. Darcy brushed back her son's dark hair. His brother was sleeping in the cradle. They were dark haired like their mother and had blue eyes like Casper. The son Darcy was feeding was the older of the brothers. He was also larger, weighting more than his younger brother.

"Who would have thought," Darcy said in bewilderment. "Two babies, no wonder I was having such a hard time." Julia could have told her Casper would not be surprised "You have been such a help. I don't know what I would do if you weren't here to help out. It seems I no sooner get one feed and back to sleep then the other one wakes up crying."

"I'm sure all new mothers feel the same way. As if their life is no longer there own. I remember Annabel saying much the same thing when each of her girls was born."

"I never will forget the first time I met Jorge," Darcy said and laughed softly. "My brother Ben brought him home. And I thought another man to look after and feed. I was seventeen and had four older brothers to boss me around and give me orders. Jorge tried to be friendly. I think he must have been attracted to me from the start. But I didn't want to be friends." She smiled as she remembered. "I did feed him supper. And I remember ma scolding me for being rude to him. He was company and I had treated him badly."

"I think it might have ended there if it wasn't for my brothers. Jorge was on his own and I think he was lonesome for company. He came around every few days just to have someone to talk too. But he pretty well left me alone after our first meeting," Darcy continued.

Darcy gently rubbed her son's back. "I think I forgave him for being so brass when he offered to carry water on washday. Because of that, he took a lot of ribbing from my brothers. But he didn't seem to mind and I thought it was too bad he was so poor. I had made up my mind I was going to marry a rich man. We were poor back in Tennessee. What you would call a dirt farm family. And I believed I'd had enough of living poor."

"I don't think Jorge had a clear plan of what he wanted to do. He worked at the Sawmill in town. The town built a school house but teachers were scarce. I was asked if I would teach

198

school because I could read and write. Since Jorge went through town every day on his way to the Sawmill, it just seemed natural for him to give me a ride each morning. He would stop at school long enough to build a fire in the stove. The school was warm by the time my first student arrived. Then in the evenings, I'd wait at school for him to quit work and bring me home. He generally ate supper with us before going home to do chores."

"Summer arrived and school closed. I missed the times we spent together. Then Ben informed me Jorge was seeing some girl in the next valley. I think it broke my heart. I didn't realize I was in love with him until then. He didn't come around much. He was still working at the Sawmill and farming. I didn't see how he had time to court a girl at the same time," Darcy confessed.

"The next time he came to Sunday dinner, I asked him if he wanted to go for a walk. He looked at me in surprise and I do believe he was about to say no. Then he changed his mind and we were hardly out of pa's sight when he kissed me. I'll confess I kissed him back. He looked at me and said, so you've changed your mind." Darcy held her sleeping son in her arms. "Jorge is such a hard worker I knew I could trust him to take care of me."

Julia could understand Darcy's sentiment. She would never be afraid of intrusting Casper with her future. Julia picked up Darcy's sleeping son and carried him back to his cradle. "You need some rest and Molly should be waking up from her nap."

It was snowing when Julia started supper. The flakes were large as they swirled around before falling to the ground. Snow was piling up against the side of the barn and outbuildings. The air was crisp and cold. She added wood to the cook stove and slid in an apple pie to cook. She stirred venison stew and mixed biscuit dough.

Molly had her baby under her arm. The doll was dressed in her new winter coat to match the one Julia had made for Molly. She was telling Herschel the cat all about the new babies. "Mommy," she asked, glancing up. "Can I have two babies?"

Julia leaned over and picked Molly up. She felt the blast of cold air and turned expecting to see Jorge but it was Casper who stood just inside the door unbuttoning his coat. She rushed into his arms. "I love you," she told him.

Casper's heart skipped a beat as he wrapped his arms around Julia. She had said she loved him. "Julia," was all he said before kissing her. He had not expected such a warm greeting.

"I wasn't expecting you back until tomorrow," Julia said, wrapping her arms about his neck and placing her cheek against his cold face.

"I decided to stop cutting trees early and come home for a few days," he explained. "Living in a tent when it is cold is miserable," he added softly. "Not to mention I'm missing you and Molly." His blue eyes were bright when he looked at her. He kissed her again holding her close. "Julia," he said again. "I love you." Julia heard the wonder in his voice as he acknowledged his love for her. She laid her cheek against his shoulder.

"Mommy," Molly said tugging on Julia's skirt.

"Hello little one," Casper greeted his daughter picking her up and raising her above his head. She squealed and giggled.

"Can I have two babies," she asked Casper.

"Two babies," Casper replied.

"Like Aunt Darcy. I want two babies."

Casper glanced at Julia for conformation. His wife smiled and nodded her head yes. "Two boys," she said, "Born five days ago." She moved back into his arms tilting up her face to welcome his kiss.

200

CHAPTER TWENTY NINE

The door to the bedroom Casper shared with Julia was closed when he walked up the stairs. Upon opening the door, the room was warm with a fire burning in the fireplace. Julia sat in a comfortable stuffed chair reading. She looked up with a smile on her lips when he came into the room.

Molly lay sleeping on the window seat where Julia had made her a bed. Casper walked over to Molly checking on his daughter first. He leaned down to kiss her on the cheek then tucked the warm blanket around her small body. For a moment, he stood thinking of the cold tenement they had shared the winter before. Molly was happy and strong and his heart filled with thanksgiving.

A book was open on Julia's lap and he sat on the floor at her feet. "Do you mind reading out loud," Casper asked. He missed Julia reading to him.

Julia read aloud the chapter she was reading and the following chapter before closing the Bible. Casper studied her fine features. He had endured heartbreaking loneliness over the past week while cutting timber. "I am building a log shed on our land," he said. "I plan to live there this winter. I bought a cook stove to provide heat and to cook meals." Julia tilted her head to one side waiting for him to explain what he wanted. "When the shed is done, do you think you and Molly might come for a visit," he asked.

"I will be happy living anyplace you are," she answered.

"I don't expect you to live in a shed," Casper retorted. He was still having misgivings about asking Julia to visit. The structure was crude and uninhabitable by civilized standards. "Just come and spend a few days. I miss you when I'm away."

"If I come for a few days, I'm sure I won't want to leave," Julia replied earnestly.

Casper took her fingers in his hand studying her features once more. "I'm remembering your grand home with its rooms of fine furniture," he admitted. "There were oil paintings on the walls and cabinets displaying crystal and fine porcelain. I believe what surprised me most was the thick rugs covering the floors," he declared. "It was the first time I visited a real home."

Julia touched his cheek. Her eyes glowed with her feelings. "I will live wherever you live," she whispered.

"It will only be until spring," Casper assured. "Mr. Russell and his sons have volunteered to help build our house. He has drawn a floor plan and made a list of lumber I will need. When I get enough trees cut, I'll take them to the Sawmill and they will start ripping boards. Mr. Russell suggested I bargain with Mr. Morton and see if he will accept timber as payment. It means more timber cutting but will save what money I have." Casper paused wondering what Julia thought about his plans. She seemed a sensible young woman. Still, she had lived without wanting luxuries or having the money to indulge in her whims.

"I was in town earlier today and mailed your letter to Mr. Forbes requesting he send us six orphans. Two boys to work the farm and four girls to help inside the house. As scarce as girls seem to be, we will probably need to have Mr. Forbes send us girls every few years. For, they will marry and start homes of their own," he said, giving Julia a broad smile. Standing, he pulled Julia out of the chair so he could sit holding her on his lap. "Tell me again," he requested. Julia was not sure what Casper wanted. "Tell me again you love me," he said

"I love you," she answered, color slowly creeping into her cheeks.

"Julia," he said after kissing her thoroughly. His heart pounded in his ears. "I love you," he whispered against her lips.

Julia slipped from his lap and went to turn down the blankets on the bed. "I was waiting for you to return," she said, reaching for his hand.

Snow was high the next morning. A wintry sun was in the sky and wind blew from the mountains stirring snow drifts. Julia lifted the whimpering baby from its cradle and carried him to his waiting mother. Darcy took her son in loving arms.

"I'm glad Casper is back for the weekend. It looks bad outside," Darcy said.

"Yes," Julia agreed. "He's built a log shed and bought a cook stove for heat. He's asked me to go live with him," Julia said blushing. Julia was really a shy person. Her shyness was natural and it complimented Casper's strong independent personality. In this Jorge and Casper were alike.

Julia cleaned Darcy's bedroom while they talked. Molly was helping her. She had her own little dust cloth rubbing the sides of the bureau dresser, occasionally the floor or wall.

"You don't need to stay and help me," Darcy said after Julia gave a long discourse on why she needed to stay and help her with the babies. "Mother is just down the road if I need help. I've been lazy. I should be up doing more. The boys are over a month old." Julia smiled taking the baby and carrying him back to his cradle. A few minutes later Darcy's other son woke crying. Julia picked up the baby and carried him across to Darcy. "It is nice having you here but your place is with Casper," Darcy stated.

Julia met Daryl Russell when he stayed for supper. He was tall and slender with reddish hair and brown eyes. He spoke in the slow drawl that Darcy used putting a twang to his words that made it hard for Julia to understand at times. He was pleasant and Julia could see he liked his brother-in-law. Though the fact, Jorge and Casper were identical twins had him a little befuddled.

But now that she was getting to know Jorge and seeing him daily there were differences. And most of the time, she could distinguish one brother from the other without checking the color of his eyes or hearing him speak. Jorge had picked up some of the slow twang Darcy and her brothers spoke.

"Daryl is good with wood. He has opened a carpenter's shop and is making furniture. Says he makes more money from his furniture then he does farming." Jorge explained after Daryl had gone home. "He made the furniture for this house."

"He did," Julia asked, intrigued.

"I said he is good with wood."

"Your furniture is beautiful." Julia added admiringly.

"I've asked Daryl to oversee the construction of the house," Casper stated, prompting Julia to wonder how much he had been paid to bring her to Oregon. "Enough if I'm fugal," Casper declared, reading Julia's thoughts.

203

"You always seem to know what I'm thinking," Julia declared, firming her lips.

"I doubt there's a man alive that can read a woman's mind all the time," Jorge declared. His green eyes glowed with mischief.

"Since apparently, I'm in the way. I will go to bed," Julia retorted, standing and leaving the room.

It was late when Casper joined Julia in their bedroom. He always checked on Molly first, kissing his daughter's cheek as she slept. Julia was a good mother, he thought. He sat at Julia's feet listening to her read until she closed the book and sat with her hand resting on top.

"Is it hard to learn to read," Casper asked with uncertainty sounding in his voice. "Do you think I can learn?"

"I don't see why you shouldn't. You're an intelligent man." Julia thought he was intelligent, this pleased him. Leaning over, she kissed Casper and he pulled her into his arms. "I'm leaving in the morning. Will you come with me," he asked.

"I talked with Darcy this morning. She assures me it is time she starts taking care of her sons," Julia paused, looking lovingly at Casper. "I would love to come," she stated.

The following morning, Julia sat on the wagon seat beside Casper. The road through the tall cedars and pines was little more than a rutted trail. She could see where trees were cut to widen the road. Trunks cut low enough the wagon passed over them.

It was above freezing and snow lay around the trunks of tall trees. She was seeing their land for the first time and kept turning her head to view new sights.

Trees gave way to a meadow. Julia looked around in surprise. The slope of the land rose gradually. Logs were piled waiting to be taken to the Sawmill and cut into lumber. The shed was built of logs and stood a short distance away from where Casper planned to build their house. He had spent the past week finishing the cabin and was anxious to show Julia her new home as humble as it was.

The bay draft horses pulled to a stop before the log shed. It really looked more like a cabin and Julia decided Casper called it a shed to let her know it was to be their temporary home. She was delighted with the way it looked and told Casper.

Waiting on the wagon seat, he described the land. Pointing to a creek, he explained it flowed into a valley where he planned to raise cattle. The creek ran across their land before flowing into the Rogue River.

He helped Julia from the wagon. "Don't expect much," he warned opening the cabin door. The room was cold and Casper knelt to start a fire in the cook stove. A pipe stuck through the roof carried away smoke. There was a bunk built against one wall and crates were used for chairs. The table was planks over two sawhorses.

"All the comforts of home," Julia said laughing. Casper frowned at her. "I had a playhouse when I was a young girl," Julia explained. "Don't worry. I don't mind living here with you."

"I'll admit it's not much," Casper apologized.

"It is home," Julia said.

Casper closed the door on the stove and took Julia in his arms. "I want you here but if you want to go back to Jorge's, I'll understand," he said before kissing Julia.

"It is home," Julia said once more. "I want to be with you and after traveling five months in a covered wagon your cabin looks nice."

Casper laughed and hugged Julia close. "I guess it is better than a covered wagon. It doesn't move," he said smiling. "The floor is dirt though," he pointed out.

"I don't mind," Julia said. "But, I do expect a real house come spring." She thought of the new life growing inside her and knew she wanted to be with Casper regardless of the condition of his log cabin.

They spent the best part of the morning hiking over their land before returning to a warm cabin. Julia asked questions and breathed deeply the scent of cedar and pines. She had laughed as she and Molly gathered large pinecones to toss playfully at Casper. Molly carried pinecones back to the cabin.

"Home," she told him with her cheek against his arm. "A home is people. You, Molly and me and the coming baby, we make a home."

"By the time the house is built our baby will be here," he said, kissing her on the forehead.

Julia sighed deeply. She was tired from her long hike over their land. She smiled as she thought of the days of trouble and toil that had brought her to this state of contentment with Casper. It had been a long battle of discouragement and set backs. Times

205

full of fear and lost hope. She leaned against him, the uncertainty of her future gone now replaced by the love they shared.

Casper picked Julia up and carried her over the threshold. The earth inside the cabin was dry and hard packed. Julia removed her warm coat and hung it on a nail drove into the cabin wall. "I am looking forward to cooking my first meal in my new home," she declared. If her voice trembled, Casper chose to ignore it. Julia always faced new challenges with hope in her heart.

CHAPTER THIRTY

Christmas morning was cold and clear. The snow of the previous days, sparkling white was sun kissed. Casper presented Julia with a rocking chair telling her all new mothers needed a rocking chair. He gave Molly a windup jack-in-the-box that popped up as music played. She jumped and giggled each time the clown sprung forth. Julia gave Molly a baby doll to match the one she had already made her daughter. Molly now had two babies like Aunt Darcy. And Julia gave Casper a new plaid wool shirt to wear while cutting trees.

The Russell's house was warm and full of cheer as the family gathered for Christmas dinner. They welcomed Casper and Julia as family. Molly at first was shy among so many strangers. The Russell children accepted her among them and they went to play.

Molly was sleeping in Julia's arms as they traveled home. Casper carried his daughter to bed. As the sun set in the west, Julia leaned back in her rocking chair and opened her letter from Sara. Jorge had collected the mail and given Julia the letter while she was at the Russell's.

Sara wrote they had not yet found a place to settle. After leaving Horn's wagon train, they had joined a wagon train traveling to California. But after being there for a few weeks decided not to settle. Nathan was working and come spring they hoped to return to Oregon. They had heard land was good in Willamette Valley. She would write again once they settled.

Julia folded the letter and slipped it back inside the envelope. As she did so, she wondered if Sara was likely to write again. Their days on the wagon train already seemed a long time ago.

The last day in December a letter arrived from Annabel. Julia knew at once how happy her sister was. Her words bubbled over with praise for Phinehas Wheeler. And Julia was in no doubt her sister was in love. Annabel wrote the girls were well and growing. They were adjusting to having five older brothers. The Wheeler household was active and a challenge but she enjoyed every minute of it.

They had settled on a farm in upper Washington and she would not trade one day for all the days she had spent in Europe. She ended stating, she missed Julia but knew Casper was taking good care of her and asking her sister to write soon.

Julia folded the letter after reading through it a second time. She dried away her tears and blew her nose on one of her dainty handkerchiefs. Casper watched as she sniffed and smiled at him. She requested simply, "hold me."

"Julia," Casper asked as she sat on his lap, leaning her head against his shoulder.

"Why couldn't she have found happiness the first time? Why did she need to suffer through a marriage with Charles," Julia asked.

Casper had no answer for her. "Be happy Annabel has at last found a man that is good to her," he said, leaning over and kissing Julia on the forehead. A smile curved up his lips. He kissed her with a thoroughness that left Julia breathless with anticipation.

* * * * *

Julia placed the basket of eggs on the kitchen table. Removed her winter coat and hung it on a peg near the door. After helping Molly out of her coat, she put her hand into the small pockets retrieving an egg from one and several chicken feathers from the other. Molly was forever picking up small items and placing them in her pockets.

"I thought I'd bake an apple pie," Julia said, thinking out loud. There was still a stack of supplies unused. The thought of Casper coming home after a day of cutting timber had her humming softly as she worked. Julia was waiting for him with open arms when he stepped through the door. He kissed her thoroughly, hungry for the feel of her in his arms.

When he raised his head, her hand rubbed against his beard. "The beard is because I spend so much time outside. I can shave if you like," he said.

"I'll get use to it," Julia answered, leaning back against his arms.

After supper, Julia stood at the window watching snow fall. Molly was playing mama with her twin babies. She had asked Julia for a box to make her babies a bed and was looking through a stack of fabric scraps for a piece of material large enough to make a blanket. Finding a soft piece of flannel, she asked Julia if she might have it.

It seemed Molly grew each day. She was getting to be a young lady and very grownup for a three and a half year old. Julia wondered if she remembered living in the east. Casper had told her very little about their life then. Only, mentioning the cold tenement in passing comments. He had also told her it was Jorge who first noticed Mary, Molly's mother.

Julia turned from the window and with needle and thread sat in her rocking chair hemming Molly's baby blanket.

"It's a real storm this time," Julia said, looking at Molly. "Spring will be here before long." She stood and walked about the room. She was feeling restless. The last few weeks she had rounded out in front. Was she near her time?

Julia sat piecing a quilt top. Time would go quicker if she kept herself busy. She wondered if she could wait. As much as she wanted to, she was not sure. Her pains had started. Surely, she could wait a while longer until Casper came in from doing evening chores.

Julia watched the room darken from her bed. Molly sat on the foot playing with her babies. Julia heard Casper open the door and come into the cabin. "In bed already," he asked as he hung up his warm coat. "Julia," he questioned when she did not immediately reply.

Casper brushed back damp hair from her forehead planting a kiss on her waiting lips. He could see Julia was in pain, dark circles were below her eyes and her face was pale. "I'll get Mrs. Russell," he said not waiting for Julia to answer.

Julia closed her eyes hoping Mrs. Russell was not in the middle of something and could come right away. It seemed forever before Darcy's mother arrived. The woman's presence stilled Julia's fears.

"Why don't you take Molly to see Darcy and the boys," Mrs. Russell suggested to Casper. "Ask Darcy to keep her a few days."

Casper did not want to leave Julia. "Go on," Julia said. "Molly is missing Herschel the cat. Take her two babies with her," she instructed.

"Men are in the way," Mrs. Russell said once Casper left. "It won't be long now."

Casper heard his baby crying before he opened the door. Seated at the kitchen table, Mrs. Russell was drinking coffee. Julia was lying in bed with his baby beside her. Julia was gently patting the baby's back trying to quiet the infant.

"Thank you," Casper whispered as he knelt beside the bed.

"You have a daughter," Julia said.

"I now have three girls to watch over," he whispered, kissing her. "Little Ann looks like her mother." Julia sighed deeply, reached up and brushed her hand against his beard.

"You need to rest," Casper told her. "I'll be here." Julia nodded her head. Now Casper was home, she was drifting to sleep.

* * * * *

Molly stood beside the bed watching Julia hold Ann. She walked over and looked inside the empty cradle before walking back to Julia. Molly looked at Ann with a frown puckering her face.

"What's wrong," Julia asked, wondering if Molly might be envious of her holding Ann. She placed an arm around Molly and drew her close.

"Where's the other baby," Molly asked.

Julia thought for a moment before smiling. "There is only one baby," she told Molly.

"Aunt Darcy got two babies," Molly declared, feeling cheated.

"There is only one you," Julia reminded. Molly's blue eyes so like her father's were troubled as she sat thinking. "Sometimes babies come one at a time. You came as one baby and Ann came as one baby," Julia explained.

"Aunt Darcy got two babies," Molly insisted still frowning. She wanted two babies like Aunt Darcy.

"Sometimes babies come two at a time like Darcy's babies," Julia explained. "But more often, babies arrive one at a time like you and Ann."

Molly reached and gently touched Ann's soft hair. "Daddy's making us a house," Molly said next. "Me and Ann and you are going to live there."

Casper, Darcy's brothers and Jorge were building the new house. The foundation was laid and they started on the walls that morning.

Darcy came into the cabin looking for Molly. She took Ann and put her in her cradle. She was a tiny baby, smaller than either one of her boys. But Ann was healthy in spite of her small size and she was putting on weight.

"I don't know how to thank you for coming," Julia said, feeling tired. Ann was two weeks old. Surely, it was time she started feeling like doing more.

"Mother has been asking me for weeks to leave the boys with her. I thought today would be a good day. She promised to bring the boys out when they got fussy," Darcy said. She took Molly's hand and asked her if she wanted to see her new house.

Julia woke to the sound of Casper coming into the cabin. He walked over to the cradle to see his new daughter. Then, he noticed Julia was awake and came to her. "The walls are up," he said, leaning over and kissing her on the forehead. "We should have the roof on tomorrow. That is if the rains hold off." He pulled Julia's rocking chair over to the bed and sat down. He reached for Julia's hand and held it as he talked. "Daryl has assured me the kitchen table and chairs are made." Casper rubbed his thumb over the palm of her hand. "We will add furniture as Daryl finishes making it."

"A home is people," Julia reminded him.

"It helps to have a stove and a way to sit and eat meals," he said practically.

Julia smiled and agreed. It was important that Casper provide these for his family. He, Molly and baby Ann were what she found important. "So, when can I move into my new home," Julia asked.

"Not for a few more weeks," Casper replied. "There is no hurry. We've lived in this cabin since before Christmas."

"I'm grumbling because Mrs. Russell says I must stay in bed for another two weeks. I want to be out in the sunshine," Julia explained.

"The sun will still be here in two weeks. Mrs. Russell is correct. You need to rest while you can. When spring arrives there will be any number of things to keep you busy out of doors."

"I'm impatient," Julia replied. "Tell me about the house since I'm forbidden to walk across the yard and see it with my own eyes."

Darcy came into the cabin carrying one of her sons. "Ma's here," she announced. "It's time I went home and fixed supper for Jorge."

"Thank you," Julia said. "Molly can bring her babies and play on the foot of the bed. I'm not sleepy."

CHAPTER THIRTY ONE

The sun was warm the day Casper helped Julia walk across the lawn to her new home. She held Ann wrapped in a warm blanket. Molly ran ahead of them chattering about all the things she had found inside the house.

The house was larger than Julia expected with gingerbread trim on the gables and a wide front porch. "The trim was Daryl's idea," Casper said. "I wanted a wide porch so we can sit outside in the evening and watch the sunset."

Casper carried Julia across the threshold, kissing her thoroughly before setting her feet on the new floor. "A husband's privilege," he told her with a smile in his voice.

Julia looked around as Casper went back to the cabin for Ann's cradle. He made several trips carrying items a family needs daily to live. Last was the rocking chair, her Christmas present from him. He sat the chair in the corner of their bedroom where the warm sun from the window fell across it.

She was cooking supper when Casper came into the kitchen. "You should be resting," he admonished.

"I feel fine," she assured. Ann was more than a month old yet Casper insisted on treating her like an invalid. She tried not to resent his attitude but she was a healthy young woman who did not enjoy being coddled.

"Just do as I ask," Casper prompted. He noticed her look of stubbornness which changed to acceptance. He slipped his arm around her shoulders tilting up her chin with his fingers. He ran his thumb over her lips. "I love you," he added softly. "Don't fight me over this. You're such a skinny little thing. I want you well and strong before winter comes again."

"Alright Casper," she accepted. "But I'm going to plant my garden tomorrow," she insisted, only to hear Casper's laughter.

The sun was warm on Julia's back as she leaned over the row of green beans she was planting. Molly was nearby talking to her baby dolls and Ann was asleep in her improvised bed. Julia had added straw to the bottom of a crate covering the straw with a thick wool blanket. She had wrapped Ann in a blanket before laying her in the crate and placing her under a shade tree.

Julia enjoyed the feel of earth on her fingers. The thought of all the good things they would eat from the garden she was planting. Julia straightened up and glanced to see what Molly was doing and that the child was still close by. Another row then she once again checked on Ann. She made hills for cucumbers, dug little hollows and dropped in the cream colored seeds. Five seeds to each hill. After covering the seeds with fine dirt, she patted down the soil.

She stood at the edge of the garden wondering how much she really needed to plant. The garden seemed small compared to the one they had grown in the east. But there the garden fed a large household. In Oregon there was only Casper and herself and the children. She went back to planting vegetables. The next rows were beets then rows of onions and hills of winter squash.

Casper stood watching Julia without her knowing. She was enjoying her time in the sunshine and watched over Ann and Molly as she planted her garden. He was undecided whether to scold her for working so hard then decided Julia was being careful not to over do. Stopping from time to time, she surveyed her surroundings or listened quietly to Molly talk to her babies.

Julia looked up feeling Casper watching her. She brushed back a wisp of hair from her face. "I'm nearly done for today," she called. "Will you carry Ann to the house?"

Casper carried Ann's improvised bed and Julia walked beside him holding onto his arm. Molly ran ahead to the porch, sat on the bottom step, and waited. The house was cool when Julia entered. It was time to feed Ann and she sat softly humming as the baby nursed.

"I'm right where I want to be," Casper thought as he went back to the garden, cleaned and put away Julia's tools. He had built the chicken house the fall before so they would have eggs over the winter. The pasture was fenced. The barn was built and a milk cow was grazing in the field beyond. Corn was planted along with potatoes and today Julia had planted their vegetable garden. Apple seedlings were coming up in the field intended to be an orchard. In a few years they would have apples. There was wild game to hunt and berries to pick in the surrounding forest. With a sense of satisfaction, Casper walked to the house. He knew they had made a good start toward having a thriving farm.

The front door stood open letting in fresh air. He stood for a moment letting his eyes adjust to the interior. Julia was holding Ann. She glanced up and watched as he came to her. He pulled up a chair and sat facing her. "Are you fine," he asked.

Julia leaned to kiss him. "I think I'll take that nap you keep pushing me to take," she answered with a smile warming her eyes. "But first will you do something for me?"

"Name it," he said.

"Get your hammer and chisel and come up to the bedroom." Casper left to do what Julia asked.

Julia placed Ann in her cradle. She fixed Molly a glass of milk and crackers, and carried them upstairs. Molly sat on the window seat watching birds in the trees outside the bedroom window. Julia was removing winter clothes from the largest trunk when Casper came into their bedroom.

"You got the garden planted in time," Casper said as he watched Julia stack winter coats and woolen skirts on the floor at her feet. "It's starting to cloud up. There's the smell of rain in the air."

With the last item removed from the trunk, Julia asked Casper to remove the trim from around the bottom. He carefully pried off the boards from the ends of the trunk and then he did the same to the sides. He set the boards on the floor wondering what Julia had in mind.

"Take your chisel and lift the bottom out," she instructed when he had finished.

Casper carefully removed the board from the bottom of the trunk. There was a covering of newsprint under the thin board. Julia removed the layers of newsprint uncovering flat round objects wrapped in tissue paper. She picked up one object tearing away the paper and handed it to Casper. It was a twenty dollar gold piece. He turned it over in his hand, remarking as he did so, "I thought you gave Charles all your money?"

"I did," Julia explained. "I gave him all the expense money I had with me. I promised Perkins I wouldn't open the trunks until after I got to Oregon Country. This money was to buy what I needed and build a house." Julia gathered up the coins and sat on the floor un-wrapping each one as she talked. "You didn't think Uncle John would allow me to travel all this way without seeing I was properly provided for?"

Casper had to agree, John Forbes was not the type of man not to foresee Julia would have needs when she arrived in Oregon Country and he would have taken great pains in providing for these needs. "There's a small fortune here," Casper declared.

Julia handed him the coins she had unwrapped. "What is mine is yours," she told him. Casper remembering the words he had spoken to Julia after Charles' death and smiled.

"Why didn't you tell me," Casper asked.

"Because I knew you wanted to succeed on your own. I never doubted you," she said frankly.

Casper put his hands on both sides of Julia's face and leaning over kissed her lingering on the mouth. Julia had faith in him. He had worked and worried while all the time she had the means to make their life easy. Would he have accepted her bounty without the work and worry, he questioned. Without the knowledge she had faith he would succeed.

"I thought we might invest in cattle," Julia said. "Or whatever you think is the wisest use of our money." Again Julia was deferring to his wishes, willing to let Casper make the decision for both of them. Julia un-wrapped the last coin and handed the twenty dollar gold piece to Casper.

"No wonder your trunk was so heavy," Casper said, looking at the pile of gold coins now on the floor between them. And added silently, this was what Charles was trying to find all those times he had searched through Julia's belongings. Charles had known John Forbes would supply Julia with adequate money and he had been trying to find out where she had it hidden.

"Perkins built my trunks," Julia said. "It was his idea. I don't think Uncle John even knew where Perkins hid the money. I made a solemn promise not to tell anyone. Not even Annabel."

Perkins was a wise man, for Annabel would have told Charles where it was hidden. He would have left Julia and Annabel destitute. Charles had taken every cent he believed Julia possessed and still it had not been enough.

Casper sat on the floor and gathered Julia into his arms. She smiled at him nestling close in his arms. The money from the

216

trunk was forgotten as he lowered his head and brushed his lips across hers.

Julia wondered if Casper had heard what she had said, "Perkins had built her trunks." She had traveled west with two trunks. She would remind him later, she thought as she gave herself up to her husband's embrace.

About the Author

Author and Artist, Kay Stuart was born December 29 in the small central Missouri town of Stephens. A few years later the Stuart family moved to Hallsville, Missouri. Her father was a farmhand and coal miner. Her mother worked as a switchboard telephone operator. Born into a large family, Kay is the middle daughter. Married, she has three children.

Ms Stuart studied journalism and commercial writing. She has worked as a librarian, teacher's assistant, floral designer, and artist.

Ms Stuart incorporates into her stories many of her experiences growing up inside a large family and living in a small community where everyone knew their neighbors. Her love of God and Country is apparent in her writings.

72909703R00122

Made in the USA
Columbia, SC
29 June 2017